CHARLES BIRKIN

THE SMELL OF EVIL

WITH A NEW INTRODUCTION BY

JOHN LLEWELLYN PROBERT

VALANCOURT BOOKS

Richmond, Virginia

2013

The Smell of Evil by Charles Birkin
First published London: Tandem Books, 1965
First Valancourt Books edition 2013

Reprinted from the edition published New York: Award Books, 1967

Published by Valancourt Books, Richmond, Virginia
Publisher & Editor: JAMES D. JENKINS
20th Century Series Editor: SIMON STERN, University of Toronto
http://www.valancourtbooks.com

ISBN 978-1-939140-74-6
Also available as an electronic book

All Valancourt Books publications are printed on acid free paper
that meets all ANSI standards for archival quality paper.

Cover by M. S. Corley
Set in Dante MT 11/13.2

A Very Elegant Cruelty: An Introduction to Charles Birkin's
The Smell of Evil

GENTLE reader, beware. Before you begin to read the stories that
follow I feel it only fair to warn you. You are holding in your hands
a book of some of the bleakest, most well-written, deliciously
nasty horror stories you will ever have the good fortune to find on
the printed page. Stories about wealthy, beautiful people capable
of the most shocking acts of cruelty. Stories where the wide-eyed
innocence of a young child can lead to the most horrible kind of
death, either for the infant concerned or the adult who has unfortunately found themselves in the most macabre of situations. Stories
of brutal revenge, of petty jealousies that culminate in the most
grimly spiteful acts.

Welcome to the world of Sir Charles Birkin.

Charles Birkin inherited his title, becoming the fifth Baronet
Birkin in 1942. Prior to this he had edited the *Creeps* series of horror
anthologies for publisher Philip Allan during the 1930s. He was
educated at Eton (1921-1926), and during the Second World War,
he served as a Captain in the 12th Regiment of the 9th Sherwood
Foresters. Following this he travelled widely, setting aside the writing career he had cultivated before war broke out.

The Smell of Evil was first published by Tandem Books in 1965
and was Birkin's second volume of horror stories (after *The Kiss of
Death*) to be published after his return to writing following a long
hiatus. Dennis Wheatley is often cited as the man responsible for
encouraging Birkin to take up his pen again, and it may well be
that we have Wheatley to thank for the wealth of Birkin fiction we
have available today.

In his original introduction to *The Smell of Evil*, Wheatley likens
Birkin's stories to those of Edgar Allan Poe. While this is high
praise indeed, it's neither a strictly fair nor reasonable compari-
son. Whereas much of Poe's work arose from that author's own
tortured imagination, from within, if you like, Birkin's fiction is
very much a reaction to the external, to individuals and situations

he must have encountered during his eventful life. Indeed, one can come away from the stories in this volume feeling as if one knows very little about the man himself, other than that he must have held a pretty low opinion of humanity. I would have loved to have met Charles Birkin, and I very much suspect that the man himself would have turned out to be far more affable and convivial than his works might suggest.

Birkin was very much a product of his education and his war experiences, and with the stories that follow having been written in the early 1960s, the reader of today is asked to exercise discretion in regard to many of the tales' treatments of the working classes and those of foreign extraction. To be fair, it is not so much Birkin's attitude in these stories that is prejudiced (unlike in the writings of Dennis Wheatley) but rather those of the characters he peoples his stories with, and which are no doubt a reflection of the times he lived in.

So what actually lies ahead of you? It would be unfair to spoil some of the treats Birkin has in store, but perhaps forewarned might allow you to be forearmed. The title story begins the book, and tells of the Baron and Baroness Lebrun, who move to an isolated cliff-top house near a Cornish village with their niece, Sari. We are informed, in typical Birkin style, that this poor young girl is unable to speak, could walk when she arrived but is now confined to a wheelchair, and was last seen at one of the house's upper windows with tears streaming down her face. Oh, and Sari just happens to be heiress to the Lebrun fortune, which the Baron and Baroness would dearly like to get their hands on. Quite what they are doing to the little girl in an attempt to get her to sign over her deeds is so horrible that I am definitely going to leave you to discover it for yourself; suffice it to say that Birkin's view of some examples of humankind is so bleak and bitter that you may well want to take a break and read something else before moving on.

I dare you to read the next story, "Text for Today," and not imagine the author in church one Sunday as the verse in question from St. Paul's Letter to the Corinthians was read out, only for him to then spend the afternoon trotting out this little tale of missionaries trying to do good on some far-flung island and causing further horror instead.

"The Godmothers" starts off innocuously enough but becomes so grim that by the time bodies are being discovered you wonder if it can get any worse. And then it does.

"Green Fingers" is a classic World War II tale. All of Birkin's stories set in Nazi Germany have a discomforting ring of truth about them ("A Lovely Bunch of Coconuts" is probably his best). What really causes the chills in this one, aside from the final revelation, of course, are the casual asides describing the "awful smell of the oily smoke" from the concentration camp crematoria "if the wind was blowing the wrong way."

"Ballet Nègre" feels like it belongs in the 1965 Amicus anthology film *Dr. Terror's House of Horrors*. As mentioned above, Birkin's story itself isn't racist, but his characters and situations definitely are, undoubtedly reflecting the mid-1960s cultural climate. His most cutting line, however, is reserved for the peroxide blonde prostitute who gets interviewed in a bar, "swinging her orange plastic handbag."

Halfway through the book we get "The Lesson," a personal favourite, and one I won't say anything about, as you should discover Birkin's deliciously observed infant-centred drama for yourselves.

"Is There Anybody There?" is about ghosts, and what makes them even scarier is that they can see and interact with you, telling poor old Millie that "they're going to get her," and they do, but not quite in the way you might expect. Even little old ladies living in country cottages are not exempt from the cruelty of Birkin's world.

Another highlight is "Little Boy Blue." Charming little sailor-suited Sammy died horribly, choking on quicksand while disobeying his mother. Eight year old Oliver now has an imaginary playmate. Is little Oliver destined to die the way Sammy did? Read on to find out.

"The Interloper" is set, rather curiously, on an island described as an "Adamless Eden." We return to the theme of the concentration camp and you can probably guess what is going to happen to the man who turns up in the middle of the story wearing only his underpants, especially when it turns out he's the son of a particular SS Commandant.

The volume finishes with one of Birkin's regular, and often

quite peculiar, science fiction tales. The only real purpose of "The Cross" seems to be to allow Birkin to go on about how nasty and unpleasant the human race is, just in case we haven't got the point from the previous twelve stories.

Now, with your loins suitably girded and your sensibilities duly prepared (or at least I hope so) I shall leave you in the capable, cruel and supremely disquieting hands of a master of the short form.

They're all yours, Sir Charles . . .

JOHN LLEWELLYN PROBERT

September 5, 2013

THE SMELL OF EVIL

CONTENTS

To
Dennis Wheatley
for all his kindly encouragement,
and for my daughter,
Mandy,
who was made to read them all.

THE SMELL OF EVIL

THE first mention that I heard of Sari Lebrun was in the bar parlor of the Golden Ball where I was drinking beer after supper on the second evening of my holiday. The Golden Ball was the center of the social life of Trezarth, a tiny and unspoiled village on Cornwall's southern coast, and it was remarkable only for having been run by the same family in whose hands it had remained for the past two hundred years. There were no innovations, no attempts at cuteness, no unfortunate contemporary influence, and no self-conscious artists' colony to ruin it with their defiant bohemianism which, to my mind, can be the most irritating factor of all.

How it had escaped the exploitation that had done so much to spoil the neighbouring villages is unexplained, except that it is by no means easy of access to motor traffic and has never been written up.

There were only four guest rooms and a single somewhat primitive bath, in which an incautious movement while indulging in one's ablutions often resulted in a scrape as from a nutmeg grater. There was always a smeared residue of sand on the peeling enamel, no matter what the season, and the wraiths of straps of dried seaweed seemed to haunt the tack marks in the recessed window embrasure which gave on to a small paved yard, nostalgic and kindly spectres of the bygone holidays of happy children.

Sam Varcoe ran the bar with the help of his son Luke, who was also a boat builder by trade, while his wife, Dorothy, and their seventeen-year-old daughter, Magdalen, did the cooking and the housework. They were a charming and unsophisticated family with whom it was a joy to stay.

It was the beginning of May when I arrived and the holiday season had not yet begun, in fact I was the sole guest. I had gone there to try and make a start on my second novel, and it was proving a difficult pregnancy. My first effort, *Nuns on the Doorstep*, had enjoyed a fair reception from the critics, if not quite so enthusiastic a one from the book buying public, and it had left me spent and drained of ideas, and my publishers had requested delivery of the new manuscript by the end of August.

Trezarth had a permanent population of about five hundred souls which increased during the summer months by maybe twenty-five per cent. The little fishing village was not spectacular like Mousehole or Helston and was, on the whole, rather down-at-heel, but for me it held great charm. There were few houses of any size in the surrounding countryside and, of the few that there were, Angdon alone was in the hands of "strangers", having been let for a year to foreigners, presumed to be French or Belgians. They were a couple by the name of Lebrun, and the girl, Sari, was said to be their niece.

They had captured the imagination of Trezarth, for no one had met them. They had been observed from a distance, and of Sari it had been reported that not only was she an invalid but she was also reputed to be dumb, a combination which, together with her undeniable good looks, had aroused the interest and compassion of the villagers. This sympathy had been heightened by an incident which Dorothy Varcoe had herself experienced. Having spent a rare day in Penzance, where she had gone to purchase wallpaper, she had been walking home from the bus stop and had taken a short cut across the fields to a minor road which passed the front of Angdon on its way to Trezarth.

She had paused at the gate of the drive to admire a display of tulips which had come into flower when, happening to glance up, she had seen the girl at an upper window with the tears pouring down her face, apparently in great distress, and while Mrs. Varcoe was watching, her aunt, or stepmother, or whatever her relationship may have been, had come up from behind her, her face perfectly livid, and had wheeled her chair back until it was out of sight from the road. Mrs. Varcoe had been much upset by the girl's patent unhappiness.

Baron François Lebrun and his wife seldom appeared in Trezarth, but the couple who looked after them occasionally toiled down the steep hill for minor purchases, although most of the supplies for Angdon were, or so it had been put about, obtained from Penzance which was some eight miles away, an arrangement which did not endear them to the locals.

"It's a terrible thing about that poor girl," Dorothy Varcoe said. "I'm always telling Maggie that good health is the chief blessing that the Lord can bestow. 'Look after your health, Maggie,' I say to her, 'and you'll have no worries that can't be sorted out. Miss Lebrun now, with all the worldly advantages and the beauty of an angel—but an invalid! So what's the use of it all?' I ask her. And she always answers: 'I know, Mother, you're quite right.'" There was no cavilling to this truism that I could think of, and Mrs. Varcoe gave a final polish to the breakfast table. "When the Baron and the Baroness first came here the girl was able to walk about with a stick," she said. "Tottery and slowly, I must admit, but she could move. Now I hear that she's in a wheel chair all the time. Sounds to me as if she's wasting." She made a tutting sound. "I suppose they have had a doctor to her, but I've not heard so. Not Doctor Marreco, that much I do know, although if it was me I'd sooner call him in than any of your smart London specialists." She seemed to be worried by this lack of elementary attention.

I was finding it hard to get started on the new book, probably because of the relentless approach of the stipulated and awesome deadline, and on the following afternoon I abandoned all attempts at work and went instead for a walk along the shore. The tide was way out, uncovering islands and archipelagos of weed-bearded rocks patterned with miniature lakes and pools that were encrusted with the pointed shells of limpets, and sea-gulls strutted arrogantly on the shining waste. It was a gray day, but warm and without a breath of wind. An hour's walking and, it must be confessed, dawdling, for the attractions of marine life on the seashore have ever proved irresistible to me since my earliest days, brought me to the foot of a pathway that zigzagged up the cliff face and which led to the garden of a big house at its top, which I surmised correctly to be Angdon.

I was strongly tempted to climb it and make some pretext for a call on the sequestered Lebruns, who had aroused my curiosity, in common with that of the remainder of the tiny community, but I could think up no suitable excuse for so doing. Accordingly, I walked on, wracking my brain in vain for inspiration and dreading my return to the typewriter, and did not get back to the Golden Ball until half past five, when I cancelled immediately the benefi-

cial effects of my exercise by consuming a whole plateful of Mrs.
Varcoe's scones which were heaped, with baneful threats to my
already expanding waistline, with Cornish cream and homemade
strawberry jam.

It was in the Public Bar after supper that the talk turned again to
the subject of the Lebruns. It transpired that during the afternoon
their French cook had come in to Trezarth in search of cigarettes
for the Baron. It was early closing day, and she had made her way
to the Golden Ball. She spoke some English and Mrs. Varcoe had
gathered that the tenancy of Angdon was shortly to be terminated,
after which they would all be returning to their own country. Made
more forthcoming by the glass of sherry which Mrs. Varcoe had
insisted on pressing on her, and becoming a victim of that good
lady's skilful questioning, she also let fall other items regarding her
employers.

The Baron, she said, had been engaged in compiling a volume
on the lost continent of Atlantis, upon the geographical location of
which he held strong views, belonging to the school that believed
the Isles of Scilly to have been an outpost, and he had come to
Cornwall to complete his treatise, a task that was all but finished.
Sari Lebrun was indeed their niece, and unfortunately her health
was failing rapidly, which was sad as she had everything to live for,
being a great heiress. The Baron and his wife had nursed her with
a devotion as if she had been their own daughter, with no thought
for themselves, but had finally been forced to admit defeat and had
decided to take her back to Paris for her last few months, a city,
which, as everybody knew, led the world in medical science. It was
true, also, that the poor Mademoiselle was unable to speak, for
she had been dumb since birth, but was, nevertheless, extremely
intelligent and of considerable education. Should she succumb to
her illness there was no doubt that her benefactors, as she was an
orphan, would inherit her fortune unless she should marry, which
was most unlikely.

"Seems odd to me," Mrs. Varcoe said after she had finished telling me this news, "their taking the poor girl all the way to Paris
just to die. Globe trotting's very tiring at the best of times. If their
doctors are as brilliant as that woman claims, why on earth didn't
they leave her over there in the first place—in a hospital or nurs-

ing home—where she could have had proper attention? If you ask me," she pursed her lips in disapproval, "there's more in it than meets the eye. I never did trust these frogs, especially where money is concerned."

Given such a promising lead speculation ran rife through the smoky bar, the upshot of it being that I, as a brother author, should be the one to call upon the Baron on the next day and report back on anything peculiar that I might learn concerning the conduct of the household.

"Yes, Mr. Ives," Sam Varcoe agreed, "Dorothy's right. You're the one to go. Being a gentleman they could hardly refuse to let you in, particularly as you're in the same line in a manner of speaking. They couldn't bar you, not without appearing more singular than they'd like, and so causing talk."

I grinned, wondering if the Lebruns were aware of the speculation about themselves which was already raging through the village. "But I know so very little about Atlantis," I protested.

Sam tucked his thumbs into the armholes of his leather waistcoat and beamed at me benignly. "That won't signify," he said comfortingly. "You've got the gift of the gab and that should see you through, and what with being of good schooling I daresay as how you speak a bit of their lingo."

"Not a word," I said untruthfully.

Sam Varcoe gave an unbelieving chuckle. He leant down to draw another pint and the big silver shield on his watch chain clinked against the bar as he did so. "Talk the hind leg off a donkey if you've a mind to, as we all know," he said cheerfully, making it sound like a compliment. "Dorothy and Luke were saying so not an hour ago," he went on. "Mind you, it can come in very useful." He pushed across the pewter mug. "This one's on me," he said, "and the best of luck to you."

"All right," I said as I raised the tankard, "I don't mind having a bash at it—but it will be your fault if I come back with a black eye for my impertinence."

"We wouldn't be put out by that, Mr. Ives," said Mrs. Varcoe. "We've seen many a shiner in this bar, haven't we, Sam?"

I felt that she might have shown more concern on my behalf.

Of course in the morning I was full of regrets for having allowed

myself to be cornered into undertaking an act of such meddle-
some intrusiveness, but knew that if I went back on my word I
would have to face a barrage of largely unspoken and sorrowful
criticism. However, it was made easier for me by the fact that the
sheet of paper in my typewriter obstinately remained unsullied,
and also by the enticement of the spring sunshine that washed
over the lime green of the bud-laden orchard beneath my window.
I decided that the afternoon would be a more civilized time for my
unwarranted encroachment into the privacy of Angdon.

I took the cliff road in preference to plodding along the beach,
intending, if all went well, to make the return journey along the
sands, and as I idled along my mission became more and more
bizarre and I felt like some silly adolescent embarking upon a foolish prank. When I came in sight of the gates my enthusiasm for the
visit grew even less, and I climbed on to a gate where I perched,
swinging my legs, and filled my pipe and planned my opening
remarks.

Like most exposed gardens, that of Angdon was not ambitious,
neither was it large, and the drive to the house was less than forty
feet in length. A few shrubs sheltered under cover of the gray stone
walls and a climbing rose had not done too badly on the house
itself, although it faced north. The tulips which Mrs. Varcoe had
admired had lost their vivid petals and stood like an army of green
and skeletal phantoms, deploring their nudity.

I rang the bell and after a pause the door was opened by a manservant who was still in the act of shrugging on his white coat. I
had my card ready in my hand and on the back of it I had pencilled:
"Dear Baron Lebrun, as a co-author I would much appreciate a
brief talk with you on the subject of Atlantis—upon which you
are such an authority." I became aware that "co-author" was not
correct, as I was not his collaborator.

The servant did not ask me to enter, but took my card and reluctantly disappeared with it towards the back of the house, leaving
the door ajar. Presently he returned, his expression wooden. "S'il
vous plaît, Monsieur," he said, motioning me to follow him. He was
swarthy and dark and I guessed that he was a Corsican. We went
through a large hall and he opened a door into a long and pleasant
sitting-room with wide windows looking out over the sea.

Baron Lebrun was busy at a writing table whose top was strewn with manuscript, but he put down his pen and rose to greet me as I came forward. He was tall and thin, with an ascetic's mouth, and what remained of his hair was blond. He gave me a faint smile and his eyebrows were arched inquiringly. "Please be seated, Mr. Ives. I would be delighted to give you any help that is within my power." He held out a gold cigarette case. "You, too, are writing a work on Atlantis?" His tone was reproachful and a shade derisive. "You are my rival?"

"No," I said. "I am a novelist, and the subject is really only incidental in my forthcoming book. But in it, during a discussion about reincarnation, there *is* a reference, and I like to get my facts right, or I will receive a lot of disagreeable letters! One of my characters argues that the capital city had four, and not three, inner walls."

The Baron laughed. "I fear that will always be a matter for surmise," he said, "at any rate until we can excavate on the floor of the ocean!" He spoke with only a vestige of accent.

Beyond the windows was a colonnaded terrace on which long chairs had been placed, and one of them was occupied by a pretty woman of about fifty years of age who lay back motionless, with her face turned to the warm spring sun. She wore dark spectacles, and beyond her, and at the far end of the flagstones, stood an invalid carriage in which Sari was sitting, her legs wrapped tightly in a cocoon of rugs. The sea and sky made a backcloth of contrasting blues. The Baron went on talking. "The popular theory is that there were three walls," he said, "and that the innermost, which contained the temples, was plated with gold or bronze. If it is not to be a serious book—a work for *les savants*—I should stick to that. I imagine it would mean but a trivial alteration?"

We discussed the matter for a few more minutes and then I got up. "You have been most kind," I said. I drifted over to a window. "Before I go might I admire your wonderful view? As a matter of fact, since it's such a glorious afternoon I thought of walking back to Trezarth along the beach."

For a moment his handsome face darkened. "You should be careful of the tide," he said. "It can be dangerous in the cove." He had spoken without thinking and stopped abruptly in case I might be aware that he was trying to put me off.

"It won't be high tide until late this evening," I said. "I was at the foot of your path at about half past four yesterday afternoon. I don't think there'll be any danger."

"You may well be right." He came over to join me. "I do not pretend to be an authority on such matters." The thin lips curved. "I am a writer, Mr. Ives, not a sailor." He flung up one of the high windows and we stepped outside. The woman on the chaise longue opened her eyes at the sound of our approach. "This is my wife," Baron François said. "Gaby, I would like to present Mr. Ives who is interested in what you regard as my boring research, in which, as I am sure he will not resent my saying, he is an enthusiastic amateur. He is also a novelist," he added drily.

The Baronne, who was maybe a year or two senior to her husband, smiled at me but did not get up. She possessed great elegance and was extremely soignée. "I would like to ask you to stay with us for a cup of tea, Mr. Ives, but I have to confess that it is one of your English customs to which I have not taken. I hope that you will excuse us? Besides," her head half turned in the direction of the girl in the invalid chair, "my niece is not well and tires easily, which is why we discourage callers. I'm sure that you will understand." It was a firm dismissal. In repose her mouth was as prim as a cat's.

"Of course I understand." I walked a few paces along the terrace, as if better to enjoy the vista, until I was standing quite near to the girl. There was a sketching pad on her knees and she was toying with a pencil. She did not acknowledge my presence, although she must have heard my footsteps, but kept her eyes resolutely down.

I complimented the Baronne on the beauty of the scene that lay before us and retraced my steps to say good-bye. "It is rumored in the village that you will be leaving here soon," I said. "Now that I have met you, may I say that I am sorry?"

The Baronne smiled in acceptance of the courtesy. "The rumor is correct," she said, "and you are most polite. It has been a pleasant interlude." She gave a little Gallic shrug. "But now we must go home." As I bent down to take her hand I saw from behind her that the girl in the chair was staring at me fixedly, and as I stared back she crumpled the sheet of drawing paper upon which she had been working into a ball and let it drop on to the paving. Her look was imploring and filled with meaning.

"It has been a pleasure to make your acquaintance," Baron François said. "Good-bye, Mr. Ives." He was obviously impatient for my departure. "I shall look forward to reading your novel."

I made him a bow. The way to the top of the cliff path was beyond where the girl was sitting and as I passed her chair I stood still for a moment to light my pipe and while thus engaged I allowed the box of matches to fall from my hands. When I retrieved them I collected also the scrap of paper on which she had been drawing and thrust it into my pocket.

At the gate I turned my head and raised an arm in a gesture of farewell. The Baronne was standing by her husband's side and both of them were looking after me. They made a distinguished couple between the pillars of the colonnade.

I waited until I reached the beach before I took the paper from my jacket, leaning back against the cliff face where I could not be spied upon from above.

Sari Lebrun had sketched a portion of the foreshore, the focal point being a triangle of large rocks surrounding deep pools, and one of these she had shaded; at the bottom of the page she had scrawled: *"Au secours, je vous implore, Monsieur. Ce soir. 22.00 heures."*

The rock formation shown in the drawing was to my right and some distance below the high tide mark. There was no mistaking it. I thought of walking down to make an inspection but rejected the idea in case there should be watchers above me at Angdon. 22.00. That must mean ten o'clock tonight. I would return shortly before that hour and discover if anything might occur to elucidate Sari's reckless and cryptic message. I saw again her alarming pallor and the desperation in her eyes. Probably she would try to send another letter. But who would be her emissary? It could only be the cook who had called on Mrs. Varcoe for cigarettes.

Back at the Golden Ball I was greeted by the entire Varcoe family, reinforced by the presence of a cousin, Jack, a young giant of a fisherman. My report of the situation at Angdon fell rather flat until I came to the acquisition of the sketch, which I produced and translated the message, at which Dorothy cast a look of great significance towards Sam.

"I knew that there was something wrong," she said, "terribly wrong. You will go back to the pool tonight, Mr. Ives, won't you?

Sam and Luke shall go with you. Jack, too. Maggie and I can manage the bar for once."

"Certainly I will go," I said, "but I don't see the need for such an escort. If it is to be an assignation with Mademoiselle Sari I don't want any competition and would be better off alone," I made a face at the good-looking cousin, "although I can't imagine how she could possibly get down to the beach unaided, unless one of the servants is helping her." I tried to sound facetious. "There's no necessity to call out the militia!" I laid the sketch face down on the bar.

Mrs. Varcoe said no more but the line of her chin was purposeful and she was quite clearly unconvinced by my nervous levity. Sam must have sensed that I thought that his wife was erring on the side of melodrama, for he said quietly: "Dorothy's not often wrong, Mr. Ives. Like a lot of us in these parts she's almost got second sight where wickedness is concerned."

I started off in what I judged to be good time to keep my watchful vigil, the Varcoes clustering outside their door to witness my departure. It would be wise to arrive well before the hour which the girl had jotted down on the sketch, for then I would know whom it was that she had enlisted for an ally.

I had omitted to allow, however, for the difference of walking on a nice afternoon and covering the same distance in moonlight, when caution had to be taken in negotiating obstacles, and my watch told me that if I did not hurry I should be late. I broke into a run, jumping from one precarious rock to another, but luck was not with me and my haste proved disastrous, for one over agile and ill-timed leap landed me on a slope of slippery weed, which brought me to my knees, and when, swearing, I managed to struggle to my feet, a sharp pang of pain made it plain that I had sprained an ankle rather badly, which so impeded my progress that when I came eventually in sight of the pool it was to find a little procession which was wending its laborious way not down, but up, the cliff path.

It was too far away for me to make out details, but I could discern that the party comprised four persons. Sari herself was seated in the wheel chair, her head bowed forward on to her chest, but her back was to me and I was unable to see her face. There were also the manservant and, to my surprise, the Baron and his wife, Gaby.

I waited in the shadows until they had completed the ascent and had disappeared through the swing gate into the garden before I hobbled forward to the pool, hopeful that Sari might have managed to leave a further message for me there, but search carefully as I did I could find nothing. I sprawled on the rocks, groping down among the seaweed in case a note could have been anchored in some container, but the pool appeared as innocent of communication as any other.

Looking up from these investigations I saw a figure of a man outlined on the summit of the cliff, and from his build and the set of his shoulders I knew it was Baron François Lebrun. I lay still, but he could not have failed to see me in the moonlight, for I had no cover. He remained as motionless as a statue and after an interminable minute he moved away.

My return to the hotel was arduous and uncomfortable and by the time that I had limped as far as the main street of Trezarth my ankle was swollen and throbbing and giving me hell. I felt that I had messed things up by my clumsiness and had been a fool in insisting on going off on my own.

The bar was closed when I reached the Golden Ball, although light shone from the windows, and I let myself in by the private door to tell the Varcoes about my misadventure and of the failure of my mission.

Mrs. Varcoe clucked maternally when she saw my drawn face, and Sam pressed a glass of whisky into my hand. The bar-room was very snug in the flickering firelight as Luke walked quietly round turning down the lamps and closing the shutters for the night. Maggie was polishing the glasses in readiness for the next day.

Dorothy settled me down and examined my injury, probing gently with firm and experienced fingers. Apparently satisfied, and despite my wincing, she made a compress and bandaged my ankle, declaring that by the morning it would be practically healed and that she saw no call for disturbing Doctor Marreco at this hour, since he was a very busy man. She also treated me to a brief homily, the gist of which was that in her opinion I should not be allowed out on my own without a Nanny. "You city-bred men are all the same," she said. "As awkward and helpless a lot as ever I laid my eyes on."

When she had finished the Varcoes demanded to hear every

detail of my evening, and I was forced to admit my folly in having by my rashness permitted the Baron to observe my examination of the pool, which must have confirmed any suspicions which my visit to him might have occasioned.

Sam was not in total agreement with this. "From that angle," he argued, "and in those dark clothes, you may have got away with it if you were lying still. But then there's no knowing how long he was waiting up there. He could have gone with the others to the house and then doubled back." He rubbed his chin. "He did not call out to you, Mr. Ives, or make any attempt to start down to the shore?"

I shook my head, and Mrs. Varcoe said: "You could well be right, Sam. Moonlight on those rocks in Angdon Cove can make strange shadow play. It seems to me that Mr. Ives should pay a further call at the house tomorrow and try to contrive another meeting with the girl." She broke off before she added brusquely: "And the three of you must go with him to the beach at night, whether the girl is able to communicate with him or no."

"Might it not," I said as I lit a cigarette, "be best to take the sketch to the police and let them deal with it?"

Mrs. Varcoe frowned. "They'd never believe us. Suspicions aren't enough to get a search warrant, and they're a canny bunch in these parts, more's the pity. We do know that something's wrong, but just what it is we do *not* rightly know." As she spoke I could not help but wonder how often it must have been that outsiders hesitated to interfere in what was not their business, when action might have made all the difference. "And now, Mr. Ives," Dorothy Varcoe turned to me briskly, "it's bed for you, and if your ankle's not down by morning I'll get the doctor to you, but it's surprised I'll be if it's troubling you by then, after you've rested it. Luke, help Mr. Ives up the stairs!"

I took her advice and went to my room, but sleep would not come and, long after the murmur of their voices had ceased, I lay on my back milling over the puzzling circumstances of Sari's frenzied appeal and the terror that she had shown when our eyes had met. In spite of Mrs. Varcoe's reasonable objections, if there was something horrible happening at Angdon, if the wretched girl were being victimized, it was not for us to take risks with her health, perhaps even with her life, by postponing the summoning of police action. Finally I took two aspirins, and the next thing I knew it was eight o'clock and Maggie was saying a soft "good morning" and putting my tea on the bedside table. Her mother had been right; during the night my swollen ankle had subsided and the pain had almost gone.

After breakfast we had another consultation, but the summoning of official assistance had been made, we discovered, far more difficult, for a further disaster had occurred. Sari's sketch had vanished. The Varcoes had thought that I had taken it up with me, and I had assumed that it was in their possession. Luke must have thrown it inadvertently into the fire together with the cigarette butts and other rubbish when he had been tidying the bar-room and, with our one piece of concrete evidence gone, it was agreed that we wait a little longer to try to strengthen our case before having recourse to the law. For a start it was proposed that I was to gain entry into Angdon upon the same pretext that I had used previously, when I would be able, surely, to discover from my reception if the Baron knew of my activities of the night before.

The door was again answered by the manservant and once more I was left on the mat to cool my heels before being granted admittance. The Baron lacked all modicum of affability. His eyes were cold and he did not rise when I was shown in, but waited for me to explain the reason for what it was obvious that he regarded as an unwarrantable intrusion. "Mr. Ives," he said, "I have no wish to appear inhospitable, but we are very occupied as we are leaving here in a few days, and I need hardly explain that we have a great deal to do."

I glanced out of the window. The terrace was untenanted. I asked a few questions, but they sounded unconvincing and lame even to my own ears. Baron Lebrun did not extend his hand when I left, but rang for the butler to let me out, and it was evident that he was making no effort to disguise the fact that he was giving me a deliberate brush-off. As well as hostility I sensed a lurking fear in his behavior. Of the Baronne there was no sign. My expedition had not been wasted.

As I reached the end of the drive some instinct made me look back over my shoulder. The girl, Sari, had propelled the wheel chair up to the window, as she had done when Mrs. Varcoe had been passing by, and through the glass I could see her piteous face as she tried desperately to attract my attention. Her right hand was tracing letters in the air. I stood still, endeavoring to understand them but I could make no sense of her efforts.

While I was concentrating on the signs that she was making I had the feeling that I myself was being watched, and from the corner of my eye became aware that the Baron had followed me to the door and was now leaning against its jamb. Caught, as it were, red-handed, and cursing myself for my bungling, I shaded my eyes with my hands and tilted my head back, pretending that I was absorbed in the passage of an aeroplane across the soundless sky. When I allowed my gaze to drop the face behind the window had gone and the panes were blank and I turned and walked slowly away.

Mrs. Varcoe listened to my account with great attention and without interruption and it was decided that her proposal of the previous evening be accepted and that I should go with the three men to the cove. My ankle no longer hurt and we set off early, allowing ample margin for possible mishaps. The night was cloudless and the moon almost full, turning the beach and the lowering bulk of the cliff into a clean-cut etching of dramatic contrasts.

We were installed in our hiding places by half past nine. The tide was racing in, but it would be another two hours or more before it reached high-water mark. It was very still and quiet and I longed to smoke a cigarette. The rhythmic music of the waves was soporific in its regular beat, and I enjoyed the eerie beauty, although the night had turned chilly.

I could not see Sam or Jack Varcoe from the eroded spur behind which I was crouching, but I knew approximately where they had concealed themselves, as we were in a rough semi-circle, and Luke, on my left, was within soft calling distance.

The waiting seemed to be endless. We all, I knew, had our concentration pin-pointed on the twisted cutting in the cliff down which the retinue would have to come, the girl in the wheel chair surrounded by her attendants, bent on a purpose that so far was inexplicable. But nothing happened and the beach remained deserted save for the occasional flitter of a bat from a hole in the granite.

Once the peace of the night was broken by the whir and chugging of an engine, and a helicopter, its jewelled lights winking, churned over our heads bound for France, a huge may-bug, black and clumsy against the nacreous gray of the sky. Twenty minutes later Luke's voice said from the far side of a neighboring mass of outcrop near to me: "They're not coming tonight, are they, Mr. Ives?" His whisper was very clear.

"Doesn't look like it," I said. He left the shadow and we walked forward openly to where Jack Varcoe had stationed himself. He rose at our approach, looming above us in the moonlight. We held a low-voiced conversation and, whistling to Sam to join us, went over in line and squatted down by the pool and leant over it, with our silhouettes reflected darkly on its surface.

The patch of water was pear shaped and deep, fringed with thick clumps of winkle encrusted weed and budded with the closed udders of puckered and stranded sea anemones awaiting the liberation of the incoming tide to revitalize them so that they could unfold their tendrils. By daylight there would have been much activity to study in this miniature world, but now all was undisturbed and there was no ripple to distort the mirror.

Jack Varcoe was wearing faded jeans and a striped singlet and he thrust one muscular bare arm into the water to plumb its depth and his fingers were barely able to touch the bottom. "Nothing there," he said, "except pebbles and sand." I don't know what it was that he had expected to find. He peered up at the cliff. From where we were squatting the gables and upper story of Angdon were just visible. No lights showed. "They've gone to bed early tonight," Jack said. He plunged his arm back into the water and, for something to do, scraped up a handful of sand and broken shell which he let dribble through his fingers on to the rock. We all sat in silence, prying down into the water like a quartet of self-hypnotizing fortune tellers gazing into a crystal. The moonlight glistened on the little mound of damp salvage. I reached forward and picked up a piece of it by way of occupation, thinking it to be a morsel of razor shell, and weighed down by the dull disappointment of anti-climax. I was looking more closely at the object in my palm when I realized that what I had been about to flick away was no broken shell but the greater part of a toe-nail—a human toe-nail.

I stared at it, comprehending at first only partly what it was. Sam Varcoe saw my attention and stretching out his hand took it from me. We neither of us spoke, unwilling to admit its possible significance. "Take a look at this, Jack," Sam said at length.

The young fisherman was peering down again into the water, parting the seaweed, his face intent. "Sam," he said gruffly, "sit on my legs, will you?" He curved his torso down over the pool until the water covered his arms and welled over his shoulders and the small of his back. I heard him give a grunt of satisfaction. "Got something," he said. "Come on, Luke, lend us a hand."

With great difficulty he pulled up a wicker cage, large and stoutly woven, and in it scrabbled two of the biggest crabs that I have ever seen. The cage had been well hidden, pushed away to the back of a submarine hollow in the rock shelf. The monstrous crabs froze for a moment into immobility before they began to lumber cumbrously round the cage, their gigantic claws clicking in agitation at this rude interruption to their existence.

An explanation of the toe-nail crossed my horrified mind. Jack Varcoe must have had the same thought for his face was grim as he regarded the loathsome creatures and he shot me a glance of appalled understanding as the truth dawned on him.

He opened the sliding door of the trap and tipped them out, flipping them over on to their backs. Then, seizing a loose stone he began to pound at them viciously, shattering the silence and battering at their armor, hissing under his breath as he tore off the waving claws. He was attacking them like a maniac and did not desist from his destruction until the crabs had become an oozing pulp of crushed shell and meat.

He sprang to his feet and, kicking aside the spasmodically twitching fragments, ran towards the foot of the cliff path, the rest of us at his heels. We were wearing rubber shoes but, in any case, there was no longer any reason for concealment. When we reached the top I was panting from the exertion of the climb as we ran diagonally across the lawn.

The door from the verandah was shuttered and bolted and we skirted the building to the main entrance, the stone chips spurting from beneath our flying feet. There was not a glimmer of light from within. I kept my thumb pressed hard on the bell, hearing the distant ring that had that special tone which makes one know instinctively that there would be no one to answer it.

Jack's tread sounded on the gravel. "There's another door round at the side," he said, "and a window beside it which I've managed to force. You wait there." He darted away and presently we heard the key of the door, before which we had grouped ourselves, being turned and bolts were shot back.

The house, as we had expected, was empty. We made a thorough search of every room, but the only sign of the former occupants was the customary debris left behind by departing tenants, screws of paper, cardboard boxes, a used lipstick and forlorn bottles and packets with only a silt of their contents remaining. It was evident that the Baron, his family and his staff had gone.

Suddenly I remembered the buzzing helicopter bumbling its way across the Channel.

We went back to Trezarth, Sam Varcoe muttering angrily to himself. "The swine. The filthy swine. There has never been such a smell of evil as there was in that house: It was . . . palpable." His tongue tripped slightly over the word as if it had been from a foreign tongue. "I'll get him for this if it means going to Paris myself to do so. And his bloody old bitch, too. The cruel devils. The filthy, filthy swine!" Jack and Luke strode on without speaking, their faces ugly.

We made straight for the police station. The Sergeant in charge was newly arrived and the Varcoes had not met him. He listened to us attentively and with infinite patience, and during our incoherent and confused story he made copious notes. He was polite and soothing and said that the matter would be looked into; but we had little testimony to back up our theory of the horror that might have taken place.

Only Mrs. Varcoe was convinced.

We heard the news the next morning on the B.B.C., and it was later substantiated and elaborated by the newspapers. A helicopter had crashed in the Channel shortly before half past ten on the previous night, to the west of Guernsey, and in deep water. There had been only one casualty. It had made the headlines, for the people concerned had been in the Big Money.

HEIRESS KILLED IN AIR DISASTER.
GALLANT EFFORT OF BARON FRANÇOIS LEBRUN
TO RESCUE HIS CRIPPLED NIECE.

The Baron and his grief-stricken wife had given their story. Sari had, of course, been trapped in the machine. She had had no chance of survival. The pilot and his four other passengers had all managed to escape and had been picked up by a fishing boat which had most fortuitously been in the vicinity. It had all been very pat, and doubtlessly scrupulously stage managed. With his connections, money and, above all, incentive, for Sari had possessed one of the biggest fortunes in France, the Baron had made good use of the time that we had unwittingly allowed him in which to make his arrangements.

There were no steps that we could take, for any "evidence" had been destroyed.

Perhaps Sari had been murdered because she had refused to sign her will, knowing that should she do so she would be signing away even that measure of borrowed time which was being permitted to her, and during which some miracle might bring her salvation from the outside, and that her signature would be the equivalent of her death warrant.

I thought of her pathetic swathed legs, wrapped to hide the bandages round her lacerated limbs, of her distorted face as her mouth stretched in a noiseless frantic scream from the atrophied vocal cords, and of the fantastic torture which she must have repeatedly endured before she had finally lost consciousness.

And now she had been sent to keep her final rendezvous with the fellows of the crabs which had been starved and trained to tear at and devour her living flesh while she had been held down on the edge of the pool on that lovely and deserted beach below Angdon; and I grew weak with the fiendishness of it.

Sometime soon, be the penalty what it may, Sam Varcoe and I are going to hunt down Baron François Lebrun, and when we find him we are going to get him alone and scare his guts out, and then we are going to kill him.

TEXT FOR TODAY

(St. Paul to the Corinthians, Chapter 14, Verse 21.)

THE Reverend Herbert Wessel and his wife, May, had lived on
Namavava for three years. It was a beautiful island, a near earthly
paradise, and lay less than a day's sail from Misima but, for all the
contact which they had with the other and larger land masses of
the group, they might just as well have been posted to Pitcairn.

Not that they minded. So long as May had Herbert, and so long
as Herbert had his work among the natives, doing God's will, they
were both of them perfectly content.

Herbert was the first resident missionary to have been sent to
live on Namavava. Formerly it had been treated as an outpost of
the D'Entrecasteaux Group, and had been visited on rare occasions by their predecessor, Cecil Oliver, who had been based on
Misima, but upon his retirement there had been a reallocation of
territory, and the Church of England had increased the numbers
of its representatives in order to combat the growing menace of
the Church of Rome, which was sending out more and more of
their militant priests, although Namavava had so far escaped their
attentions.

Herbert and May Wessel were of the same age. They had been
married for twenty-five years, and had seen much of the world, generally in the more remote and unattractive corners of Africa and
China, before this Melanesian appointment had been given to them,
and a very pleasant one it had turned out to be. The climate was, for
the greater part of the year, ideal, the inhabitants were cheerful and
easy going, and there were no poisonous snakes or insects. True
there was a species of large cockroach of which May had an unrea-
soning horror, and against which her carefully hoarded supply of
Keating's Powder seemed to have very little effect. Nevertheless
they referred to Namavava as their Garden of Eden.

Herbert sometimes thought that his career had been an undis-
tinguished one and that now he could never expect to rise to any

23

great heights. When this feeling of failure came upon him May would become as impatient with him as it was possible for her to be. It was not, she said quite forcibly, necessarily the Bishops and the high dignitaries of the Church who undertook the most important work, although she could not but agree that they were all of them fine and upright men. It was someone like Herbert who really counted in the eyes of God, a man who was selfless, and who asked for nothing for himself, one who had dedicated the whole of his life to the spiritual and physical well-being of the backward communities among whom he had been sent, and whole sole desire had been to serve. "And no one," she would say, "no one is more self denying than you, and no one has a greater gift for making converts enjoy their religion. Under your guidance Christianity is for them a case of Te Deum rather than, as is so often the case I am afraid, one of tedium." She used to smile brightly when she made this little joke.

They were the only white people on the island. When Queen Victoria had died during the previous year it had taken the news six months to reach them. Although they had not visited England for a decade they felt the loss as keenly as if it had been a personal bereavement, and Herbert had made the deceased monarch, with her many admirable virtues, the subject of his next address in the rickety corrugated iron church that he had caused to be built on the outskirts of the main center on Namavava, which was merely a straggle of extremely primitive dwellings that housed some six hundred souls.

Herbert's thick fair hair was already graying, while May's had been for a long time a mixture of pepper and salt in which the latter predominated. In appearance they were strangely alike, both being on the heavy side, both constantly smiling with a sincere and determined benignity, both viewing the world through thick spectacles. Despite the tropical sun there was scarcely a line on their faces, which resembled ripe and downy apricots.

Their own house had been erected on a narrow plateau about a hundred yards from, and fifty feet above, the winding village. It was perched on a forest of squat bamboo stilts and encircled by a shaded verandah to which access was given by half a dozen steps. The walls were of woven bamboo and the roof had been thatched with palm. In addition to the verandah, where the majority of their scant free time was spent, there was a bedroom, a living room and, built on to the back, a more spacious annex which served as May's workroom and dispensary, where she did her best with inadequate equipment to attend to the health of any who might be ailing.

A short distance from this were the cookhouse and the lean-to where their two "boys" slept. May had to laugh when Herbert referred to them as "the boys." It always seemed to her so comical for in fact they were handsome young men in their twenties, brothers, and as broad shouldered and impressively muscled as gladiators.

The one who did the cooking was married. Herbert had conducted the ceremony a few weeks after they had moved in, and had at the same time taken the opportunity of baptizing the three children, when he had baptized their parents. Their father had chosen the name of Zebedee, and after some argument Herbert had given in to this wish. He would himself have preferred to bestow upon him the name of one of the disciples or apostles but had unwillingly allowed that Zebedee was perhaps near enough.

Zebedee's brother, not to be outdone, had requested Boanerges, and this demand, although their relationship was scripturally wrong, had also been granted. Zebedee's wife had been content to become Mary. Their Melanesian names had been quite unpronounceable, and so this solution had been simpler for all.

May was uneasy that Zebedee insisted on sleeping in the lean-to rather than in his own hut on the shore of the lagoon. Marriage was sacred, and surely his proper place was at his wife's side? She had resolved many times to speak to him about it, and had tried once to get Herbert to do so but he had been embarrassed by the idea. Zebedee would want to know why, and they neither of them had any desire to embark upon so delicate a topic.

It had been a matter of nagging distress to May and Herbert that they were such very poor linguists. Maybe, Herbert thought, if he had possessed a better ear for languages he might have advanced further in his vocation. It had been a tremendous handicap and one that probably had held him back. May, however, in an attempt to remedy this weakness had trained herself to become an excellent, if unorthodox, teacher of English. She was blessed with patience and humor and had a talent for pantomime which had stood them in good stead. Nor had their frequent transfers been helpful. Sierra Leone, Uganda, Kweichow, Kansu and finally Namavava had made it difficult for them to become completely identified with their surroundings, since they had never had the opportunity of putting down roots, not strong tap roots, which were so essential in their life.

They hoped that they would be permitted to stay on Namavava for many years. After all, May told herself, it was Herbert who had started the mission. It was his creation, and she considered and also prayed, that they would be allowed to remain there until the time should come for their retirement. The islanders were so charming and lovable, as naive as children, of course, but friendly and biddable children, and from a total of the two thousand scattered population they could already lay claim to at least a quarter of that number as converts.

Wisely, Herbert had not, upon their arrival, insisted on the destruction or disfigurement of the idols which they had found. Rather had he sought to wean away their worshippers by treating the images as interesting antiquities whose interest could be compared to those on Easter Island. He had taken immense pains to put over this viewpoint.

They had encountered no trouble. There had been no unpleasant incidents, that is to say, there had been none until a month before. Then, unhappily, there had been a murder, a crime which was unheard of on the island.

When they had been informed of it they had hoped, at the beginning, that it could have been treated as a case of assault but, as a result of the injuries which had been inflicted, the victim had later died. It was, or so Herbert had been told, the sole case of its kind to have happened on Namavava within living memory.

Mahele, who was one of the innumerable nephews of the Chief, had enticed a girl into a cave which was in the Bay of Shells, and there he had raped her. She had been betrothed to Ke-Kulah, who was related to Zebedee. Through the ages rape on Namavava had been taboo, especially where a betrothed girl had been involved. The girl had immediately confessed to her father what had occurred and Ke-Kulah with the assistance of her brother Manè had waylaid Mahele, and after beating him almost senseless had clumsily castrated him and had then left him for dead in the cave where his offense had been committed. It was fortunate, May thought, that none of those concerned was as yet a Christian.

Mahele had been found on the following morning and carried back by members of his family to the missionary's house and May had done her utmost to save his life. It had been the day that the schooner from Misima had been due for its monthly call with the Wessels' mail and supplies.

Herbert had not made an official report to the schooner's Captain, and in failing to do so he might have been wrong, but he had hoped that Mahele would recover and had wanted to postpone any action for as long as it could be arranged, and to avoid, if it were possible, the necessity of the men having to face a capital charge. But soon after the schooner had sailed, when the victim had died, Herbert had had a case of murder or, at the best, of manslaughter, on his hands.

Accordingly, since there would be no communication with the outside world for a further four weeks, and as the island possessed neither a gaol nor a police force, Herbert had put Mahele's assailants under arrest in a hut which he had ordered to be converted into a makeshift prison, and had appointed a roster of guards to ensure that they did not escape. Both May and he made a routine visit twice daily to the prisoners in order to satisfy themselves that they were being well treated until the date when they could be sent to Misima to stand their trial.

He was most upset by this outbreak of violence, and his anguish was made the more acute as he was unable, to any appreciable extent, to communicate with or to comfort the accused men, and their bewilderment at having been apprehended for doing only what they had conceived as being their duty was another cross for him to bear, since he could not explain to them the error of their thinking.

Herbert's depression was in no way shared by the islanders, to whom the affair was fraught with drama and excitement. As capital punishment at the hands of white men had been hitherto unknown, the prisoners came to be regarded as sacrificial animals who would be called upon to expiate their misdeeds for the sake of the community, and once they had been enclosed behind bars they

enjoyed that odd veneration accorded to the doomed, being regarded, to all intents and purposes, as already convicted and waiting for the hangman's noose.

This aspect of the situation Zebedee and Boanerges endeavored
to put forward to Herbert, and they were at a loss to comprehend
why he should continue to be so cast down and to worry himself
about their fate. It had been an exciting event, a welcome break in
the monotony of their uneventful lives. The target of their criticism had been shifted from Mahele to Manè and Ke-Kulah for their
bungling in not having finished off the culprit cleanly and throw-
ing his body to the sharks, a course which would have avoided all
the fuss and interference from outside authorities as well as obey-
ing their ancient and unwritten laws.

The two houseboys, in common with Herbert's regular congregation, were devoted to their employers and were proud of
the cachet which their positions in God's House endowed them,
for the missionary's home ranked equally in their minds with the
precincts of the church. So far as it lay in their power they were
determined to help him in his tilling of the Lord's vineyard, and
none were more active in canvassing and gaining new proselytes
although, it must be admitted, conversion was looked upon more
in the nature of being allowed into a select Club than of embracing an uplifting creed.

They had done their best to increase and widen the Wessels'
grasp of their dialect and so improve their potentialities for free
expression, but it had been uphill and unrewarding work and they
had begun to despair of success.

The day before that of the schooner's expected return fell on a
Friday, and Herbert was seated on the cooler side of the verandah
wrestling with the weekly problem of Sunday's sermon, which
had to be elementary, basic, and intelligible. He had given them
The Ten Commandments repeatedly and in varying homely guises,
and was planning to discourse once more on Thou Shalt Do No
Murder, both to point Manè's and Ke-Kulah's crime and to try to
make his listeners understand the justice of retribution. He gazed
thoughtfully at a lizard plastered motionless on a newel post near
to his elbow. The task which he was setting himself was a sad and
a difficult one.

By reason of their mutually limited vocabularies his flock's perception was confined to bare essentials, and the stirring events in the Old and New Testaments had to be recounted as one would tell them to infants in a kindergarten. The Flood, The Tower of Babel, The Fall of Jericho and above all the life of Jesus Christ had come to sound in his own ears like far away fairy stories, while confusion was apt to take place over such differing injunctions in the Holy Book as demanding an eye for an eye and, alternatively, meekly turning the other cheek.

Herbert put down his pencil and decided that he would go and see Ke-Kulah and Manè once more after he had revised his sermon, and that Zebedee should go with him to act as his interpreter. It would be in the nature of a farewell for he might not be seeing them alone again. The men seemed to have no idea of their predicament or of the prolonged proceedings which were awaiting them, and their families had cast them off in new found horror when they had realized that Captain Marriott's schooner and the important island of Misima were to be involved. It would be a public scandal and would bring shame upon them all.

Herbert's visit was not a success, and despite the blood bond between Zebedee and one of the accused, it rapidly deteriorated into a slanging match, for the houseboy resented bitterly the discredit which had been brought down on them all and which had reflected not only upon Namavava but on The Reverence as well.

The evening was sultry and suffocating and the sky was obscured by a mass of leaden clouds. The rainy season was due to start, but Herbert thought there would be several days of this breathless and unbearable heat before the weather finally broke.

He was writing in his diary when May emerged from her dispensary to summon him to the evening meal. Each night he confided to the pages in his neat hand exactly where he considered that he had failed in his calling, often when he had been needed most. Tonight he had written that he should have been more resolute in the guidance of his people by setting them a more combative example in the Christian cause. If he had done so, the murder of Mahele, and even the rape of the girl, might never have occurred. He blamed himself for having been too lax.

There was no breath of wind to stir the oppressive humid air, but the table had been laid as usual on the eastern side of the veran-dah. Apart from her modest store of tinned foods, which May doled out herself with strict economy, she left the housekeeping to Zeb-edee. Their menu was supplied from such bounty as the island could provide, eggs, scrawny chickens, goat meat, and fish and fruit in abundance.

Tonight Zebedee had given them a clam soup followed by a stew of tongue with which he had served sweet potatoes. A basket of multi-colored fruit, arranged by an artist's hand, stood upon the little wicker side table.

Herbert did not say a great deal during dinner, and May told him of her own afternoon's activities. Three more of the women had come to her and had asked if they could have cotton dresses, which was a minor triumph, for they preferred to leave their breasts bare. She had lanced the festering finger of a small boy. She had written a long letter to her sister Hilda in Essex, where she was married to a farmer and was the mother of four sons. May would have liked to live near her when they returned to England. She often discussed this possibility with Herbert. She wondered why the Lord had denied issue to themselves. No doubt He had His own reasons for having done so but it had been a great disappoint-ment. May said that she hoped that Captain Marriott would bring sorely wanted medical supplies. There was hardly a drop of iodine left and her stock of aspirin and bandages was dangerously low. Besides which, they were nearly out of tea.

At the end of the meal Herbert returned to his task of record-ing the day's doings and to smoke the second of the ration of three pipes which he allowed himself. Before he went to bed he would try again to communicate with Ke-Kulah and Manè and this time he would ask his wife to accompany him.

May left him to his labors and went over to the cookhouse. Really Zebedee and Boanerges had excelled themselves. The soup had been delicious and the tongue had been more like that of a calf than of a goat. He must have simmered it for hours to make it so tender. He was a born cook and one to whom she had at once admitted that she could teach nothing. She gave grateful thanks to her Maker for having allowed them such a luxury.

"The boys" were together, talking in low voices and squatting upon their heels on the ground. Boanerges had stripped off the loose coat which he had worn while serving them and they were both of them clad only in abbreviated loincloths, one of scarlet, the other of patterned green and blue, that left their magnificent torsos and well developed limbs exposed. They leapt to their feet at May's approach.

They were delighted by her appreciation, towering over her and grinning with pleasure. "It was good, Missah?" said Zebedee eagerly. "Good, eh? But no goat, Missah. No goat." He clapped his brother on the back. "See, Boanerges, the Missah liked! The Reverence too? Now we shall see, Missah! Now The Reverence happy he will speak Namavan like native man. They will all see. Is not that so, Boanerges?" He swung round to his brother for confirmation. "Now everyone will understand what he is trying to tell us."

"Yes, Missah," Boanerges said. "As The Reverence gentleman told us in the church in the words of the Mighty Saint Paul," he frowned in an effort of memory. "'With other men's tongues and through my lips will I speak unto this peoples.'" He quoted the text with great pride. "My peoples, they shall all hear," he said. "On Sunday they shall all hear."

May was puzzled. Surely it was Corinthians 13. "Tongues of men and of angels." No, that was not right. Boanerges had been correct. What had the text actually been? "With men *of* other tongues and *other* lips will I speak unto this people." Still, Boanerges had made a gallant effort and she beamed her approval at him.

"God will speak to you in His own way," she said.

"Yes, Missah," replied Boanerges. "God will now be able to speak to us. It will be made easy for The Reverence."

Zebedee was smiling, showing his magnificent teeth. They had held a meeting last night down in the village and they had all been in agreement. "Those no good men down there won't need them no more, Missah," he assured her. "And they can now take their part in the spreading of the Gospel to the whole of our peoples. Even to those savages from Bwago and Zagu." These were two remote villages on the island's northern tip. "Even they will understand," he said scornfully. "Will they not, Boanerges?"

"Praise the Lord they will," said his brother, "now that The Reverence has had the gift of tongues!"

An icy fear struck at May. "What do you mean, Zebedee," she said. "What do you mean? What is it that you have done?"

The young giant grinned down at her. "We ain't done nothing wrong, Missah. Just turned those lazy wicked-bad murderers into good Christians. They going to die by execution when they go Misima, so why should they not help The Reverence and Missah before they are taken away?" He spoke reasonably as if May were being rather dense.

She stared up at them unable to speak, her mind battling against the implication of what she had heard. Then she turned away and holding up her long white skirt hurried past the house and down the rough path in the direction of the stockade where the two men had been imprisoned. Her plump erect little figure in its unyielding blouse and wide starched belt with the square silver buckle stood out against the background of palm trees whose leaves hung limply under the threatening sky which had drained all color from the sea. As she stumbled through the brief tropical twilight strands of hair escaped from their confining net and caressed her skin.

She would have to discover for herself what it was that had taken place before she sought out Herbert. She remembered his fears that he spoke above the heads of his congregation. Whatever the misunderstanding that might have arisen it was not his fault. He had felt it incumbent upon him that he should explain about the Holy Ghost, for was not that the corner-stone of their faith? He had had to try to share with them that glory of the Spirit which was God's most important gift to His followers. What could they do to Herbert, should something ghastly have happened? Could that saintly man be pilloried? Would he be dishonored and disgraced? Pray God that it would not be so.

At the entrance to the stockade which surrounded the hut three men lounged on guard. They were not regular attendants at the services and she saw that she scarcely knew them. They stiffened at her approach and drew closer together, for it was their obvious intention to bar her way.

"Let me pass," she called out. May did not slacken her pace until she had drawn level with them. She held out her hand for the key.

The oldest of the men gave it to her, but reluctantly. "No go in there, Missah," he said. "No go in there."

"Rubbish!" she said. She motioned authoritatively for them to stand aside and they looked at one another in some confusion.

One of the guards put a hand on her arm as if he would restrain her. "Sick," he said, nodding towards the opening of the hut. "Bad men's very sick. No go in there, Missah."

She brushed away his hand and unlocked the gate. A sound of moaning came from the interior of the hut. She took the few steps to the entrance and peered into the gloom inside. Ke-Kulah and Manè were hunched on the beaten earth of the floor, their backs resting against the wall of packed mud. Their expressions were vacant as they turned their heads to look at her with the frightening and blank vacuity of idiots.

Blood still trickled from their mouths, ebbing over that which had congealed in ridges on their chins and prior flow ebbed down upon their naked chests. Their lips sagged slackly, torn and bruised when their tongues had been hacked out. Already the flies were clustering greedily upon their bodies.

Sickened by what she saw May Wessel swayed, and steadied herself by an effort. From behind her, outside the stench of the hut, came the rumble of thunder, and lightning forked down, violating the mass of darkening clouds.

"With other tongues . . . will I speak unto this people."

THE GODMOTHERS

"Run along now, Elsie, it's your bedtime." Mrs. Donaldson glanced over at her husband, Kenneth. "Say good-night to your Uncle Ken. Quick-quack!"

"Quock!" said Elsie, completing the time honored formula. She began to tidy up the elaborate cardboard wardrobe of the cut-out doll which she had been engaged in dressing, the comprehensive changes of garments brilliant with the strident colors of the German dyes. She was sitting crosslegged on the tufted hearthrug that was spread in front of the coal fire, her black strap shoes projecting stiffly from under her petticoats. Without hurrying she deftly packed away the pieces of the toy and, with the box tucked under her arm, pecked her uncle on the cheek.

"I'll be up when you're settled," said Amy Donaldson. "No reading, mind, or you'll wear your eyes out!" She gave a smile as she listened to the child's footsteps running up the steep staircase. "There's an improvement in her already, Ken," she said to her husband, "and she's got far more roses in her cheeks, don't you think so, dear?" Ken grunted his agreement.

Elsie had been with them for nearly two weeks. Amy had gone over to Billingham Street to collect her as soon as she had been notified that her father—who was Elsie's grandfather—had been told that he must go into hospital. The neighbor who had told her so had said that it was appendicitis. So naturally she had hurried back with her. Her informant's name was Mrs. Bentley, and they had seen the old man off in an ambulance, and Amy had brought the child home. She'd visited St. Luke's as soon as he had been allowed visitors and had taken him grapes, and he'd been quite cheerful and glad that it was over, and all being well was due to return home on Saturday.

It was a bit of a squash having Elsie with them, for it meant that Edith had been forced to share her room with her, and her bedroom was small enough in all conscience, but the child had nowhere else to go, and she was a dear little thing. Three years had passed since she had been orphaned, since Alec, Amy's brother,

34

and Maisie, his wife, had been killed in that awful rail smash. She had never been able to understand why Alec had chosen Maisie, who had been both featherbrained and flighty, not to say fast. Thank goodness that Alec's daughter had taken after his side of the family. At any rate in appearance.

At first she had had qualms about letting Elsie live at Billingham Street, but the old fellow had been so set on it and had the space, after all, and they were company for each other, and Elsie knew that she could pop round to them whenever she felt like it. Not that she did so very often, only at Christmas and birthdays really, or when Jack went over to fetch her on his bike, but she seemed well cared for and in good enough health and spirits, a trifle pale, but lots of children were on the pallid side, and she would soon be starting school and getting out and about more.

Dad's flat wasn't exactly ideal, being a semi-basement, but it had water and gas laid on, which was more than a lot of places could boast, and there were three decent-sized rooms besides the kitchen; and where he had put ferns and potted plants by the area steps he had made quite a gay little garden. He was a perfectly adequate cook, and adored the companionship of children, played with them for hours on end whenever he got the chance—and the tales he made up—he was a regular Grimm or Hans Andersen, if you were to ask her opinion!

Of course he was getting on, seventy-five next March, and sooner or later other arrangements would have to be made. Maybe after Edith married Jack Stock then Elsie could move into her room permanently, and her own sister, Aggie, in Leicester would have to give their father a home. It was time she took on her share of the family responsibilities. Admittedly Aggie's accommodation was limited, but now, she would just have to face up to it, there were only herself and the two boys left there. She'd have to write to her about it one day.

"Quite a card, isn't she?" remarked Ken indulgently from the depths of his armchair. "It's as good as a play to listen to her!"

Amy began stacking the tea things on to a tray preparatory to carrying them out into the scullery. "She's quaint," she allowed, "and full of fancies. Enough to make a cat laugh sometimes!" She was pleased that Elsie had won Ken's heart. Men were inclined to get set in their ways. "I'm glad you two get along so well," she went on. "Dad's not growing any younger." After so many years of contented marriage further elaboration was unnecessary, but just to make sure she added: "Edith won't be with us for ever."

Ken took out his watch. "Where is she?" he asked. "Isn't she late in coming back, 'specially as it's early closing and all?"

"She was meeting Jack at six." Amy Donaldson smiled. "I thought I'd told you. He's taking her to the moving pictures and then she's bringing him here for supper."

"Moving pictures!" exclaimed Ken. "Whatever will they think up next!" His look was almost boyish, reminding her of the young man of her courting days. "We might go along one night, Amy," he suggested. "The two of us. Got to keep up to date!" It was the first occasion when this novel form of entertainment had been shown in their town. Ken broke off to fill his pipe. "Do you think Jack's popped the question yet?" he inquired.

"I think he will have done so by the time they get back," she said knowingly. "He's a good lad, and it will be nice having a police-man in the family." She carried the tray out of the room and Ken had to raise his voice to continue the conversation through the open door. He liked Jack Stock. He was the local light-heavyweight champion, a lively clean living youngster and, what was more, he had some money of his own in addition to his pay. Edith could do a lot worse for herself.

"What are you giving them for supper?" he called.

"Pork pie and biscuits and cheese. You got in some beer, didn't you, dear?" She knew that he was in fact in as close touch with the situation as she was herself.

"You'll find it in a paper bag under the sink."

There was a clatter of crockery. "I don't want to spoil the girl, Ken," Amy said, "but as she's that fond of Jack I've a mind to let her stay down with him for a while."

Her husband laughed, pulling at his moustache. "Which girl?" he said teasingly.

"Don't be silly," said Amy. "You know quite well which one I mean. Elsie."

There came the splash of running water and Ken Donaldson picked up his evening paper, but he found it hard to concentrate on the news for he also had given consideration to Albert Piers, who had never been any trouble to them, never intruded. In spite of his ease with, and fondness for, young society, he was, in some ways, a withdrawn individual, who might be leading the Lord knows what sort of a private life. Ken realized that harboring such thoughts about a man in his seventies was ridiculous. In all probability his father-in-law was a model of rectitude. Surely? Or was he, as Ken had suspected in the past, a man of strong sexual appetites driven underground by the Pharisaic code of the reign of the late Queen Victoria? He gave a mental shrug. It was all too idiotic. Old Albert Piers was as respectable and above reproach as was Queen Alexandra herself.

But could one ever judge, or know the temptations, concealed and not admitted, of one's fellow men? Ken Donaldson had, with a sad twinge of self scorn, forced himself to review in retrospect his own blameless past. He might have had his moments if he'd wished to take advantage. But then, he'd got Amy, and one can't have everything. All of a sudden Ken recollected an occasion when he had called on his father-in-law unexpectedly. It had been a good many years ago, and he had found him alone. He must have been reading by the gas fire when he had been disturbed, and after the two of them had returned to the sitting-room he had tried to conceal the book in which he had been engrossed by covering it with a cushion; but before Ken had left, and while Albert Piers had been out of the way getting glasses from the kitchen, he had lifted up the cushion and taken a quick look at the volume.

It was not at all the sort of thing that he'd have dreamed of having in his own house, pure pornography, that is what it had been. He remembered wondering if there was a cupboard filled with similar literature. If so, with a child around, he hoped sincerely that it was always kept locked. Bachelors and widowers had funny weaknesses sometimes. Naturally he had not mentioned the matter to Amy. She would have been extremely upset. He pushed aside these somewhat disturbing thoughts.

After a while his wife returned and settled herself opposite to him with her knitting. "It is rather nice, dear, isn't it," she said. "About Edith and Jack?" Her husband growled his agreement. The heaped coal fire gave out such a heat that she was forced to move back her chair farther to one side. Save for the clicking of the needles and the occasional rustle of a turning page there was a contented silence in the small room.

An hour later they heard the opening of the front door and the murmur of voices from the passage where Jack must be hanging up his coat and hat. Amy put her knitting down on the arm of her chair and stood up. She glanced quickly into the glass of the over-mantel above the ornament crowded chimney-piece and patted her neatly braided graying hair. "Get your coat on, Ken," she said urgently. "They're here."

Her husband grinned. "Get myself all dressed up for young Jack Stock?" he said indignantly. "He won't mind. Sits around of an eve-ning in his shirtsleeves in his own home, I'll bet. And will continue to do so when he marries our Edith, or I'm much mistaken."

"That's as may be," said Amy briskly, "but tonight he's 'com-pany', so do as I ask, dear." Ken gave an ostentatious sigh of mar-tyrdom as he obeyed.

The door to the living room was pushed open and Edith came in, Jack hard on her heels. She was bright-eyed and excited. "'Eve-ning, Mrs. Donaldson. Good evening, sir," the young man greeted them.

"Good evening, Jack. Hello, dear," said Amy to her daughter. "Had a good time? How were the Pictures? A bit jumpy, I'm told."

"It was ever so thrilling," Edith said. "All about a train robbery. It was so real you might actually have been there. And before that there was a comedy with Charlie Chaplin. Such a funny man with baggy trousers that are always about to fall off. A perfect scream!"

"Seems dangerous to me," Ken said. "All that there celluloid," he explained in case of misunderstanding. "Very inflammable stuff, celluloid."

"Crossed my mind, too," Jack said. "So we got seats right in the back row by the door." He smiled at Edith as he spoke. "And very cosy they were, weren't they?"

"Dad," said Edith, and she sounded rather breathless. "Mum! We've got something to tell you."

"Really, dear?" Amy asked, trying hard not to show her amuse-ment.

"Yes," said Jack. He turned to the other man. "I've asked Edith to marry me, Mr. Donaldson, that is . . . with your permission."

"And what did she have to say to that?" Ken inquired.

Edith laughed and ran over to him, putting her arms round her father's neck. "I said 'Yes' of course, stupid. What else did you think my answer would be?"

Ken Donaldson frowned at her. "You did, did you, young lady? If you want to know what I think," he paused before he grinned, "I think that you did quite right!"

Amy smiled happily and went over to Jack. Standing on tiptoe she rested a hand on his wide shoulder. "She's a very sensible girl," she said. "We're both of us delighted, Jack." She half pushed him away from her. "I believe that it's usual to kiss the bride's mother!" She giggled as he obliged. "Ken," she continued, "what's needed here is a celebration toast, and beer's not good enough!"

"You're right, at that, Amy, it's not," Ken said, "which is why I brought in a bottle of wine. Port wine." He was pleased by his foresight. "Just to be on the safe side as the saying goes."

"Oh, Dad!" said Elsie, and she blushed with pleasure and embarrassment. "Whatever will Jacko think of you!"

"Sit down, Jack, and make yourself at home," Amy said. "I'll give Elsie a call. She'll be so excited. A mite jealous, too!" She went to the foot of the stairs. "Elsie! Jack's here. You can come down and see him if you like."

There was an immediate scamper of feet from above, and a small figure in a long white nightdress hurtled through the doorway and flung itself in the direction of the seated Jack. Although, apart from the last two weeks, their acquaintanceship had been rather tenuous and spasmodic he had become the target for her affections. "Jack's going to be your new cousin, Elsie," Edith said a little smugly. "We're going to be married."

"And you must come and see us often," said Jack, as she perched herself on his knee. "How would you like to be a bridesmaid?"

"In white?" inquired Elsie. "And carrying flowers?"

"White with blue ribbons," the young man promised, "and a posy of primroses and lily of the valley. That suit you?"

"When?" Elsie demanded. "Tomorrow?"

Jack Stock cleared his throat. "Not quite so soon, I'm afraid." He looked up at Amy inquiringly. "What am I to tell her, Mrs. Donaldson?"

"Primroses are plentiful in April," Amy said, "and I don't think Edith could possibly be ready before then."

"But that's over four months away!" protested Elsie. Edith bent down and gave her round bottom a none too gentle smack.

"If I can wait until April," she said, "so can you." Edith could not help but feel rather vexed. Elsie was a little madam, running after all the men, already trading on her studiedly winning ways. Not as guileless as she pretended. She'd grow up into the kind of woman who caused mischief, the sort that egged men on, and then got insulted when they responded. Edith told herself that if she had the rearing of her she would turn out very differently.

Elsie sat up. "In the morning," she announced, "I must go home so that I can tell the Godmothers."

Ken and Amy exchanged puzzled looks. "Not tomorrow, dear," the woman said. "Grandfather won't be coming back until Saturday, and I'm not taking you over to him until Monday. He'll have to take things easy at first." She spoke firmly. "I'll be getting supper," she said. "No, stay where you are, Edith dear. I can manage quite well by myself." She hurried out.

"What Godmothers?" asked Jack, raising a black eyebrow.

"The ones who leave presents for me in Billingham Street," the little girl said. "They live there, but Granfer never lets me meet them. I call them my Aunts although they're not really. I think I like Aunt Madge the best of all. She's the one who gives me toys."

"One of my father-in-law's games," Ken explained to Jack quietly. "He's a great hand at story telling."

"Do they live next door to you?" inquired Jack, entering into the make-believe. "Sisters, perhaps?" he suggested. "How many of them are there, and what do the other ones give you?"

"They're not exactly next door," the child said. "They live on the other side of the walls of our sitting-room, but you can only get to them by finding the secret passages. And they're not related. At least, I don't think they are." Edith's lips formed the word "neighbors", while Ken mouthed: "Through The Looking Glass," and he winked. Elsie's fingers were plucking at the large gold chain that stretched almost in a straight line between the upper pockets of

Jack's waistcoat. His head was bent and he was smiling down at her, the flesh of his neck creased over his high constricting collar. His thick dark hair was brushed into a quiff. "There are three of them," Elsie said. "Granfer says I can meet them one day but not quite yet—when I'm a little older. Aunt Selina leaves sweets, usually gumdrops and jelly babies but sometimes penny bars of milk chocolate. Penny ones," she emphasized grandly, "not halfpenny ones."

Amy came in and began to lay the table. "I hope she won't ruin your teeth for you, dear," she said practically, resolving to speak to her father on the subject.

Elsie did not rise to this implied criticism of her benefactress. "And Aunt Dorothy," she said, "leaves me picture books. Some of them are rather babyish, but she means to be kind."

"I'm sure she does," said Ken. His attention began to wander. He was thinking about Edith and Jack. He could not have wished for a better chap, but even so he would miss her when she had gone.

"They're not really old," said Elsie. "My Godmothers, I mean. Granfer sometimes calls them 'the girls'. About your age, Cousin Edith. He once told me so." She was proud of having won their attention and was determined to hold the floor. "Aunt Dorothy's fair and pretty and Aunt Madge has wonderful red hair and Aunt Selina's a bit on the plump side, but she's ever so jolly."

Amy Donaldson put the pork pie down on the tablecloth. "That's enough, Elsie," she said.

The little girl clapped her hand to her mouth guiltily. "Don't tell Granfer what I've been saying. It's supposed to be our secret. Cross your heart?"

"Say goodnight now and run along," Amy said. "I'll come and tuck you up in a few minutes." Somewhat to her surprise the child carried out her instructions without argument. Ken was kissed, a cheek proffered to Edith, and Jack was the recipient of a bear hug and a close and damp embrace.

Elsie paused in the doorway. "It's not another secret, is it?" she asked. "About you and Edith, I mean. I can tell my Godmothers if I see them on Monday? Granfer told me he might arrange a party with them when he came out of hospital."

"It's not a secret," said Edith pettishly. "Who shall we ask to be the other bridesmaid . . . Winifred Tetley?" She straightened the yellow rosebud in Jack's buttonhole.

"No," said Elsie decisively. "I want to be the only one." She made a great labor of climbing the stairs, and pretended sleep when Amy crept in to turn out the gas; but after she had left Elsie lay awake for a long time staring into the darkness and listening to the muffled talk and laughter from the room below. She heard Amy and Ken come up to bed, and after that there was only the deep and intermittent rumble of Jack's voice. She did not hear him go.

It was a most unpleasant mixture of rain and sleet that rattled this Wednesday afternoon against the window panes. The twisted clay-like pillars of the gas fire glowed and popped, but failed to make the sombre room cheerful. Enforced confinement had made the child restless and bored.

"Granfer," said Elsie, "have you forgotten your promise?" She peered down at the stencilled shamrock which she was embroidering with big clumsy stitches.

The old man knocked out his pipe. "Have I ever done so?" he asked seriously.

"No," the child admitted reluctantly. "I suppose not. Then when can I?"

"Can you do what?" asked Albert Piers, smiling.

"Meet my Godmothers. I want to thank them. I'm sure they'll be fun." She gave him a seductive look.

"Oh yes, they're fun," he said. "They're fun right enough."

"Then can I? Today?" she persisted.

He was a large and square-shouldered man and he stood staring down at her. He had startlingly blue and innocent eyes, and his hands, although the finger joints had thickened, were still strong, and his carriage as straight as that of a man many years his junior. He had been a widower for sixteen years. "Are you ready, do you think?" he said at last. "Well, time goes so quickly, maybe you are." He went on softly: "I'm getting on, Elsie. I won't always be here to look after you, and, whatever you may hope, I shouldn't rely too much on that young chap of Edith's, if I were you. He won't have a lot of time for you, not after they're wed. He allowed his eyes to rest on her and his tongue passed over his lips as if his mouth were dry. "It might be best for you to get to know the girls," he said at last. He seemed lost in thought and after a minute had gone by he said: "I'll ask them to tea, shall I, say, in an hour's time?"

"Will you, Granfer? You are a duck!" Elsie bit off the green thread which she had been using, peeking up at him from under her long lashes.

"If you wish it." He stood with his legs apart, his hands balled deep in his trousers pockets. "And now you run along to your bedroom and tidy up, and don't come back until I call you. It'll be a surprise party and there are a lot of preparations that I have to make."

"What fun, Granfer!" Elsie stood up and looked around the room critically. Now that the day for which she had waited so eagerly had arrived she was rather nervous and obscurely dissatisfied. "We're a bit shabby, aren't we?" she suggested. "For a grown-up tea party, I mean? Didn't you tell me that you were going to finish putting up the new wallpaper when you came out of hospital?" Already she had a hostess's pride in her surroundings.

"The aunts won't notice," said her grandfather. "They're used to humble surroundings. They never spend much money on themselves." During his working life Albert Piers had done expert plastering and painting. "Be off, Elsie, and make yourself look extra pretty for me . . . and for the girls. Put on the new dress that Amy gave you, and tie a ribbon in your hair." He watched her as she left the room and he seemed to catch her anticipation and excitement.

When she had gone he closed the shutters against the lashing of the rain, turned up the gas and locked the door.

Sergeant Edward Tomlinson was due shortly for retirement. Not that he wished for it. He had lived the past twenty-three years of his life in Midhampton and, despite his origins having stemmed from East Anglia, he had made the grimy industrial town his own and it was there he intended spending the rest of his days.

On this, a Friday, afternoon, he had dealt with the routine business of the station and was now sitting tipped back in his chair, his thumbs tucked into his belt. There was no one in the inner office with him except Constable Stock absorbed in paper work. He pondered this young man with approval. Finally he said: "What's all this that I heard from my Missus last night?"

Jack raised his head, his brown eyes alert. "All what, Sergeant?" he asked.

"About your deciding to get yourself spliced, young fellah-me-lad. That's what!"

"Any objections, Sergeant?" Jack was grinning, his forehead creased. "Not against the law, is it—even for a bloody copper?"

Sergeant Tomlinson grunted. He had a weakness for this boy. One of the best lads in the district. At his age he was lucky to be able to afford to get married, but then he'd been told that he had private means, about a hundred a year, or so it was rumored. Very useful. He was in favor of young marriages, kept a man out of trouble. "According to my Missus you've picked yourself a nice girl, not like some of those empty headed flappers you see about nowadays. Mrs. Tomlinson knows her mother." He said this as if he were conferring an honor.

"Yes, Sergeant."

"Yes, what?" demanded Edward Tomlinson in pretended disgruntlement. "That's no answer."

"Yes, I have," Jack agreed mildly. He picked up his pencil and resumed his labors. He was all right, was old E.T. Pity they were going to lose him. They all of them regretted it. Called him The Walrus behind his back. It had become a term of affection.

"You might bring her round to the house one of these evenings. I'd like to meet her."

"Righto, I will. Thanks, Sergeant." Jack's tone of voice told the older man that he was being gently ribbed.

"She's an only child, I'm told. Edna. Isn't that her name? Pretty name, Edna." In the atmosphere of the strictly masculine surroundings in which they were sitting Sergeant Tomlinson's clumsy playfulness sounded false, and he was made vaguely aware of it.

Jack closed the book in which he had been working. "Edith," he said.

"Ah, Edith," repeated the sergeant. "That's right. I remember now. You can have a fag if you feel like one," he encouraged.

"Not during working hours." Jack Stock got up and took the register over to a filing cabinet. "Yes," he said, "Edith's an only child, but there's a kid cousin who's been staying at the house temporarily. Rum little thing! Going to be our bridesmaid. Lives with her grandfather in Billingham Street. Attractive. Full of—what do you call it? . . . whimsy. Told us a story when I was last there about a lot of imaginary godmothers who came when she was asleep and left presents for her. Her Grandpa fills her up with all that stuff. His name's Albert Piers. Queer sort of a cove from all accounts. Used to be in the building trade."

"Albert Piers?" said the sergeant. "It was more decorating," he corrected. "Had his own business up to about six years ago."

"That's right," said Jack.

The sergeant lit a cigarette and Jack followed suit, his prim resolution forgotten. He perched on the edge of a table and contemplated his polished boots. "Ah!" said Edward Tomlinson, more to keep the conversational ball rolling than for any other reason.

"Let me see," Jack said, "what did she call those fictitious characters?" He felt rather than saw the sergeant's quick glance at him. He chuckled silently, knowing the other man's aversion to what he thought a lah-di-dah manner of speaking. Jack snapped his fingers. "Got it," he said. "Aunt Madge, Aunt Dorothy and Aunt Selina. Selina, I ask you! One dark, one fair and one redhead. The Three Graces. Lovely girls, all. Not wizened old maids as you might have thought! Wonderful what you can do with a bit of imagination, isn't it? She keeps on pestering the life out of the old fellow to let her meet them, but no, it must be their secret, and she can't be allowed to do so until she's older, although he hinted that she might not have to wait long."

Edward Tomlinson frowned. Somewhere at the back of his brain a muted bell was ringing. About what? Jack had been saying something that had once been familiar. "Go on, Jack," he said. Constable Stock was a Londoner originally, although he'd been in Midhampton nigh on four years. He, himself, could cast his mind back a great deal further than could young Jack, especially where Midhampton affairs were concerned. "Go on, Jack," he said again quietly.

"It's all a lot of nonsense," the young constable continued, "but children enjoy it. I've not seen Edith or any of them since Saturday, been kept on the hop here," he said pointedly, "but I'm calling round tonight."

"We've all been busy," the sergeant said. "Two men off sick. It happens sometimes, but I won't forget it. Carry on with what you were saying."

"That's about all," said Jack. "I expect Elsie's back with her grandfather by now. She was going on Monday, after giving him a chance to settle down." He flicked the ash from his cigarette into the saucer of his tea-cup. "He's been ill. Why, what's the matter, Sergeant?" he asked.

Sergeant Tomlinson was staring at him fixedly. "Tell me those names again, lad," he said.

"Which ones? The godmothers'? Dorothy, Madge and Selina?" He regarded his superior in astonishment. "They're only made up. No surnames." He gave a brief laugh. "It's a kid's story, there's no more to it than that."

Sergeant Tomlinson was on his feet, his hands fastening the collar of his tunic. "Perhaps there is, lad, perhaps there's not. Tell Parkins to bring in the files for 'ninety-four and 'ninety-five—and look sharp."

"Right you are, Sergeant." Jack hurried out. A few minutes later two men sat beside one another at the table, the dusty files opened between them, with Jack Stock standing attentively at their side. The sergeant's face was grim as he looked up. "When did you say that the little girl was being returned to Billingham Street?"

"Last Monday, Sergeant."

"And she went there?"

The young man shook his head. "I couldn't rightly say."

"What number is the Donaldsons' house?"

"Sixty-two, Radcliffe Grove, Sergeant."

Edward Tomlinson said abruptly: "There's no telephone, of course?"

"No, Sergeant."

"Then get your bicycle and pedal over there like hell, and if that kid is still with them tell them to keep her. Then report back to me at Billingham Street, to the old man's flat."

"Very good, Sergeant." Jack opened his mouth to ask a question. Then shut it again and, reaching up for his helmet, went out.

It took him seven minutes to reach the Donaldsons'. He strode up to the door and banged on the knocker. He waited, but there was no sound of movement so he knocked again. Edith would be at work, and his future mother-in-law probably out shopping. He fumbled under his coat for his watch. It was half past four and already dusk. Mr. Donaldsons' printing works were, he knew, in Ruddington Street, not more than a few hundred yards away, and usually he did not leave until a quarter to six. He would go there to inquire about Elsie. He ran back to his bicycle, wondering what had made the sergeant so grave. At the bottom of the road he encountered Amy as she turned the corner carrying a shopping bag. Jack swerved over to her and dismounted.

"Why, hello Jack," she said, "found no one at home?"

"That's right." He hesitated. "Where's young Elsie?"

"Elsie? I took her round to her grandfather's on Monday, didn't you know? He's made a wonderful recovery. They're off on a holiday together on Saturday, so I don't expect to see them for a while. They're going for a month. He's taking Elsie to France. Abroad," she explained. "It's a marvellous opportunity for her, but personally I think she'd appreciate it more when she was bigger. When you think of his age, it's ever so good of Dad." She moved her basket to her other hand. "I'm going in now, if you'd care for a cup of tea?" She fell silent and then said: "Why did you ask about Elsie? Is there something wrong?"

Jack Stock did not know what to answer. "Sorry, Mrs. Donaldson," he said. "I'm on duty." He rubbed his chin thoughtfully. "Can't stop. Look in later if I may?" He remounted and rode off, leaving Amy staring after him in slight bewilderment.

A quarter of an hour's hard exertion and he reached Billingham Street where, outside number thirty-three, the station wagon was standing. A knot of spectators had assembled and a uniformed man stood on the pavement by the door, whom Jack recognized as Charlie Morland, who had been posted recently to them.

"Sergeant Tomlinson here?" he asked him.

The other man nodded. "Proper lark, this is!" he said.

"Why, what's going on?"

"You'd better go in and see for yourself." The boy's bland face went deliberately blank.

Jack walked up the steps. When he reached the hallway he halted. A grey-faced old man whom he would scarcely have known to be

Albert Piers was coming towards him flanked by two stolid constables and followed by a detective in plain clothes. Jack stood close
to the wall to give them room. He saluted Detective Inspector Rowe
as the group passed by. If Foxy Rowe was here it must be something important. He watched them enter the waiting wagon and
then ran down the stairs into the basement flat. He was haunted
by the stunned pole-axed look of the man in custody, whose expression had been that of one who had been confronted with a
forgotten horror, the impact of which had been all the more dev-
astating because it had been denied and veiled by a refusal to admit
its existence. The china blue eyes had been clouded and only half
comprehending.

Albert Piers' home seemed to be full of men. Besides Sergeant
Tomlinson and Parkins there were two of their own constables and
a further one whom Jack did not know, as well as a police photo-
grapher and the doctor and another plain clothes officer in a brown
bowler hat and a striped suit which was too tight for him. They
were congregated in the living-room, which was hazy with dust.
The policemen's faces were set as they went about their appointed
tasks. Two pickaxes were propped against a Windsor chair.

One wall was in the process of being hacked to pieces; it had
recently been partly repapered with a thick flock pattern of crim-
son and gold, oddly pretentious for its surroundings, its glossy
freshness accentuating the discolored chipped paintwork. Rolls of
the wallpaper and size were stacked in a corner of the room by a
second wall which had been prepared for redecoration, together
with brushes and a step-ladder.

Jack looked at the cluster of absorbed figures. In two of the
apertures which had been revealed were hunched the bodies of
young women, embalmed grotesquely by the action of the lime
in which they had been embedded, the skin stretched tightly over
their bones. Their legs had been forced up nearly to their chins, like
those of skeletons in a prehistoric grave, and as Jack stared at them
he saw that the stuff of their garish garments were the tatters of a
fashion of twelve years ago or more. The clothes had been bundled
in beside them, and were rotting, and rusted with dried blood.

Between them gaped a smaller opening in which lay the corpse
of a little girl, flaccid as a sawdust doll. She was wearing a white

frilly party dress and a spotted bow was in her hair, and her face was dark and swollen, the tongue protruding from between the congealed lips, as if in lewd mockery of what had befallen her. For some reason Elsie had been permitted to retain most of her clothing.

Sergeant Tomlinson turned round as Jack came in. "You were too late, lad," he said. "We were both of us too late." He left his companions and came across to where Jack was standing in the doorway. "There was a lot more to it than a child's game," he said. He indicated the excavated alcoves. "Dorothy and Madge," he said quietly. "As yet we've not found Selina, but we shall do so." Jack was gazing aghast at the rubble where Elsie lay. "When you mentioned their names and their descriptions," Edward Tomlinson went on, "it came back to me and I remembered them as if I had heard them yesterday. Selina Boucher, Madge Burke and Dorothy Johnson, three prostitutes in the files of missing people. They weren't none of them over eighteen. Well, they're missing no longer, poor little devils." He blew his nose loudly. "She was violated too," he said, nodding towards the wall. "The old bugger must have been as mad as a hatter. He could never have hoped to have got away with it again, not with that child, he couldn't." A flash bulb exploded, blinding them. "Those girls there," he went on, "were long before your time, lad, you must have still been at school. Caused quite a stir, their disappearance did. On a national scale. And to think it was old Albert Piers! Only goes to show, doesn't it?"

"So those were the . . . 'the godmothers'?" Jack said.

Sergeant Tomlinson laid a hand on his sleeve. "There's nothing for you to do here, Jack," he said. "Our men are too thick under foot already. Look, lad, you'd best be getting along to Mrs. Donaldson and your Edith. They'll be needing you more than what I will."

"Very good, Sergeant. Thank you, Sergeant." Jack marched up the stairs and walked heavily along the hall and down the steps to the street.

White with blue ribbons and carrying a posy of primroses and lily of the valley.

Now that the wagon had gone the bystanders were beginning to disperse. The street lights were softened by the first fingers of a fog. "Move along there," P. C. Morland was saying authoritatively. "Move along, now, there's no more to see. Move along, please." He glanced round at Jack. "Told you it was a proper lark, Stock, didn't I?"

Jack did not answer. He found his bicycle propped up against the railings and began to wheel it slowly up the road.

GREEN FINGERS

HILDE BERGER refilled her guest's cup. It was such a treat to drink coffee again, real coffee, after the meagre ration of that horrible ersatz stuff which tasted more like ground acorns. It had been kind of the Herr Major to give it to her, and had been even more kind on her part to share some of it with Elsa.

They were sitting one on either side of the card table which she had brought out on to the porch of the neat doll's house in which she lived on the outskirts of Krandorf, a house sheltered on three sides from prying neighbors by high brick walls against which she had trained peaches and plums and pears. In springtime their blossom was a sight to see, and when they fruited they were acknowledged to be in a class by themselves. Hilde knew that some people laughed at her for being so extremely house proud. She paid no attention to the scoffers. The floors and windows gleamed, the whitened steps were always freshly done and immaculate, the lace curtains, newly starched, were reflected as dim ghosts in the high polish of the furniture.

The garden, too, which was spacious, covering as it did more than an acre, was a credit to her industry. The closely weeded gravel walks enclosed oblong or triangular beds of roses, while during the summer months a hedge of sweet peas at the end of the main path of shaven grass shut off the vegetable section from view. On this July day both roses and sweet peas were at their peak.

Hilde leant forward, her full bosom resting on the table's top. Her large pale blue eyes considered her guest. Elsa was the exact opposite to herself, a spare dark woman with a brown and wrinkled face who might have belonged to any European country. Her niche in life had always been that of friend and confidante, despite the fact that she was a married woman of many years standing and one who undoubtedly had problems of her own.

"This is good coffee," said Elsa. "I have not drunk such coffee since the invasion was started in France." She waited expectantly for her hostess to reveal the source of this luxury.

Hilde smiled but did not reply at once. "I am afraid," she said after a noticeable pause, "that I cannot provide you with any white sugar to put in it . . . as yet." She knew that in all probability Elsa's curiosity would not allow the topic to drop.

But her question, for once, was not a direct one. "You will sweep the board as usual?" Elsa inquired. "It is becoming quite monotonous. First prize for roses . . . Frau Berger; for sweet peas . . . Frau Berger . . . for the best mixed bowl and for the largest strawberries . . . who else will it be but Frau Berger again?" Her smile was a little pinched. "There is no doubt at all that you have green fingers." What made it the more annoying for her was that she herself was by no means to be despised as a gardener, frequently carrying off third and sometimes even second prizes at the local shows, but she had never as yet succeeded in defeating her friend in any category. "If we should lose this war," she lowered her voice instinctively, "it will be women like you, my dear, who will secure the affections of the conquerors. You have all the virtues which they so much admire, domesticity, artistry and," she hesitated briefly before adding with a touch of acidity, "nice blonde looks. In you they will recognize the true peaceful Germany, you will give the lie to much of the disgusting and lunatic propaganda that has been spewed forth by the Communists and Jews and others from among our enemies."

"Lose the war?" Hilde raised her eyes to Elsa's in shocked surprise. "What are you talking about? How could we lose the war?" There was no note of warning or reproof in her voice as she repeated the words, only astonishment. In anyone else except Elsa Stein she would have regarded such a supposition as being dangerous and subversive talk.

Hilde shifted in her chair, an uneasy movement which Elsa noted. She saw her glance unobtrusively at her watch. It was clear that Hilde wanted to get rid of her. Perhaps she should have telephoned in advance before dropping in. No doubt she was expecting a caller . . . perhaps Karl Schultz? It must have been Herr Hauptmann Schultz who had been the supplier of the coffee, of that she was sure. He must be well placed for obtaining extra delicacies. Still, she must not be censorious. Hilde had been a widow for a long time now, for her husband had been killed right at the beginning of hostilities, when the army had gone into Poland.

At first, Elsa remembered, there had been a period of intensive mourning of her "dead hero". His room must be kept unchanged, inviolate, just as it had been when he had left it. His photograph, in uniform, had been draped in crêpe, and Hilde had been inconsolable. But so violent a grief naturally could not be maintained and gradually the bereaved widow had recovered. She had declared it to be her duty to take her part in entertaining soldiers who were stationed in Krandorf, far from their homes, and the crêpe had been removed, and the photograph itself had been taken from the bedroom and now stood in the front parlor. Well—why not?

Elsa got to her feet and leant forward to give her friend a kiss. "Good-bye my dear. We will meet again on Saturday at the flower show—the day of your anticipated triumphs." She walked away down the path that bisected the arrangement of flower beds. They were filled at this season with floribundas, fine enough but not comparable with those to be found at the back of the house.

She had left her bicycle propped against the knee high aubretia-bearded stone wall by the newly painted gate. As she wheeled the machine into the roadway she turned to wave.

Hilde was something of an ostrich. When she had made the remark to her about the possibility of defeat she had been personally affronted. Hilde had never been able to bear to face disagreeable facts. Anything unpleasant was pushed away into the back of her mind like discarded objects that are pushed into an attic, and the door is then closed and the contents forgotten.

Elsa had not been pedalling for more than five minutes when a small closed lorry passed her. It was one of those used by the Camp. A prisoner with the prominent cheekbones of a Slav was at the wheel and by his side, his arms folded across his broad chest, she glimpsed Herr Hauptmann Schultz. Elsa knew him well by sight although Hilde had never seen fit to arrange for them to meet one another.

Elsa smiled to herself. No wonder Hilde had been rather fidgety. There had not been a wide time margin. Suppose she had not taken the hint and had lingered! He was a well set-up fellow was the Herr Hauptmann and she could not find it in her heart to blame Hilde at all. She would have behaved in precisely the same way herself had she been given the chance, but then she was not a glamorous widow and had no opportunities for such pleasurable diversions. The presents, she acknowledged, must come in so useful, too.

On Saturday, as Elsa had foretold, Hilde carried all before her to a ripple of enthusiastic applause and merriment. She had looked very nice in a new blue spotted dress and a big straw hat which had matched her eyes exactly. She had smiled and been maddeningly gracious as she had accepted many congratulations, and had kept on explaining: "Flowers always grow well for me. It must be because I am *kind* to them!"

Standing at a short distance from the complimentary group Elsa had thought that Hilde might have been the prima donna of an operette—in a touring company of course.

Karl Schultz waited for the "kapo" who was with him to jump down from the lorry and open the door on his side of the vehicle before he himself got out. When that had been done the Major had smoothed his tunic and buckled his belt, and the man had saluted smartly and had climbed up once more to his seat, after which, as a matter of practiced routine, he had driven the lorry round to the back of the villa by the empty garage.

The Herr Major lit a cigarette and went up the path to the front door. He was aware that Hilde Berger was watching for his arrival from behind the lace curtains in the front room. She was a great comfort to him. Whenever he was able to visit her it was like stepping into another world and for an hour or so the Camp, in which he was the Second in Command, faded away into a temporary unreality.

Frau Berger had really been more than kind and had proved herself most grateful for the favors that he, in his turn, had been able to bestow upon her. His wife, Irma, was in Berlin and he saw her only when he was on leave which, if he was to be honest with himself, was no hardship. Hilde Berger was younger than Irma, more appreciative, and far better company. His rendezvous with her ordinarily took place after dusk, but lately he had been kept busy, work had grown increasingly heavier, and it had been more than two weeks since last he had seen her, and so he had seized this chance to come along in the afternoon. He tapped discreetly at the door.

It was opened immediately. Hilde made a show of surprise at seeing him at such an unexpected hour, although he had telephoned during the morning to tell her that he hoped to be able to get away. She led the way into the sitting-room and he put down the parcel which he was carrying on to the table. "For you," he said.

Hilde stood on tiptoe and brushed his cheek with her lips. She smelled strongly of "Chanel 5". "You spoil me," she said, "and I love it!" Her plump white fingers undid the string and she uttered subdued and appreciative cries as the contents of the package came to light. Sugar. Margarine. Biscuits. Coffee. A half bottle of French brandy. Two pink cakes of soap. She arranged them in a circle around an embroidered mat and stood behind them beaming with pleasure. "You spoil me, Karl," she said again.

She turned away to the sideboard upon which she had put out a dark green bottle of hock and two tall glasses, with a silver-plated bon-bon dish in the shape of a shell, which was overflowing with salted almonds, an earlier gift that she had resolutely kept hidden from Elsa and her other friends.

She poured out the hock and came towards him. When he had taken his glass she raised her own. "To my very good . . . friend!" she said with a bewitching moue. Her fat ankles bulged over the sides of her shoes. Her legs were not her best point. There came the chink of glass on glass as he joined her in the toast. "I have made a cake," she told him, "and there is also a can of beer for Zelini. He, too, is so kind to me, so helpful." She twinkled up at Karl with arch coyness. "Shall I leave them for him in the kitchen?"

"Zelini?" said Karl. He gave her a playful slap on the bottom. "He is not so very kind." He made a grimace. "He is a 'kapo', which is self-explanatory. Obedient, yes . . . but a loving heart? That I would question!" He crushed out his cigarette. "I should leave them for him now, then we can forget all about him and he can enjoy his reward when he has finished his task." Karl was faintly uneasy when he employed a prisoner on any ex-curriculum job. He was by nature law abiding and observed regulations. He could not get accustomed to the idea, as all his fellows had done so quickly, that the Camp inmates were, in fact, slaves devoid of any rights and to be used for any purpose.

Hilde went out of the room. When she came back the Herr Major had emptied a second glass of hock. He raised his eyebrows and glanced suggestively towards the door. He loomed very large as he climbed ponderously behind her up the narrow staircase. Three of the treads creaked under his weight. Hilde had been meaning to have them repaired. Every blind on the upper floor had been drawn. After all, it was natural for her to close them in order to protect the furnishings against the summer sun and it would cause no comment. Like so much else textiles were in short supply.

Stanislav Zelini put away his spade in the tiny elaborately carved chalet at the end of the garden which served Frau Berger as a tool shed. He had worked hard and he was sweating, but his labors, he realized, could have been a lot more back breaking had not Frau Berger's soil been cultivated for so long and with such intensive care.

Still, accustomed as he was to physical labor he had had enough, and he decided to peer through the kitchen window to see whether the Frau had remembered to leave out something for him. It was understood between them that anything that might be left on the shelf under the window would be intended for his consumption.

As he stood making his reconnaissance with his hands on his hips and his muscular torso bent slightly forward, his slate-grey eyes narrowed. The preparation of the ground had taken longer than he had thought. He expected every moment to hear the Herr Major's jovially shouted summons but there was no sign or sound of life from the house. He stared up at the curtained windows, his mouth bitter. Then he lifted an arm in its striped sleeve and pushed gently, probing against the window of the kitchen, which yielded to his touch.

On a metal tray on the shelf below and within easy reach lay a bottle of beer and a sponge cake sprinkled with icing sugar. Savoring the promised ecstasy he gazed at the offerings for a few moments before he reached through to stroke them with his thick spatulate fingers. Frau Berger might be a greedy and self-seeking whore, but at least she realized that people, even prisoners, were human beings.

Everybody needed friends, even Frau Berger might be grateful for one before the whole story was told. He was willing to help her only for as long as it paid him to do so, and she must know it. Was she being amiable out of benevolence—or was it a form of insurance? He was inclined to think that Frau Berger and himself were two of a kind. She had left a knife on the side of the plate upon which she had placed the cake. It was a refinement which he appreciated, and by cutting it into thin slices it could be made to last longer. He wondered as he lifted the tray through the window if she had done so in order to restore a modicum of his dignity as a man, or if the action had merely been the automatic one of any tidy *hausfrau*.

He ate the cake slowly and drank the beer with a lingering appreciation. Then he ran a spittle dampened forefinger over the crumbs and replaced the empty plate and bottle on the enamelled shelf. Next he went to relieve himself behind the tool shed, cleaned the rake before putting it back beside the spade, and walked across to the lorry to await the Herr Major's call.

He sat apathetically behind the steering wheel. His past life had paled into an unreal limbo, and his future was nonexistent. He was doomed forever as a slave laborer, utterly dependent on the whim of whoever it might be who was in control of the Camp. The Herr Major was tolerable, a weak character who would never dare to stand up to the Herr Oberst, but who knew when he might be transferred? It was paradise just to be on the outside of the electrified wire fence, away from the squalor and the suffering, irregular though such procedure was, even for a "kapo"—"trusty". It was blissful to leave its confines, and the dreary countryside around Krandorf, a hideous modern town which tentacled from a medieval nucleus, appeared to him to be as beautiful as Arcady.

He had to wait for a further twenty minutes before the Herr Major made his appearance. During their drive back he was extremely affable, even joking with his driver, and only relapsed into a stiff official silence as they approached the skeletal watch towers which were spaced out along the perimeter of the Camp's boundaries.

After the Herr Major had been driven away Hilde went out into her garden on a tour of inspection. She gave a murmur of satisfaction. The piece of ground with which Zelini had occupied himself was raked carefully into a smooth carpet of dark unmarked tilth. Later on she would lime it and then leave it fallow until the time came for autumn planting.

She had been taken a little unawares when Karl had mentioned that the "kapo" would be accompanying him. During the summer months over the past two years he had been wont to come by himself. It had been generally in the autumn and early spring that Zelini had been his accepted companion. It had been such short notice that the cake had been still warm when they had arrived.

What a dear fellow was Karl Schultz! She was distressed that he had looked so pallid, for when she had first met him he had been so robust. It was caused by all the paper work and filing that he had to attend to and which kept him chained to his office. He had told her that he hardly ever put his nose outside. Running a Camp or, to be accurate, helping to run a Camp was, he had told her, similar to running a business. He had said humorously that his job was a cross between those of an accountant and a store checker, and was concerned chiefly with turnover. His chief, the Herr Oberst Frederick laid down the discipline, and the junior officers were responsible for carrying it out, leaving him to occupy himself with the records. Confidentially, he had confided, the Herr Oberst was a bit of a bastard.

She mused sometimes about Karl's wife and could not help but be a shade jealous of her. He was so handsome and gentle and amusing, and was so methodical. He should have been the head of some important commercial enterprise. He was not really suited to war but, she thought regretfully, when finally the war was over she supposed that he would have to go back to Berlin and out of her life. He would return to that wife of his . . . Irma.

It was odd that up there in the bedroom he had sighed and said: "If we should chance to lose the war, Hilde, you, anyway, would have nothing to fear." The look which he had given her had been quizzical. His words had been the same that Elsa had used earlier in the day. How could they talk so when the Luftwaffe, the Army, the Führer himself had all proved to be so invincible? As he had spoken there had been a hidden fear behind his eyes, or had it been in her imagination? Was it possible that the civilians were not being told the whole truth?

For Hilde it had been a dreadful spring. It could no longer be hidden that her country was going down to defeat. Hamburg, Berlin, Hanover and others of the larger cities were being shattered into shapeless mounds of rubble, and the bombers and fighters that patterned the sky were invariably those of the enemy.

Karl Schultz was dead by his own hand. He had been found slumped over his desk with a bullet through his head. He had taken his life the day before the English armor had reached the Camp. She tried so hard not to think of the Camp. During February and March and well into April the people of Krandorf had been unable to close their minds or their eyes as to what might be going on there. There were horrific tales of starvation and disease, and even rumors of cannibalism, and columns of oily smoke had risen unceasingly from the squat buildings on the far side of the serried ranks of huts behind the barbed wire, making vast and wavering pillars in the frosty air, and when the wind blew from the west the stench from them had been intolerable. She supposed that the cremation of the dead had been necessary. There would have been no time for decent Christian burial.

On the last occasion that she had seen Karl he had looked ghastly. He had arrived alone. He had not made love to her. He had not wished it. So they had sat in her sitting-room and suddenly he had told her a little about his work and of the appalling conditions which shortages and fear and broken communications had fostered. "Everything is chaotic," he had said. "It is like the Black Death. It is not the Russians and the Jews that I mind. They are, after all, sub-human. It is the Hungarians, and some of the Poles, and the gypsies—especially the gypsies. Their children and their girls were so pretty, so appealing and . . . bewildered. They have always touched me deeply, but there was nothing that I could do . . . nothing. A few I managed to have drafted into hospital, until I learned that it was worse for them there." He had given her a swift tortured glance. "You understand, Hilde, don't you? The ovens . . ." he corrected himself quickly, ". . . the crematoria . . . and the mass graves . . . for them it did not seem to me to be right. They deserved better . . . a chance of reincarnation into another form of beauty . . . that is why when they had been . . . when you . . ." He had broken off abruptly and had shaken his head as if to rid himself of a nightmare. "But I don't have to explain to you, do I?"

She had been puzzled, but in his overwrought state she had not questioned him. Instead she had stroked his hair and soothed him and had made him a cup of hot chocolate and tried to entertain him with more pleasant topics.

Her garden had been her one consolation in those depressing days. She used to sit and gaze out at it from her bedroom window and had drawn some comfort from the early bulbs which were thrusting up through the thawing earth, starring the drabness with patches of color.

For the first time, too, since the war had begun, she had known hardship. She had nursed her store cupboard with enormous care, but its contents had not been extensive, and after Karl was dead and the English installed everywhere, there had been no acceptable presents coming in, and she had been forced to live on the same frugal scale as did her neighbors.

But now it was August and the situation had somewhat improved. The sky was emptied of hostile aircraft and gradually life was struggling back to a more normal tempo.

Frau Berger bicycled the two miles to the field where the flower show was being held. This year it was a month later, but the British had not withheld their permission. They encouraged such activities. Her exhibits had been collected on the evening before by Hans Stein, Elsa's young nephew, who had been young enough to miss the last call-up, and he had wheeled them away in a handcart, and she had gone up to the tent to arrange them after breakfast. The sweet peas were past their best, but the roses were still splendid as also were the early dahlias. She had every hope that she would meet with her habitual success. It would have pleased Karl, she thought nostalgically. He had been proud of her achievements.

When she arrived on the scene of action a crowd of people had already assembled. Upon a decorated rostrum a rather elderly five-piece band was spiritedly playing a Strauss waltz. She noticed at once the portly figure of Burgomeister Stockey in top hat and morning coat. He was engaged in earnest conversation with a British officer in the doorway of the main tent. It was the Burgomeister who had consented to open the show.

Hilde wheeled her bicycle over the trampled grass to the space which had been reserved for their accommodation and received a numbered ticket from the attendant in charge. Hilde had chosen to wear the same blue spotted dress that she had bought for the previous occasion, but she had freshened up the becoming straw hat by trimming it with a wreath of gardenias. She had grown thinner and the dress had had to be taken in at the waist, although her ample bust still strained against the confining silk. She was turning away and putting her ticket carefully into her bag when she was greeted by Elsa who, she observed, was unsuitably clad in a baggy tweed coat and skirt. Hilde pursed her lips in disapproval. Now more than ever one should try to look one's best. There was no need to be shabby in adversity. They walked together towards the tent. It was a glorious summer afternoon, hay scented and tranquil.

Elsa was full of information. "That officer over there," she said, "is the new Town Major. His name is Clarke. Major Clarke. His German is adequate, and they tell me that on the whole he is quite reasonable. When I am introduced I intend to practice my English on him, rusty as it is!" Smugly she was aware that Hilde was a poor linguist and had not had the advantages of her own education. She suspected that, although she now had money, her origins, before she had married Otto, had been quite humble. "I talked it more than passably well when I was a girl," she went on. "We had an English 'Miss' at the school that I attended. Her name was Angela Laycock. I can see her face to this very day. She was a fool of a woman, timid and yet bossy, a fatal combination, and she was absolutely useless as a disciplinarian. She used almost to defy us to attend to her, knowing that it was a lost cause and then, when we failed to do so, she would get hysterical."

"That must have been very thwarting for her," said Hilde in an abstracted tone. She had no patience with Elsa's airs. She caught the Burgomeister's eye and he beckoned them over to join them.

"I would like you ladies," he said, "to meet Major Clarke. Major, this is Frau Berger, one of our keenest, and I may add, one of our most invincible competitors. And Frau Stein," he added almost as an afterthought. The Major bowed in acknowledgement of these introductions. The Burgomeister produced a gold watch on the end of a thick cable chain. "With your permission, Herr Major," he suggested, "I think that we might begin?"

Major Clarke had a large brown moustache, and his gleaming Sam Browne served to emphasize his girth. He reminded Elsa of a benign porpoise. "By all means, Burgomeister," he agreed.

He accompanied the women into the tent and stood with them while they listened to the Burgomeister's lengthy speech which was larded with praise of the contributors to the show who had put on such a marvellous display under conditions that had necessarily been far from ideal, and also spiced with compliments to the members of the Military Government with whom it was his duty, and indeed his pleasure, to cooperate.

There followed the prize-giving and Hilde won two first prizes and one second for her entries, which provoked good-natured laughter. Elsa was highly commended for her mixed arrangement of wild flowers. The Burgomeister had invited them afterwards to his private tent for refreshments, and it was while they were making their way there that Elsa said: "I caught sight of a familiar face this morning coming out of their Headquarters building." She laughed lightly. "Perhaps it was one that was more familiar to you than it was to me! It belonged to that sinister looking Czech, that prisoner with some outlandish name who used to drive your . . . your good friend Major Schultz when he came to call on you." It would do Hilde no harm to know that she had been *au fait* all along with her intrigue. Elsa bowed to a passing acquaintance. "I hear that inquiries are being instituted," she continued, "as to the running of the Camp, and that many of the surviving inmates are to be called upon to give their testimony." She allowed a significant pause and shrugged her shoulders. "Personally I think it would be wiser if they let the dead bury the dead and let by-gones be by-gones. I am told that everyone is likely to be questioned, however remote their connection with the unfortunate affair." Weighed down by her bunchy costume Elsa was uncomfortably hot, her forehead beaded with sweat.

Hilde walked with her in silence to the Burgomeister's tent. She might have known that nothing could be kept a secret in a place like Krandorf. It was certain that she herself would be interrogated about her friendship with Karl, who had been an important figure and who had held such an important administrative post. It was as well, she decided, that he was dead. He had been a good man, whatever people might say now, and she was glad that he had put himself beyond their reach.

Only Elsa made a pretense of enjoying the Burgomeister's reception, and Hilde took her leave as soon as she could do so without seeming impolite. It had been stilted and boring and no one had felt truly at ease, and she had been absent from her beloved house for nearly three hours. Her departure broke up the gathering, for Major Clarke also pleaded a further engagement, with the result that Elsa arrived to collect her bicycle just as Hilde, who had been waylaid by Hans wanting to offer his congratulations, was in the act of collecting hers.

Since Elsa had to pass by Hilde's door on the way to her own home they set off together, and Elsa suggested that she might break her journey and come in for a quiet talk. It seemed ages since they had had a gossip. There was so much to discuss these days, wasn't there? What had been Hilde's opinion of their new Town Major? It was evident that she had made quite a hit with him, and such contacts could be useful. She was, Elsa declared, in no hurry at all, as her Heinrich was working late and she did not expect him back until seven at the earliest and there would be plenty of time before she had to prepare his simple supper. Hilde had no desire for company but it would be difficult to refuse Elsa's proposal or she would appear churlish and unfriendly.

The road took them into the sinking sun, which was blinding, and Hilde was further discomfited by the difficulty she was experiencing in supporting in the crook of her left arm the massive silver challenge cup which, by reason of her having won it thrice in succession, was now her property. In addition she was burdened with a smaller bowl and a large square of pasteboard to which was attached a blue rosette, an award for the sweet peas. She found it awkward having to steer with only one hand.

As they neared Hilde's gate they were astonished to see a knot of spectators gathered before it. There was also, they saw with disquiet, a British staff car and a truck parked in front of it, and two tall thick-shouldered soldiers with bands on their sleeves who were stationed, standing at ease, one on either side of the entrance.

"What is this?" exclaimed Elsa excitedly. "For the love of God what is going on here? Those men—surely they are army police-men?" She turned her ferret's face to her companion. "Military policemen!" she repeated.

The two women halted and dismounted and noticed as they did so that a sergeant was coming briskly down the path. He spoke to one of the men on guard who at once began to urge the bystanders to disperse. Hilde pushed her way with determination through the sightseers, Elsa hard on her heels. The sergeant stepped hurriedly forward to bar their way, the sunlight glinting on the brilliant black polish on the bulbous toecaps of his boots. "No one's allowed in here," he said firmly.

Hilde regarded him with coldness. "This is my house," she said in her own language. "I live here."

He gave her a blank look. "*Verboten!*" he said. "Now off you go, lady. I tell you no one's allowed in."

Elsa translated. "This is Frau Berger," she said. "She is the owner of the house."

The sergeant examined Hilde with interest, and hesitated. Then he said curiously: "So you're the owner, are you? You'd better fol-low me."

An English officer stepped, frowning, out of the front door. The sergeant saluted and went over to speak to him in an undertone and they both glanced at Hilde and Elsa.

The officer came down towards them. He was young and stern and his eyes were as hard as basalt. "Frau Berger?" he said, and took a pace to one side to permit them to pass, motioning in the direction of the hall.

"What is happening?" said Hilde, and to her vexation her voice trembled. "What are you doing in my house? What is it that you are searching for? I have done nothing wrong."

He did not answer, but waved them on into the kitchen. Through the windows they saw that the garden was milling with soldiers. They appeared savagely determined and had spades and shovels, working in silence, and with them, dressed in civilian clothing, stood Stanislav Zelini. As Hilde watched him, hypnotized, he lifted his head and his expressionless eyes met hers. She stared at him, uncomprehending. She had not thought of him in months and had had no idea until today that he had survived. He had been a minor character in a chapter of her life which was closed. She had imagined that there had not been many who had lived to see the "liberation".

At first all that she could take in was that her garden, her precious garden, had been ruined. The rose bushes had been brutally torn out by their roots, the sweet peas had been dragged up and thrown in a heap against the wall, where they lay in a cascade of broken flowers and foliage among a tangle of splintered canes. Trenches had been gouged out everywhere. Her darling garden resembled a battlefield.

And along the path of mown grass there had been tidily lined up what appeared to her incredulous eyes to be skeletons, to some of which gobbets of mold, hanks of hair, and in one instance, fragments of striped material still clung, the teeth in the skulls grinning bleakly from their disintegrated jawbones.

Hilde gazed at them, stunned, unable to take in what it was that she saw. She had never admitted to herself what the contents of the lorry might have been, never even allowed herself to make a surmise as to their nature. She had refused to dwell on it. It had not seemed important. She had always been determined to live her life on a "light" note. She had said once to Karl that gardening was impossible without sufficient fertilizer, just as she had complained about other shortages. She had not complained exactly, but she had bewailed the inconvenience. That had been all. She had asked him for nothing. It had not been her fault. She had not been responsible. She was innocent, completely innocent. She might have suspected, but she had not known. She had not paused to think. Who *had* known what went on in the Camp? No one. It was none of their business. It was nothing to do with the civilian population. In any case they would have been powerless to interfere.

Why had Zelini behaved like this to her? She had been good to him, hadn't she? She had given him cake and cheese and biscuits and beer, hadn't she, when such things had been hard to come by? She had never actually witnessed the digging in of whatever it had been that he had brought with him, why should she have done so when the "kapo" had been there? Or had something warned her to keep away? She had trusted Karl. She had detested the Camp and everything to do with it. She had thought that the lorry had brought ordinary compost, swill and rotten cabbage leaves. Of course she had!

So that was what Karl had meant by his talk of reincarnated beauty, of those gypsy girls and children—and he must have thought all along that she, too, had known and had been a willing party to it. How could he have done such a thing? How could he?

She swayed and steadied herself by clutching desperately at the back of a wooden chair, and the silver trophies which she held in her arms slipped from them and fell with a clatter and rolled around on to the oilcloth of the floor. Elsa stood rigid and did not bend down to pick them up.

The British officer's face was hard and fixed as he waited for her to speak. At last he said: "You may sit down, Frau Berger." He had about him an aura of indescribable contempt as if she belonged to a completely alien and loathsome species. It was infinitely harder to bear than if he had evinced horror. He seemed to have become inured to every abhorrent possibility, having probed into the abyss, and was past showing repugnance.

Elsa looked from one of them to the other, her eyes bright and expectant. So this had been the secret of Hilde's green fingers! A jingle that she had learned all those years ago from Miss Laycock throbbed unbidden through her head. "How does your garden grow?" That was it! "With silver bells and cockle shells . . ." She closed her eyes. ". . . and pretty maids all in a row?" She could imagine the headlines in the Press, in Germany as well as in the papers of foreign countries. The scandal would raise more of a stink than that of Belsen. Hilde must be a monster. She would never have believed it of her.

And yet was what Hilde had done so unreasonable if one considered it dispassionately? Was it not preferable to be laid to rest in a private flower garden rather than to be flung into a communal grave and covered with quicklime?

"It is women like you, my dear, who will secure the affections of the conquerors." It was less than a year since she had said those very words to Hilde, to plump and pretty Frau Berger who was so kind to her flowers . . .

Shuddering, she made herself look out of the window to where the men were still grimly excavating. The Herr Major Schultz had had an original idea in gifts. If those . . . those "things" had once been pretty maids they were certainly not so any longer despite the neat arrangement of their row. *"Oberleutnant,"* she said, "you must believe me when I tell you that I, that none of us, had any idea of what was going on . . . We were in complete ignorance about . . . about all of this. Frau Berger was never one to confide . . ." Her voice petered out.

The young captain paid her no attention. "Sit down, Frau Berger," he said, and he spoke in perfect German. "Sit down, please. You must realize that there are questions which it is obvious that you will have to answer."

Hilde's knuckles showed white through her thin cotton gloves as she lowered herself slowly into the kitchen chair.

BALLET NÈGRE

THEIR seats were of the eighth row of the stalls, well placed in the exact center. Simon Cust and David Roberts had arrived early, earlier than they had intended, for the traffic had been less heavy than they had anticipated and they had misjudged the timing.

The theatre was filling up, but although it lacked only five minutes to the rise of the curtain, the audience continued to obstruct the foyer rather than take their places. It was the première of the Emanuel Louis' "Ballet Nègre du Port-au-Prince" and the majority of the seats had been allotted to those on the First Night list of the management. These favored personages included politicians, duchesses of a slightly raffish nature, kings of the property market, shipping moguls, and gentlemen who had amassed vast fortunes by sagacious take-over bids. There were also members of the theatrical profession, both on their way up, and also down, together with a sprinkling of model girls and of those "confirmed bachelors", who take such an immense pleasure in the display of black and muscular torsos.

The first warning bell rang in the foyer and there was a movement in the direction of the aisles. The Duchess of Dumfries and her tiny simian escort took their places in front of the two men, Her Grace demanding in plaintive tones to be told in what precise section of Africa Haiti was to be found.

Simon Cust looked up from his programme. "What language do these people speak?" he asked David.

"In the country districts a kind of French-Creole patois."

"Intelligible to a Wykehamist?" the young man asked.

"Yes, if you try and take it slowly," said David. Simon gave a sigh of relief. He was covering the evening for a colleague who was away on holiday.

"It should be good," David Roberts said comfortingly. "They're natural dancers and absolutely uninhibited. Or they used to be when I was there before the war. Of course it's more than possible that their travels have degutted them," he said, surveying the sophisticated audience.

The token orchestra, which was white, and composed largely of earnest ladies, was playing a spirited selection from recent American musicals which sounded oddly at variance with the evening which lay ahead. The bell gave a second and more imperious summons and the audience began belatedly to queue, jostling in the gangways to claim their places. In order that they might be able to do so the music continued for a further period before the house lights dimmed.

A tall young man stalked to a seat near to the front, stepping as delicately as a flamingo, and David nodded in his direction. "James Lloyd," he said, "the impresario."

The curtain rose on a riot of color. The backcloth was of a nebulous plantation, sugar-cane or banana. The front of the stage was a clearing in the jungle. At either side a group of musicians squatted in loin cloths crouched over their drums and primitive instruments. After a studied pause to erase the former tinklings, the drums began to throb.

The first number was spectacular but unexciting, a dance concerning the cultivation of the crops, stylized and formal, and accompanied by muted chanting. Next came a homage to "Papa Legba", one of the more benevolent of the voodoo hierarchy. This was succeeded by a tribute to "Agoué," the God of the Sea, with a magnificently-built negro playing the part of the deity, a scene during which the company warmed up, and which ended to considerable applause.

The final item of the first half of the bill was devoted to the propitiation of "Ogoun Badagris," the most feared and powerful of all the Powers of Darkness in the sinister cult of Voodoo. The scene had been changed to the interior of a "houmfort" or temple. Against one wall stood a low wooden altar bearing feathered ouanga bags, a pyramid of papier-mâché skulls, and a carved symbol of a hooded serpent in front of which burned coconut-shell lamps with floating flames. On the floor before the altar were calabashes brimming with fruit and vegetables, adding a deceptively peaceful note.

Simon had been able to study the programme with its explanatory notes, and so recognized the characters as they appeared, such as "Papa Nebo," hermaphroditic and the Oracle of the Dead, dressed as part man, part woman, top-hatted and skirted and carrying a human skull. This figure was accompanied by "Papaloi," crimson-turbaned and sporting a richly embroidered stole, and by "Mamaloi," glorious in her scarlet robes, and surrounded by their male and female attendants and by dancers disguised in animal masks as the sacrificial victims, sheep, kids, goats and a black bull, that had surely but recently taken the place of human beings.

The stage was crowded with a motley of old and young, weak and strong, and the tom-tom drums increased the pace of their rhythm and their volume, building up into a crescendo. "Damballa oueddo au couleuvra moins." It came as a mighty cry.

Simon glanced sideways at David. "Damballa Oueddo, who is our great Serpent-God." He whispered the translation.

And now came the offerings of the sacrifices and the complicated ritual of voodoo worship, in which terrified animals had been substituted for the boys and girls of yesterday. The propitiation over, there came the celebration dances to the deafening clamor of the drums and gourd rattles, the tempo ever increasing, ever mounting, until the scene was awhirl with lithe black bodies, some practically nude, others with flying white robes and multi-colored turbans centered round "Papa Nebo," curiously intimidating, the smoked spectacles which were worn emphasizing the significance of the blind and impartial nature of death.

The dancers were becoming completely carried away, shrieking and sweating, degenerating into a beautifully controlled but seemingly delirious mob, maddened into a frenzied climax of blood and religion and sex.

The curtain fell to a thunder of appreciation, and the house lights went up. As they struggled towards the bar David Roberts said: "I have to admit that they still appear to be totally uninhibited!"

The second and final half of the programme consisted of a narrative ballet based on a legend lost in folk lore. The story was that of an overseer who, with the help of his younger brother, hired out workers to till the fields. In order to augment his labor force he took to robbing the graves of the newly dead to supplement the quota of the living men with zombies, their identity being no secret to their fellow workers, who were themselves little better off than slaves and so too afraid to inform.

After a while the younger brother, overcome by pity for the zombies' misery, for his former love had been included in their ranks, broke, from the softness of his heart, the strictest rule which all must observe, that which forbade the use of salt in their spartan diet, for having partaken of salt the zombies would at once be conscious of their dreadful state and rush back to the cemetery in an effort to regain the lost peace of their violated graves.

Included in this saga was a stupefying dance, when a man and a woman swayed and postured in a lake of red-hot ash and, so far as the audience could see, this is precisely what they did, in fact, do.

It was the crux of the ballet, which was itself the high spot of the evening, and the leading players had not appeared during the previous act. Their extraordinary performance and gaunt and ghastly make-up was breathtaking, and they seemed indeed to have strayed from another world, filling the most blasé of the spectators with a profoundly disquieting sense of unease.

Simon struck a match to see who they might be. Mathieu Tebreaux and Hélène Chauvet. At curtain fall he turned to David. "This is it!" he said. "It's quite incredible. Don't you think so? How in God's name did they fake the fire?"

"Perhaps they didn't." David smiled. "They were probably drugged or doped. Narcotics are not unusual in those voodoo rites; and the soles of their feet are as tough as army boots," he finished prosaically.

"Be that as it may," Simon said with enthusiasm, "I'm off to get an interview and," he glanced at his watch, "I'd better be jet propelled about so doing or I'll be given no more of these assignments. Not that I've designs on Baring's job. Don't think that! But I must get back to the office. Will you come along with me to interpret?"

"If you'd like me to do so," said David. "My Creole dialect may be a bit rusty. It's been a long time since I've used it."

Simon presented his Press card to the stage doorkeeper and, after a few minutes wait, the two men were escorted up to a dingy functional room where the manager of the Ballet Company was awaiting them.

He was a short fat Negro, and was wearing a dinner jacket with a yellow carnation in his buttonhole. He advanced to greet them, his gold teeth gleaming. "Mr. Cust?" he asked, looking from one to the other, Simon's card clutched in his left hand and with his right outstretched. "Mr. Lloyd has already left. He will be sorry to have missed you."

"I am Simon Cust. This is David Roberts who knew your country well at one time. We were both of us deeply impressed by the performance tonight."

"My name is Emanuel Louis," said the Negro. He shook their hands in turn. "Shall we speak in French? I regret that my English is very halting. I cannot express myself as I would desire."

"By all means," Simon agreed. "You will have noticed from my card that I represent the *Daily Echo*. I would like to have the pleasure of meeting some of your cast, in particular Monsieur Tebreaux and Mademoiselle Chauvet."

Emanuel Louis gave an apologetic smile. "I am afraid, Monsieur, that that is not possible. My dancers give no interviews. I discourage strongly the star system. We work as a team. Personal publicity is strictly against my rules. I would have liked to co-operate but I cannot make exceptions. In any case it would be useless, for neither Mademoiselle Chauvet nor Mathieu Tebreaux speaks one word of English, and very few of French." He shrugged apologetically. "They come from a remote and backward part of my island."

"Mr. Roberts," said Simon, "could translate. He could talk to them in their own patois."

Monsieur Louis seemed taken aback by this suggestion and the look he gave David was speculative. "In the patois of La Gonave?" he inquired incredulously. "That is indeed unexpected."

David shook his head. "La Gonave? I'm sorry. No."

"And I regret, Monsieur, that I can make no variations to the regulations. It is not in my province to do so. You will understand. It is to me a great pleasure that you have enjoyed the show. My poor children are exhausted by their efforts. It is very tiring. Haiti is one thing. A large capital city is another thing altogether." He was shepherding them towards the door.

"I feel still," said Simon obstinately, "that I might get somewhere with them by mime, despite the language barrier. I could telephone my copy through to you for your approval."

Emanuel Louis' face set. "I have already told you, Monsieur Cust, that what you ask of me is absolutely impossible. May I wish you both a good evening?" His dismissal was curt. Simon opened his mouth, but decided against further argument.

"I'll drop you off," David volunteered as they stood waiting for a taxi.

As they neared Fleet Street Simon said: "I wonder just why that fat little bastard wouldn't let me go back-stage. I've half a mind to double back and have another try at reaching them by by-passing the so-and-so."

"I don't think you'd succeed," said David as he lit a cigarette. "And how about your deadline?"

"Bugger my deadline," said Simon robustly, "and the same thing goes for Monsieur Louis."

David laughed. *"Chacun à son goût,"* he said, agreeably, as the taxi drew up at Simon's office.

The "Ballet Nègre du Port-au-Prince" received fantastic notices, and by the afternoon all bookable seats had been sold out for the six weeks' season, for the telephones of the agencies had been ringing since early morning. Overnight it had become a "must" for London's theatregoers.

More than ever Simon fretted about his failure with Emanuel Louis, nor was he at all mollified when he learned that the representatives of rival papers had been equally unsuccessful. During the day he telephoned David Roberts, finally locating him at his Club. "After the performance tonight," he told him, "I'm going to follow that loathsome black beetle back to where they're all staying. He can't possibly stick with them every moment, and tomorrow I'll shadow the place and wait my chance. Care to come?"

"Certainly not," said David. "The wretched fellow has a perfect right to run his own business according to his own views. And you must be aware," he added in an over-polite voice, "of my feelings regarding newspaper men, yourself included, and their thrusting ubiquity!"

Simon delivered himself of a few blistering remarks on the subject of the lack of helpfulness of the public in general and of David

Roberts in particular, to struggling journalists, and rang off before David could have a chance to elaborate his theme.

At eleven o'clock that night, having contrived to fold his long length behind the driving seat of his turquoise blue Mini-Minor, and with his lights turned off, he sat watching the stage entrance of the Princess Theatre.

He had learned from the doorman, after a friendly talk and a cigarette and the passing of a pound note between them had created the right atmosphere, that the Company was called for each night by two buses, but the man did not know, or had been unwilling to divulge, their destination, beyond the fact that it was an hotel somewhere in the Notting Hill direction which catered for "coloreds". "Accommodation is always their problem," he had said. "We had the same thing when the "Hot Chocolates" were here, and a nicer bunch you couldn't wish to meet"

Simon peered at his watch. It was nearly half-past eleven, and the transport, two thirty-seater charabancs, was in the process of backing-in to the narrow cul-de-sac. The dancers, on cue, were coming out into the street, some in their native clothes hidden under coats, others in European dress, and were starting to climb into the vehicles. They talked softly among themselves.

Emanuel Louis stood by one door checking a list, and a gigantic Negro in a light grey suit was similarly engaged by the other. When the buses were full they both jumped in and the vehicles moved off.

Simon had no difficulty in trailing such a convoy and kept at a discreet distance. In Holland Park they left the main road, and after five minutes or so came to a halt before an hotel, which had been made by knocking together two lofty Victorian houses. It had "The Presscott" painted in brown letters on the glass of the fanlights, and was sorely in need of renovation.

He was unable to pick out either Mathieu Tebreaux or Hélène Chauvet. Louis and his giant aide-de-camp were the last to enter, the latter slamming the door behind him.

There was nothing more that he could do tonight. Simon drove away, making a note of the name of the road as he turned the corner. He would be back in the morning.

Alice Linley was always glad of a talk, especially with nice-looking young gentlemen who had the time and inclination to spare to take her for a Guinness. She was established by Simon's side in the Private Bar of The Cock Pheasant, perched on a high stool.

"They get all sorts at 'The Presscott'," she said. "This district isn't what it was, not at all it isn't. Gladys, that's my friend, Gladys and I are seriously thinking about leaving our flat and moving to somewhere more select. Those Jamaicans started it. The whole place is becoming just like the Congo if you ask me. Not that I've got any personal feelings against colored boys. Some of them are very nice really, but it's no longer such a good address, if you see what I mean."

Simon drained his bitter and ordered another round of drinks. "That 'Presscott' lot," he asked, "do they get around much?"

"Thanks," said Alice. "It's hard to say, I'm sure. They moved in last Friday, I believe it was. Stacks of baggage they brought. Props and things, I expect. Great boxes and I don't know what. They're theatricals. Seem to keep pretty much to themselves. There's a short chap, the head one he seems to be. He does go out sometimes with a big fellah, black as coal. They've got a limousine car." She compressed her lips in mock disappointment. "Wish I had! Maybe some day I will. It's a long lane, I always say."

"Where do you suppose they go?" asked Simon. "I heard somewhere that they were French Colonials," he added inconsequentially.

"Couldn't really say." Alice sounded disinterested. She smoothed the cream silk of her blouse over her full breasts, and Simon could not but observe that she had dispensed with a brassiere. "It's usually in the afternoon," she went on. "Being theatricals, I'd say they'd need their rest in the mornings." Her eyes traveled with approval over Simon's athletic and square-shouldered figure. "Like to come back to my place?" she asked pleasantly.

"I'd like to very much," he said, "but I'm afraid I can't. My office calls."

"Oh well," acquiesced Alice obligingly, "perhaps another day. I'm nearly always there until the evening, and you'd be welcome." She smiled at him. "It might even be 'on the house'. I think you're sweet. Most of my . . . my boy friends are such weeds," she said, "or else they're Grandpas with pot bellies. It would make a change. I've quite fallen for you. Really I have." They emptied their glasses and stood up, going together into the street. "Ta-ta," Alice said. "Thanks ever so for the Guinness. Don't do anything I wouldn't do! I live round the corner over the paper shop if you want to find me." She walked away, swinging her orange plastic handbag, the beehive of her peroxide hair glinting in the sunshine.

Simon went back into the pub and purchased a pork pie which he took with him into the car as he settled down to begin his vigil.

The day was bright and warm. Soon after two o'clock a limousine stopped at "The Presscott," and shortly afterwards Monsieur Louis and the large Negro came out of the hotel and drove away. Simon watched the car until it was out of sight, deciding to remain where he was for a spell longer.

Presently, in twos and threes, other members of the Company emerged to take the air. The girls were mostly in flowered or patterned dresses, the men in tight suits with elaborately decorated shoes or sandals; but neither of the dancers for whom he was searching was among them.

And now a woman came out by herself. She was taller and broader than the other girls, and her carriage was splendid, and Simon thought that she it had been who had taken the role of "Papa Nebo" in the principal ballet. He pulled the crumpled programme from his pocket, scanning the names of the cast. Here it was: "Papa Nebo" . . . Marianne Dorville.

She was standing on the pavement at the foot of the stone steps enjoying the sunshine that was hardly more than a vitiated version of her own. Simon swung his long legs out of the tiny car and straightened up. Casually he walked towards her. As he drew level with her he stopped and raised his hat. "Mademoiselle Dorville?" he asked.

The woman glanced up at him in some surprise that he should know her name; or could it have been in fear? "Monsieur?"

"You speak French?" asked Simon, using that language.

"I do," she admitted, still ill at ease.

"I much admired your performance," Simon said. "I was at your opening night."

"You are very kind."

"I was," said Simon, "enchanted. I am the drama critic of the *Daily Echo*," he went on untruthfully, "which is the most powerful of the English papers, and I have come here by arrangement with Monsieur Louis to interview Mathieu Tebreaux and Hélène Chauvet . . . and naturally yourself," he finished gallantly.

Marianne regarded him with some doubt. "That is not possible, Monsieur. We never give interviews. It is not permitted." She turned away.

"I assure you that it is all arranged," said Simon. "Monsieur Louis has made a rare exception in my case. If you will take me to him he will tell you so himself."

"He is not here. He has gone out."

"Not here?" repeated Simon in dismay. "He must be." He pulled back his cuff to look at his watch. "But that is a disaster. I have to turn in my copy by four o'clock. My paper is giving your show a tremendous boost. I would be greatly obliged if you would be so kind as to lead me to Monsieur Tebreaux. Otherwise," he said, relapsing into English, "there will be hell to pay. Hell for us all."

Marianne's large black eyes clouded. "Monsieur," she said, "you are talking nonsense. No interviews are permitted, particularly with Tebreaux and Chauvet. They would be unable to answer you." She hesitated and went on: "They are talented, yes—but they are also dumb, and comprehend nothing of the outside world."

"Dumb?" He searched her face. "How do you mean, dumb? Stupid?"

She shook her head and indicated her own tongue. "They cannot speak. They have suffered from this affliction since their birth. Unhappily there are many such in my country." Her gaze was as impassive as that of an image.

"I see," said Simon. So they were dumb, were they? And Louis had told him that they could speak only some obscure dialect. It didn't tie up. It didn't tie up at all. Regarding her pensively Simon realized that she was beautiful. She hailed from Byzantium or from the land of the Pharoahs or from the drowned continent of Atlantis. She came entirely from the past. "Where are they?" he shot the question at her abruptly.

"In the room next to Monsieur Louis'," said Marianne before

she could stop herself. "But you will not be admitted. You can
spare yourself the trouble."

"I thank you," said Simon. He ran past her and up the steps into
the lobby of the sleazy hotel. Marianne watched him go in a state
of considerable distress. Then she followed him into the house,
and darted into the telephone booth which stood in the hall.

Simon took the stairs two at a time. He had no way of knowing when Emanuel Louis would be back. Halfway up he nearly
collided with a child that was on its way to the street. It could not
have been more than ten years old. Simon took a shilling from the
pocket of his trousers. "Monsieur Louis?" he inquired. The information would confine his quest to the two adjoining rooms.

The little boy took the coin, regarding him seriously out of
huge dark eyes. "You will find him in Room 12, Monsieur."

"Thank you." He found himself on a landing crowded with
doors. Their positioning made it clear that the big rooms of the
old house had been divided and sub-divided, again. The numbers
ranged from one to ten. He listened, but the house was quiet save
for a muted crooning from a room on his left and the murmur of
women's voices from further down the passage.

He tiptoed to the floor above, which was a replica of that which
he had just left. The same walls of arsenic green, the same cocoa-
brown dados and surrounds, and all around like incense was the
sweetish smell of colored people, which was vaguely reminiscent
of musk. Simon found it at once both repugnant and exciting.

From the end of the corridor came the sound of imprecations
and the rolling of dice. The ejaculations were agitated and guttural.
He knocked on the door of number 11. There was no answer. He
knocked again. Dead silence. He tried the door-knob and rather to
his astonishment it opened at his touch. There was no one there.
So it must be number 13. Twice he knocked and once more there
was no sign of occupation. There were footsteps coming up the
stairs. He could not risk discovery. He went in. The room was high
and narrow. At one end an altar had been erected, a twin of that
which he had seen in the "houmfort" at the theatre, except that he
had an idea that the skulls which he was seeing were not made of
papier-mâché.

There were two mattresses thrown on to the floor, and lying

upon them were the couple for whom he had been searching. They lay there motionless, arms to their sides, and their eyes, turned to the ceiling, were filled with sadness and desolation. They made no movement at his entrance nor gave any acknowledgement of his presence. Their clothes were those which they had worn in the ballet in which they had danced.

Simon froze where he stood, unwilling to go further. "My apologies," he said, "if I am disturbing you. I am a Press reporter and have come here at the request of Monsieur Emanuel Louis. I represent the *Daily Echo*." Still there was no reply nor reaction and he stepped forward. "You do not understand French?" he asked. Only their eyes registered that they possessed a semblance of life. At closer quarters their faces were hideous and heart-breaking, the lips drawn back from prominent teeth, the skin taut over jutting cheek bones. "You are ill," he said gently. "Shall I get you a doctor?" He received no answer and walked forward once more until he stood gazing down at the emaciated forms. "You are hungry?" he suggested. "Is that it? You are hungry?"

And now the girl spoke, and her voice was as soft as the wind blowing through willow trees. "Yes," she whispered. "We are hungry. Oh, so hungry." Her jet black hair hung in ragged pennants to her shoulders. Simon dropped to his knees beside her and groped for her pulse. The grey skin of her wrist was as cold as that of a dead fish.

At his back the door was pushed open unobtrusively, but it gave a slight creak which was sufficient to make him turn his head. The doorway appeared to him to be filled and crowded with people. Emanuel Louis, who was grasping a revolver in his hand, the immense Negro in the pale suit, Marianne Dorville, saucer-eyed with apprehension, and behind her the craning necks and dusky terror-stricken faces of a tableau of other men and women.

Emanuel Louis' face was stiff and contorted by rage. "Get out!" he said. "Leave this room immediately. I will not have my artistes upset by such behavior. If you must know, they are suffering from fever, from grippe, but it is not serious. It has happened before, and they are under my personal supervision. You are committing a trespass, and if you refuse to take yourself off at once, I will summon the police. Your actions are insupportable—beyond all reason. Get out! Get out! Will you leave, or must we throw you into the street?"

Simon got to his feet. "That will not be necessary, Monsieur Louis," he said. "And you can put that thing away," he added, pointing to the revolver. "I must warn you, however, that it is illegal to carry weapons in this country. And also that you have two very sick people on your hands."

"Go," said Louis, "and should you try to return I warn *you* that I will not hesitate to have you arrested." He was so choked by his fury that he could scarcely speak.

Simon said no more. He walked over to the doorway, and the rows of black faces divided to let him pass. He was shaking as he got into his car.

In the evening he visited the Princess Theater for a second time, standing at the back of the dress circle. Both Tebreaux and Hélène Chauvet were dancing, and their performance was as good as the one which they had given on the first night.

David Roberts must have been right. Perhaps, after all, they were dope addicts. But Simon was by no means satisfied. There was a story here, and he was determined to get it.

It was after midnight when Simon reached "The Presscott." No lights showed, and he walked round to the tradesmen's entrance and down a flight of steps leading to an area. Here there was a glow from a curtained window of what he took to be the kitchen. There was a bell in the surround and he pressed it.

It was opened by a mulatto in his shirt sleeves and a tattered pullover, who stood there waiting for him to speak.

"I know it's very late," Simon said, "but I wondered if you could by any chance oblige me by letting me have a room? It would be for tonight only. I arrived from Cornwall an hour or so ago and I can't get a bed anywhere."

The mulatto stared at him with mistrust. "No," he said, "I can't. I am full up. This hotel is for colored people." He made as if to shut the door in Simon's face.

"I don't mind that at all," Simon said. He produced his wallet, from which he extracted a five pound note. "I only want somewhere to sleep, and perhaps a cup of coffee in the morning."

The man eyed the note. Then he turned away. "Olive!" he called. "Come here a second, will you? There's a bloke out here who wants a bed. He's a white feller." He pushed the door nearly shut once more, and Simon could hear a muttered colloquy coming from behind it. There was a lighter step, and through the crack he was aware that a fair-haired woman was inspecting him.

Apparently satisfied by what she saw, she said: "Come in, won't you? As my husband told you, we are full up, but if it's only for one night, and you don't mind roughing it, I daresay we could let you have Ivy's room. She's my living-in maid, and a lazy slut. Her mother's been taken poorly, or so she says, so she won't be coming back until tomorrow afternoon. 'Clinging Ivy' I calls her, the way she throws herself at those black chaps. She'll get what's coming to her one of these fine days if she doesn't look out. They're only human, aren't they, same as the rest of us? Girls are so inconsiderate these days. But you can't pick and choose, more's the pity, you can't by any manner of means, and well they know it! No luggage?" she finished sharply, looking at his empty hands.

"I'm afraid not." Simon thrust the note towards her. "Will that do instead?"

"Not on the run, are you?" she asked him suspiciously. "We don't take that sort here."

"No," said Simon, "I'm not on the run."

Olive's hand closed on the five pounds. "It's just to oblige," she said. "We don't usually accept men without any luggage. Certainly not at this time of night. If you'll follow me I'll show you your room. It's nothing very grand." He went up behind her to the top floor, and to a door that had no number. "The bed's not bad," said the woman defensively. "And it's clean. You'll find no bugs in my house. What time would you be wanting calling in the morning?" They had encountered no one on their way up.

"Half-past seven?" Simon suggested, knowing that long before that he would be gone.

"Righty-oh. Whatever you say." She glanced around her. "Ivy's left her things, I see. Still, you won't be needing cupboard space, having brought no luggage. Well, good night." Her pin heels clattered away down the staircase.

Simon took off his coat and removed his shoes, and stretched

out on the bed, which protested loudly under the weight of his
fourteen stone. He would give his landlady and her husband half
an hour in which to retire. He must have dozed, for when he
looked at his watch it pointed to a quarter to three.

Jumping up he crossed in his stockinged feet to the peg on
which he had hung his coat, and took from its bulging pocket a
packet of sandwiches, which had been thickly stuffed with nearly
raw beef. He had remembered the whisper of the girl in room 12.
"We are hungry. Oh, so hungry."

Their room must be on the floor below his own. He stuck his
head over the stair-well. There was a dim bulb burning on each
landing. Cautiously he made his way down, hoping that there would
be no loose treads. On the landing he stood listening. From behind
the door nearest to him came the noise of rhythmic snoring.

He reached number 13 and slipped inside, for it was not locked.
It was in darkness, but he could hear no breathing. He might have
been in a tomb. He had satisfied himself that there was no tran-
som, so he fumbled for the switch and turned on an unshaded light.

The man and the girl were lying just as he had last seen them.
"Do not be afraid," he said in a whisper. "I was here to see you yesterday and this time I have brought you food. There is no reason
for you to be afraid of me." He leant down and closed first the
girl's cold fingers and then those of the man round the gift that he
had brought them.

Their fingers gripped like pincers into the soft bread, and slowly
they raised it to their mouths. Simon looked at them with compassion. Drugs, he thought, that is what it is. The pupils of their
eyes had dwindled to pin-points. They were chewing on the meat
convulsively, their mouths crammed.

And now they were stirring and raising themselves up from the
mattresses, and their eyes were changing. The sadness and hope-
lessness was fading, and a fierce intense hatred was taking its place.
Appalled by what he saw Simon jack-knifed to his feet, but quick as
he had been, they too had leaped up and were upon him.

Mathieu closed with him and his scrawny arms had in them
all the strength of steel. Exerting every ounce of his considerable
force Simon was barely holding his own with his assailant. And
then the girl, uttering a piercing shriek of passionate and diabolical

rage, snatched up a curved knife from the altar and clawed herself up upon his back.

Simon knew that he was being overpowered and had no chance and, weak with fear for the first time in his life, started to shout for help. The girl had twisted her hand into his hair and was forcing back his head, exposing his throat. And the knife flashed once in the light from the unshaded bulb. Simon's cries ceased, smothered and silenced by the bubbling blood that gushed into his windpipe.

There came the patter of running feet, and of calling, and amid a great confusion and tumult the door was burst open and Emanuel Louis ran into the room. Almost at his feet lay the body of Simon Cust, the throat from which his lifeblood was pouring had been slit from ear to ear like that of a sacrificial animal.

Emanuel's eyes passed on to the dirty matting on the floor where a beef sandwich was oozing from its torn wrapping. It was clear to him what had taken place. His charges had been fed meat. Meat and salt; those were the forbidden foods of zombies, the keys which would give them back their memories, and the interfering fool had not known it. So they had turned and rent the first man they had seen, judging him to have been responsible for their final degradation.

The two occupants of the shabby room, blood spattered and with their arms hanging loosely by their sides and nearly to their knees, brushed past him blindly. Along the passage, lined with horrified Negroes, they went, and passed unmolested down the stairs and out into the deserted street.

Emanuel Louis let them go, for it was useless to try to stop them, and then in his turn he paced through the waiting and watching men and women and went down the hall and to the telephone. As he reached it a woman began to wail from above and soon all had taken it up in a weird and uncanny lament.

Having made his call, Emanuel Louis sat on a hard chair by the booth and waited. He had not long to wait. In a very few minutes there was a screech of tyres as a squad car braked to a halt in front of the house and there was a roar of motor bicycles, and the hall became filled with policemen, two of them middle-aged and in plain clothes, and a uniformed constable, and a young Hercules in crash helmet and leather-encased legs who stood behind them with his hands planted on his belt. From the street more men could be heard arriving.

Emanuel Louis led them up to the room where Simon Cust was lying, and for a moment the men stood in a shocked semi-circle eyeing the body. The smaller of the plain clothes men was the first to speak. "Stop those damned niggers making such a bloody din, can't you?" he said. "It's enough to turn your stomach."

His companion also swivelled round to face Emanuel Louis. "Well," he said, "are you going to tell me which one of you is responsible?"

The plump little man stared back at him sorrowfully. "I am going to tell you," he said. "Those who have done this thing have gone. They have gone I do not know where, but it will be to the west."

"What's that?" demanded the police officer. "You admit that you know the identity of the murderers? Why the hell did you let them get away?"

"They will be making for the west," said Emanuel Louis once again, scarcely seeing the stern and stolid faces that surrounded him, "for when the Living Dead realize what they really are, they always head for the graves from which they have been dragged."

THE LESSON

THE party had thinned out, as well it might, since the hour was past nine o'clock, and the invitation had clearly stated "Cocktails 6.0–8.0." However, a hard core was apt to remain, and in this case the lingerers comprised Waveney and Milton Payne and "Mumso" Vivian. And Oscar Landmore.

Oscar had become extremely drunk. He had long since taken over the duties of host from Rupert, and seemed to be ever present at somebody's elbow with a freshly made jug of Martinis in his hand, or else hovering by the table on which clustered bottles of whisky and half emptied siphons, exhorting one and all to refill their glasses with that warm and enveloping hospitality shown by a fellow guest who has no plans of his own for the evening.

He weaved up to Mrs. Vivian. "Can I get you another 'mumso,' Bloody Mary?" he inquired with cheerful solicitude.

Mrs. Vivian was not amused. She did not care for drunks, whom she found tedious. She considered that Gina and Rupert should make a point of discouraging such conduct as Oscar Landmore's. The handsomely beautiful woman gave him a look which would have gone far towards quelling a mutiny. "Nothing more for me," she told him coldly. The Paynes were saying good-bye. She was dining with them and playing bridge, otherwise she would have taken her leave long before. She wondered how Bobby Clarke, who was to make their fourth, had liked being kept waiting.

"On Thursday, Gina," Waveney was saying, "and no more grumbling about the stairs! If Honor can manage them then so can you. It's not absolutely necessary to have had a sherpa's training if you lunch with me!" she finished with a touch of tartness. They moved together into the red papered hall, raising a hand or nodding to Oscar as they collected their coats and prepared to go out into the rainy November night.

"I'll come down with you," Gina said. "You'll never find the lights. They're automatic and turn themselves off. It's one of the management's economies. A sort of battle of wits and mobility—a

85

combined operation which a novice has no chance of winning."

Rather to her astonishment Rupert followed them into the lift. It was a tight squeeze. Grouped in the doorway and peering out into the rain they saw that it had increased in density and was sheeting down. They stayed bunched together and talking in the lobby for quite a long time, hoping that it would ease off, for the Paynes had been forced to park their car on the other side of the Square. Finally Milton said to his wife: "I'll go. It's useless waiting any longer. You girls stay here." He turned up the collar of his coat and plunged gallantly into the deluge.

As they turned away from seeing off their departing guests Gina said: "We'll have to ask Oscar to dine, darling. He's nowhere to go, and is really in no fit state to be turned loose."

Rupert groaned. "I thought we'd arranged to eat out," he said. "I'm not taking him with us to 'Umberto's'. He'd tack around it like an out of control sand yacht."

"We'll have to get something from the delicatessen," Gina said, "and stay here. It's not very far and doesn't close until ten. I'll fill him up with black coffee, so for God's sake don't give him any more booze." She discouraged Oscar's visits from becoming too frequent, for when he came to see them Rupert, under his friend's influence, was inclined to drink too much himself. In fact, glancing at him, she thought that her husband was a little high even now.

"What a bore he is!" said Rupert, oblivious of Gina's unspoken criticism and more than half to please her.

They had known Oscar Landmore for many years and known him well, Rupert especially, in fact the two of them had been together at Harrow. As a young man Oscar had been gay and amusing and greatly in demand, but at forty a large and regular daily intake of alcohol had become a "must" to keep him going, and not just a pleasurable social stimulant. He had remained kindly and obliging, and was totally ineffective, and children were still able to appreciate his innate goodness and gave him their confidence and love. He was usually hazy and rather fuddled, a happy prisoner in a world of his own, unconsciously trading on the memories of days gone by.

He had been married at one time to a rich and attractive American wife and their union had lasted for six years, but his lack of ambition and his unreliability had wearied her and she had left him and subsequently remarried, and his existence now had grown aimless and a shade pathetic. If one were lucky enough to catch him sober he possessed a lot of his former charm, but such occasions were becoming less and less frequent, yet for old times sake it was impossible to shrug him off uncaringly. His boyish good looks had vanished, and his laughing eyes, which had been of a bright blue and which had been his chief attraction, were faded and slightly milky, and sad and affectionate and compassionate in the puffy face.

As Rupert unlocked the door of their flat and fumbled with the key in the lock there came the sound of scampering feet from the direction of the small bedroom to their left. "Milo!" called Gina. She tried to sound stern. The child should have been asleep an hour ago, although she had to admit that the racket of the party would have made actual slumber difficult, if not impossible, but tomorrow was a school day, which had been one of the reasons why her seven-year-old son had been packed off to bed early. It had been arranged for him to go to his grandmother in Felixstowe for the week-end, but Rupert had grown stubborn and had said that he must wait until Saturday. Already he had started to fuss about the child missing his lessons.

Milo adored Oscar, which was another factor for his having been confined to his room—to save both of them from mutual embarrassment. It would distress the boy to see his idol staggering and behaving foolishly, and for the same reason Oscar, too, had a right to their protection.

Gina went into her own room to comb her hair and Rupert crossed over to the bed in which the little boy was lying with screwed-up eyes and as rigid as if held in the grip of rigor mortis rather than in the more relaxed one of sleep. Beside him on the pillow reclined Penny, an ancient broken-beaked and battered penguin that had lost most of its stuffing, and to which Milo had been fiercely attached ever since babyhood.

His father pulled out his watch and saw that they had been away for more than twenty minutes. He wondered how much more of his whisky Oscar had managed to consume. They would have to hurry if they were to get to the shop before it shut. Rupert prodded his son with his thumb. "You're not fooling me!" he said. "What exactly have you been up to?"

Milo kept his eyes closed, but he could not help smiling. "Um?" he said, and gave a prodigious yawn.

"You've been to the drawing-room," said Rupert accusingly, "to see Oscar. Haven't you?"

The little boy sat up abruptly, his face bright with excitement. "Yes, Father. We've been playing at space warfare. He was a wicked Martian and I was Jeff Hawke and I captured him with my deadly paralyzing ray-gun and made him my prisoner, and I tied him up with a helmet over his head as our atmosphere is too strong for him, and now he can't move at all as I've trussed him up so well," he finished with satisfaction.

"A helmet?" queried Rupert.

"Well," Milo admitted reluctantly, "I broke my proper one, so it was a plastic bag really, the one that Mummy's new yellow jersey was packed in. It's a bit crinkly, but it does O.K. for a space helmet if you're not too fussy. And then just as I finished I heard you coming back so I jumped into bed so that you would find Oscar as a surprise. We arranged it between us. I had to climb on to a chair to do it," he went on, "but I must admit that he was quite copulative," he added graciously.

Rupert grinned. "I think that 'co-operative' is the word you mean," he said, "and it was wise of you to get back into bed," he added drily.

"Why, what does the other word mean?" Milo inquired.

His father laughed. "It is capable of several interpretations," he said.

Gina joined them and bent to tuck Milo up and kissed him good night and then lingered, while Rupert went on to the scene of rather squalid chaos that is the aftermath of cocktail parties.

He found that the Martian prisoner had been roped to one of the three pillars which separated the dining alcove from the drawing-room, and that Milo had made a professional job of securing him. As Rupert came in Oscar inhaled and blew out his cheeks, unable to speak owing to the balled up handkerchief which had been stuffed into his mouth. Being a natural comedian and greatly addicted to playing the fool he rolled imploring eyes desperately at his host, who professed to ignore his presence.

Rupert lit a cigarette before going over to release him, then, when he was reaching out to do so, he changed his mind. "You can stay right there where you are, old fellow," he said, "and sober up." He glanced meaningly at the drink table. "We're generously inviting you to dine and we've got to go out and get the food, so be a good fellow while we're gone. We won't be more than ten minutes, and you're staying trussed up until we return." Rupert shook a clenched fist at Oscar in mock anger. "It will serve you right for over-exciting Milo, who was given strict instructions not to get out of his bed!"

Gina caught a glimpse of part of the captive from where she was standing in the hall. "There's no need for you to come, Rupert," she said. "Take the dirty glasses and empty bottles into the kitchen for me and start tidying up, there's a darling."

"I want to come," Rupert insisted. "I could do with a breath of fresh air."

"Then untie poor Oscar first."

"The hell I will!" Rupert inspected his son's handiwork. "Oscar must be taught a lesson." The knots were tight, but not so tight as to be painful. He straightened up and brushed a scatter of cigarette ash from his waistcoat. "He'll do," he said with quiet satisfaction. He gave a friendly grin to Oscar, who was growing alarmingly red in the face with his futile efforts to communicate. "'Bye, old boy!" he called. As they passed Milo's door he said: "That child is wonderful with his hands. Even Houdini would have had a problem getting out of that lot!"

"'Night, Milo," Gina called out. "If you get up again I'll skin you alive. 'Night, ducky."

"'Night, Mummy."

The rain was not quite so heavy, and they hurried across the pavement to where they had left their tiny Austin, and Rupert laboriously arranged his long length behind the steering wheel, jabbing with impatience at the lever with which to push back the seat for extra leg room. The windscreen wipers went into valiant frenzied action. He engaged the gear and the car jerked forward. Gina looked at him anxiously, "Would you sooner that I drove?" she suggested.

"No, thank you. I'm perfectly capable of driving." He spoke

shortly, annoyed by her implication that was a questioning of his sobriety.

Gina compressed her lips and said no more until he had over-shot the turning which he should have taken. She sat tensely, aware now that she should have insisted upon driving. Rupert swerved violently to avoid a wavering bicycle that had no rear light, and the front wheel of the Austin bumped jarringly against the kerb. "Do be careful, Rupert," she said, then added: "You'll have to take the second on the right. Macey Street has been made one way."

"We've got to step on it," Rupert said. "They'll be shut in five minutes."

"For God's sake!" said Gina as an island with concrete defenses veered towards them. "Rupert, *stop!* Let me drive. Don't be so idi-otic. The road's like glass. What's so important about buying a tin of tunny fish and a packet of spaghetti compared to *life?*"

Rupert did not answer. He kept his eyes straight ahead, the line of his mouth sullen. They arrived at the delicatessen just as the shutters were going up. Gina hurried in. A few minutes later she returned carrying her parcel. Rupert had not got over his annoy-ance and began to drive away with exaggerated caution. While they waited for the traffic lights to change to green he relented and said: "Milo's certainly an imaginative little beggar."

"Yes," said Gina. "I think that he is." She was always ready to discuss her child. "In what way in particular?" she asked.

"Using your plastic bag as a space helmet," said Rupert laugh-ing. "The one that your jersey from Harrods was packed in."

"Helmet . . ." she said. "What do you mean, 'helmet'?"

"The bag. He crowned Oscar with it!"

"Was that what it was?" Gina was silent for a moment and then drew in her breath and laid a hand on Rupert's sleeve. "Rupert," she said urgently. "He'll be in danger. Oscar. Was it tied round his neck? If so, he won't be able to breathe properly—there'll be no oxygen."

Her husband did not answer immediately. "I believe that it was," he said thoughtfully. "What a bloody fool I've been!"

"Then for the love of Christ hurry!" said Gina. "I read only the other day that a baby had suffocated itself in that way—in a matter of minutes."

Rupert looked at her appalled before putting his foot hard down on the accelerator, and the small car shot forward out of the side turning which led on to Chelsea Embankment.

A van had been parked on the corner, obscuring their view of the road, and as they shot forward past it they saw too late that an enormous lorry was bearing down on them at speed from the right. The driver of the vehicle was perched in his cab far above their heads. The immense wheels loomed over them. There was the tear of crumpling metal, a screeching of brakes, and Gina instinctively raised an arm to try and shield her face as a shower of splintered glass fell in from the shattered windscreen. The Austin turned over onto its side, entangled with the lorry, and was dragged along. Then there was nothing but confusion and agony and darkness.

Sister Carstairs raised her eyebrows at Nurse Butlin and then bent lower over the narrow bed. The patient was in great distress. Although her face had been deeply cut, and despite the fact that she was badly concussed, the poor dear was obviously endeavoring to tell them something.

Sister Carstairs trusted that it would not fall to her to have to break the news of the husband's death when the patient had recovered sufficiently to be informed of it. She pursed her lips. Of course it was always possible that his life might be saved. They were working on him at the moment in the theatre, but he had grave injuries, very grave indeed.

Gina's head turned from side to side on the pillow. Her eyes were open but unseeing, and she was talking quickly, her words slurred and run together. Nurse Butlin whispered: "I think, Sister, that she's worried about the loss of her handbag."

Sister Carstairs gently touched Gina's forehead. "It's quite safe, dear," she said. "Your handbag is being looked after for you. You had it with you when . . . when you went out. Don't worry, dear, nobody will steal it. Everything is being taken care of, and there's nothing at all for you to be anxious about. Just try and rest."

"Bag . . ." repeated Gina. "Somebody must . . . remove the bag. Important . . . dangerous . . . Miloscar . . . life or death . . . the bag . . . it must be taken . . . it must . . ." She made an effort to raise herself in the bed.

"There, there, dear!" said Sister Carstairs soothingly. "You have not lost your bag. You must believe me. We have it here. You can see it if you like. It's in the office. I will go and get it for you." She nodded to Nurse Butlin to stay with the patient and walked briskly away.

What a terrible waste of human life these car crashes caused. It was pitiable, and a large proportion of them were so unnecessary since they were caused by drunken driving. Not that she had proof that Mr. Cumberland had been drunk, but tests had shown that he had lately consumed a quantity of alcohol. After their identities had been established the young police constable had gone round to the Cumberlands' flat. Naturally the hospital had telephoned there at once, but there had been no answer. Like most people nowadays they had probably no living-in domestic, or perhaps it had been the maid's night out.

Fortunately identification had been easy. Mr. Cumberland's name and address had been on the driving license in his notecase, and his wife had been carrying among her effects a letter which had been addressed to her. Sister Carstairs sighed. When would people be made to realize the criminal folly of driving when they were not sober? Why had they to be in such a frantic hurry? "More haste, less speed" was a truism if ever there had been one. She hoped sincerely that there were no children to whom it would have to be broken that they had lost their father.

As she sailed back down the ward with Gina's bag in her hand she saw Nurse Butlin smile and raise a cautionary finger to her lips. The sedative had taken effect and the patient was sleeping.

Milo could hear the shrilling of the telephone. He opened his eyes weighed down by fatigue and groped for the flex of the lamp by his side. It was a quarter past eleven. He had been dozing. Gradually memory returned. Surely his parents must be back. Perhaps they had already gone to bed. Anyway it was none of his business whoever it might be.

The dual summons continued. No one was answering it. There was an extension in the hall as well as one in his parents' bedroom. Milo was wide awake. Maybe, after all, he should see who it was. As he lay there listening and making up his mind to get up and do so, the ringing stopped.

He began to wonder where his mother could be. He had over-heard his father saying, presumably to Oscar, that they were off to buy something for dinner but that they would be back soon. Surely that must have been hours ago? And he hadn't heard Oscar leave. His father must have untied him and he had slipped out quietly without his hearing him. He decided that he would run along and see.

All the lights were on. He buttoned up the jacket of his pepper-mint-striped pyjamas and went out cautiously into the hall. The drawing-room door was ajar and he caught sight of Oscar who was, to his surprise, still tied to the pillar, just as he had left him. He felt a spasm of guilt. Why had he not been released? It had been a game that they had been playing, that was all.

Milo put his head round the side of the doorway. Apart from Oscar the room was unoccupied. He walked in with dragging footsteps and stood eyeing the bound figure. "Oscar?" he said ten-tatively.

The figure did not stir and Milo swaggered twice round the pillar, hands on hips, inspecting his prisoner. Then, with arms akimbo, he stopped directly in front of him. "Hello," he said. "Hello, Oscar."

He noticed with dismay the lolling head and the congested blue-lipped and blood-suffused face. The body drooped forward against the restraining cords as limply as a straw-stuffed effigy. "Oscar . . ." Milo said again and more loudly, and this time his voice quavered.

He stood staring at the man's body without making a move-ment. From the Square below the curtained windows there came the sound of a car driving away amidst a chorus of shouted "good nights".

The child did not know what to do. He remained gazing sol-emnly up at the figure in the transparent helmet, his expression worried and puzzled. He could not bear the silence in the room and he began to talk to himself in an authoritative voice. "Don't be frightened, Oscar," he said reassuringly. "I've come back and now I'm going to let you go. I must have forgotten all about you. You made a wonderful prisoner, really you did, and it was such fun our playing together, wasn't it?"

He did not want to have to look at Oscar. He went over to pick up one of the chairs that circled the dinner table, glancing back over his shoulder in spite of himself as he did so, as if his little head was being pulled round against his volition, like a puppet's. He would not allow himself to admit what he knew must be true. "Wait a minute," he said, "and I'll take off your helmet, and then we can talk for a bit until Mummy comes in." He studied his naked toes and then said again: "I'm sorry I forgot all about you, Oscar."

He kept his eyes averted from the sagging shape behind him, and all at once he could think of nothing more to say. Yet there must not be a silence between the occupants of this familiar room. He abandoned the chair which he had been about to move and turned on the tape recorder which his mother had been playing to herself while she had awaited the arrival of her friends. It was an old tape that they had made years and years and years before, shortly after his fourth birthday. This evening when they had been listening to it he had laughed himself silly.

The voices began to speak from the limbo of those past days. "Sing it for me, Milo," his mother was coaxing. "Come along, you remember it!" There was a hiatus and she began to sing the song herself. "'And if one green bottle should accidentally fall . . . there'd-be-how-many-green-bottles hanging on the wall?'"

And it was his own voice, and it seemed to him that of a baby that had eventually chimed in. "'Four green bockles hangin' on the wall . . .'" Milo smiled to himself. Imagine his having said "bockle" instead of bottle!

A little reassured he turned back to deal with the chair and lugged it over to Oscar's side. If he went on listening to the tape recorder, in some curious way he wouldn't really be here, he would be in another place and in another time. He would be back in the cottage in Kent with his mother on that autumn afternoon when they had made the recording.

"'There were *no* green bockles hangin' on the wall!'" he heard himself asserting triumphantly. There followed a burst of delighted laughter and a new voice had broken in, Oscar's, and it was saying: "Well done, Milo! That was a splendid effort. Before you're through you'll be another Einstein!"

Milo climbed up on to the chair. The piece of pink string around the bottom of the plastic bag had been tied around Oscar's neck in a simple bow. He undid it, trying not to touch his skin, and lifted the bag carefully over the man's head and removed the bunched up handkerchief from his mouth. Oscar's voice on the tape was saying: "Young Milo's got tenacity, Gina, and a good ear. He made a jolly good job of that. I envy you that boy . . ." The tape became a meaningless jumble of conflicting noise. There were snatches of singing and spurts of disjointed argument and a lot of gobbledi-gook, and that was the end.

The telephone broke into the quiet. Milo hesitated and climbed down from the chair. He had a hunch that it must be his father or mother, and that they wanted to speak to him. He knew that it would be his mother on the line. He lifted the receiver, glowing with relief.

"That you, Gina?" asked a woman's voice. Without waiting for a reply she went on: "Sorry to disturb you at this ungodly hour, but like a blasted fool I left my diary in your flat earlier on this evening. It's got all my telephone numbers and dates and what have you in it, and frankly I'm sunk without it. Would you be a lamb and post it to me the first thing in the morning? I may have left it on the arm of the sofa. It's black and has my initials in the corner. Sorry to be such an atomic bore!" Milo said nothing and the voice asked more sharply: "Who is it I'm speaking to?"

"It's Milo," he said.

"And what are *you* doing out of your bed in the middle of the night?" the voice demanded. "It's 'Mumso'. 'Mumso' Vivian. You are a bad boy! Isn't your mother in?" she asked.

"Not yet," said Milo.

"Oh!" said Mrs. Vivian. "Apologies for waking you up. You might give her my message tomorrow, Milo, will you?" She coughed. "Too many cigarettes!" she said in explanation. "So they've left you to hold the fort?" she asked.

"What?" said Milo.

"Left you all alone," persevered "Mumso". "Well, never mind, they're bound to be back soon."

"I'm not all alone," Milo said. "Oscar's here." Immediately he regretted having told her.

"Is he?" said "Mumso" disapprovingly. "Perhaps I'd better have a word with him."

"He can't speak at the moment. He's . . . he's sort of funny."

"Oh!" said Mrs. Vivian, and she sounded even more disapproving, her fears realized. "You're quite sure everything's all right, Milo?" she demanded gruffly, but with concern. "I mean you wouldn't like me to look in on my way home to . . . to tuck you up, or anything of that kind? I could be with you in a few minutes."

"No, thank you," said Milo politely. He didn't want anybody "looking in". Not until his mother or father came back. He said a meticulous good-bye and put down the receiver with care.

"One spade," said "Mumso" when she had settled herself down at the table. "Those Cumberlands are honestly the bottom!" Her clear and indignant gaze settled on Waveney Payne. "They've no sense of responsibility whatsoever. They've gone off on the tiles leaving Milo by himself in the flat with that ghastly Oscar Landmore who, from what the boy told me, has obviously passed out!" She clicked her teeth disparagingly.

Waveney minutely considered her cards. "No bid," she said. "You don't know Oscar Landmore, do you, Bobby?" she inquired. "He's an adorable old soak. If I were Gina I couldn't wish for a more beguiling baby sitter!"

Milo pushed the chair to the wall and stepped round to the back of the pillar. The knots round Oscar's waist and those on the cords that bound his hands proved obstinate, but finally he succeeded in loosening them. He was breathing quickly. "Done it!" he said. He took a swift pace forward as Oscar began to sway alarmingly before slumping ponderously and face downward on to the floor, his buttocks raised above the level of his head and shoulders by the skipping rope which still bound his ankles, forcing his body to take up a grotesque position of humble obeisance.

In the lull that followed the impact of the leaden fall came panic. The little boy knew that Oscar wasn't pretending, that he wasn't even ill, but that he was dead. He had known it from the beginning, when he had first said "Oscar". He was alone with a dead man, and the dead man was Oscar, and he didn't look at all the same as he had done when he had been alive. Somehow he had been responsible for Oscar's death, for the death of his friend who had been always so willing and eager to play with him, and who had understood everything so well.

But people often died when they grew old, didn't they? It hadn't been his fault when Leila, Mummy's spaniel, had died when she had been twelve, and Oscar must have been much older than that. Much older.

He stood gazing down at Oscar. What action should he take? Should he make himself undo his feet and try to get him on to the sofa and then telephone for a doctor? But he didn't know Doctor Standen's number, wasn't even sure how to spell his name. And did doctors come out at night? He'd never seen one. He regarded in dismay the fifteen stones of the man's body which was prostrated in servile worship below him.

No, he decided, it would be better if he went back to bed and waited there for his parents to come home, and they would know what to do. They could arrange anything. He took a cushion from the sofa and, raising Oscar's head, which he found very heavy, he eased the cushion beneath it so that the tormented and congested face, from which the tongue protruded, would not have to come into contact with the discomfort of the hard parquet flooring.

He turned out the lights in order that Mrs. Vivian, should she arrive after all, might think that everyone had gone to sleep and would then drive off. Standing in the doorway between the drawing-room and the hall he was suddenly desperately afraid. Should he go back and try once more to free Oscar's legs? He looked so . . . so horrid lying there like that, as if he was imploring some king or judge for mercy. No, he could not enter that room again. He did not dare to make a further approach.

Milo turned off the switch in the hall. He would get back into bed with Penny and wait, and in the morning everything would be all right. A wedge of light showed from his bedroom. As he reached its security the front door bell rang unexpectedly and imperiously.

His heart leapt. It must be Mummy and Father, and they had forgotten their key. It had happened once before, and they had been full of excuses and shamefaced for having woken him up. It had to be them. But then again it might not. He remembered the many cautions that he had been given about admitting people into the flat if he should chance to be alone there.

There was a spyhole sunk into the door and he tiptoed softly towards it, standing on the balls of his feet so that he could peep through. On the landing outside there stood a policeman. Milo could see his chin and his collar and tie and the silver chain that looped down on his chest before it disappeared into the pocket of the blue uniform that was framed by the glistening cape draped over his wide shoulders. There would be a whistle on the end of it, or so he had been told, and if he opened the door he would be certain to make a search, and he would find Oscar, and then he would blow the whistle and more policemen would arrive.

His thoughts fled to the drawing-room. How could the police-man have known about Oscar? Milo wanted to let him in, but if he did so the policeman would think that he had killed Oscar, and in a way he would be right, and he would arrest him and he would be taken away and shot or hanged, and no one would know where he had gone.

He would stay quiet as a mouse and pretend that there was no one at home, and then the policeman would get tired of keeping his thumb on the bell and he would go away, and when Father returned he would tell him all about it and he would know what steps to take. It had been an accident. He would never have done anything to hurt Oscar. What he must do now was to go back to bed, and if by any chance he should drop off, then when he woke up it would be morning and he wouldn't be alone any more, for his parents would be here with him.

He crept back to his bedroom where he lay stiff with fright, and after what seemed to be a long while the trilling of the doorbell ceased.

"No," said Dick Persse to Constable Gerrard, "there's no one up there. The kid went off to stay with an aunt or grandmother or some such relation. He often does that of a week-end. They think the sea air does him good, and of course they're right. Can't tell you where, I'm sure. Comes back on the Sunday evening. Mrs. Cumberland happened to mention it to me early on in the week. Now I think of it I believe she mentioned something about Suffolk. Nice breezy county Suffolk." Dick Persse paused. "She's a nice lady is Mrs. Cumberland, and he's not a bad sort of a chap. Bit of a one sometimes when he's had a couple. You know, the larky kind. I'm sorry to hear that they've met with an accident. Where was it you said they'd been taken? My missus will be sorry, too. I shouldn't wonder but if she'd like to go along with some flowers." He picked at a front tooth with his thumbnail. "They don't leave a key with me like most of the tenants, not except when they goes away for their summer holidays. But there's no one up there, that I can tell you. I saw 'em all leave. They'd been having a bit of a do. Mrs. Jackson will be along at nine in the morning. She's their daily. If you likes to call back then she'll be glad to take you over." He frowned, trying to think of something helpful. "There's a Mrs. Vivian who visits them a lot," he said. "She might know where the kid's gone, if it's all that urgent. Intelligent little chap. Full of beans!"

Constable Gerrard thanked him. There did not seem to be much that he could do until the morning. He walked down the steps and swung a sturdy black-gaitered leg over the saddle of his motor bicycle. The machine roared into life and he headed through the rain to the station to make his report.

Milo held Penny tightly to him. There were smudged bluish shadows under the little boy's eyes. He stared up at the ceiling, his ears straining to catch any sound that might come from the landing . . . or from the drawing-room. He would leave the bedside light on until he felt sleepy.

It was still burning, wan and almost killed by the daylight, when Mrs. Jackson arrived to begin her work.

"IS THERE ANYBODY THERE?"

"Is there anybody there?"

Millie Ackland knew that she was all alone in the cottage. It had been stupid of her to call out, but she could not help feeling nervous. She had pretended to Ida that she had not minded her going off to London for two nights. She had told her that she did not mind in the very least, and that of course she would be all right, perfectly all right she had repeated with emphasis. What could possibly happen to her? She appreciated her solicitude, but honestly there was no need for it.

She had said what Ida had wished her to say, and had felt a little heroic. It was unfortunate that Ida was ignorant of the extent of her heroism. No doubt she had reassured herself about Millie's safety with the fact that their neighbors, the Kearnons, lived only a few yards away, to the left of the blue gate at the bottom of the path. Blue had been Ida's choice—everyone else had their gates painted green or white, so why should they not show some originality? Then there was Monica Findhorn, whose house was on the other side, and who could actually look into their garden from her bathroom window. There was no reason for apprehension, how could there be? Ida must go off to her cousin and enjoy herself as she had arranged, and there was no more to be said.

Millie Ackland and Ida Rankin had shared Rosemary Cottage for the past two years, and they had done a great deal to improve it, more, in fact, than they had been able to afford. They had installed a bathroom and an up-to-date kitchen and had built on a lean-to glasshouse on the south side, and they had hermasealed the warped windows, which nobody could deny had been essential for health as well as for comfort, and which could not be regarded as having been an extravagance.

Millie had known Ida since they had been at Hatchdean together more than fifty years ago. It sounded so antediluvian when she said it aloud, which she did sometimes, to hear the gratifying astonishment that was her listeners' reaction. "Ida and I," she would boast, "have known one another for more than half a century, since we first met in the Lower Fourth at Hatchdean in nineteen hundred and six!" And it was true. They had always "kept up", and when the time had come for their respective retirements from the scholastic careers which each had chosen what could have been more natural than for them to decide to enjoy the closing years of their lives in one another's company. "Ida may have her shortcomings," Millie often said with a twinkle, "but then so have I, and we have no unpleasant shocks in store for one another as sometimes happens to newlyweds!" She meant nothing peculiar by this announcement.

Ida had been headmistress at Moatlands, an expensive and rather snobbish school which had grown even more militantly exclusive after the arrival there of several of the European princesses. Millie herself had never been officially a headmistress, but on occasion had acted as such at Charleville House when there had been illness among the staff. Charleville House had been intended originally for the daughters of the clergy and professional classes and Millie considered it to be, both in education and in games, far in advance of Moatlands. She did not of course say this to dear Ida. The majority of the Charleville girls had had to work in later life and had been trained to become useful, self reliant and cultured citizens.

Rosemary Cottage had, to begin with, been a laborer's dwelling with, in house agents' parlance, "two up and two down". That was before they had added the improvements. The "down" which had been the former kitchen, was now the dining-room, and the new kitchen, with a communicating hatch, had been built on at the back underneath the bathroom. It was all most convenient.

They had bought the cottage for fifteen hundred pounds which, in view of its deplorable condition and lack of amenities, they had considered to be daylight robbery, but they had been assured that it had in point of fact been a bargain. Millie gravely doubted if her father, the Reverend Maurice Ackland, had he been alive, would have regarded it as such, but then values had changed and everything had become so terribly dear.

Monica Findhorn had had the nerve to tell them that they had managed to get it so "cheaply" owing to its "reputation". Ida had looked at her with quizzically raised eyebrows waiting for her to explain herself, and when she had failed to do so she had said humorously: "Are you implying, dear Miss Findhorn, that our sweet cottage used to be the local house of ill fame?"

Miss Findhorn had smiled and shaken her head, sharing in the joke. "No, Miss Rankin, I am not! It is supposed to be haunted. A young ploughman is said to have murdered his wife soon after the end of the first war. It was before my day. There was a lot of speculation, and although some people declared that he was innocent and that it was a case of *cherchez la femme* he was executed for the crime, and is said to be "earthbound"! Since then Rosemary Cottage has changed hands no less than three times. You know how superstitious villagers can be about such matters, especially in East Anglia." She had busied herself with the teapot. "For you ladies," she went on playfully, "the idiotic tale has proved most beneficial for, as you know, the price of property around here has risen scandalously! He worked for the Fillingham family," she finished inconsequently.

"I am not likely to lose any sleep over your revelations," Ida had said. "There is not a house in the country that has not been the scene of a death, and the older the building the more of them it must have witnessed."

"But not deaths by violence," Millie had put in. "When did it happen, Miss Findhorn?"

"In twenty-one . . . twenty-two? I'm afraid I can't tell you the precise date. But it was on Midsummer Eve. And please will you call me Monica, both of you. I hope that we may be good friends as well as near neighbors."

Ida had laughed about it on their way home. "We are apparently indebted to Piers Plowman for getting us a real bargain!" she had said. "It's an ill wind . . . not that it was not bad luck on the wretched victim." She had no patience with the psychic world. She had once misguidedly attended a séance and it had been perfectly obvious to her that the medium, a woman, had been an outrageous fraud. Tommy-rot!

She was not certain that Millie altogether shared her views, for, although the dear thing had known better than to express openly any such beliefs, she had been known to drop hints. Ida suspected that Millie thought herself receptive to vibrations from the Other

World and that she was rather proud of it, as it made her feel superior, like claims of being "old souls" always heartened reincarnationists and made them quite insufferable. Millie naturally refrained from parading her fanciful theories for she knew that if she did so they would inevitably receive short shrift.

Millicent Ackland had, with difficulty, kept her accomplishment to herself. She was devoted to Ida and would do nothing which might annoy or vex her, or which could endanger the harmony of their lives together, and it was for this reason that she had resolved to hold her tongue.

She had begun to hear things the very evening after they had been to tea with Monica Findhorn. Perhaps, she thought, it had been Miss Findhorn's disclosures that had opened the door of her awareness, had tuned her in to the right wavelength. She would have known in any case that the house was haunted, but the knowledge might not have come to her so soon.

At first she had caught only a few disjointed and whispered words, and weeks and sometimes months had gone by before she had heard more; but with the passing of time the voices had grown gradually more distinct and had come to her with more regularity, and recently she had begun to think that if she were to turn her head quickly enough she would be able to catch sight of the speakers.

She tried to do so now. "Is there anybody there?" she called. She knew that with the supernatural one must never show fear.

There were four of them; she had discovered that very early on. A man, two women and a child. When they spoke to one another Millie was usually alone in a room, but of late they had started to do so even when Ida had been seated opposite to her, reading or knitting or engaged in solving a crossword puzzle, but invariably Ida had appeared sublimely unconscious of anything untoward and Millie had hesitated to alarm her or to draw down upon herself the pungent dryness of her tolerant rebuke.

Beyond Miss Findhorn's somewhat vague statement that a murder had taken place in their cottage Millie had had no very clear picture of the personalities concerned, but by now the characters were familiar to her to the extent that she was sometimes tempted to take part in the dialogue.

There was Adam Loft, the dominant figure who, from what she had heard and subsequently observed, had been a handsome, conceited and hard-drinking man with a controlled but bullying nature. There was his wife, Nancy, a young woman of dull mind who subconsciously rejoiced in being downtrodden, and who gave every evidence of being a mental and physical slattern. Then there was their child, Lucy, a tiresome little girl who was alternately spoiled and punished by her father and nagged at by her mother.

Millie found Judith Cromer the most interesting. She was having an affair with Adam. She lived in the village, was unmarried, and was obviously terrified that her family would discover the liaison in which she was engaged. She was quite intelligent, but her judgement had been clouded by her overwhelming sexual desire. She had been trying to persuade Adam to emigrate with her to Australia. Millie knew that he had no intention of doing so, and she knew also that he was a man of considerable obstinacy. All that he wanted to do was to continue his cohabitation with Judith in his own house and on his own terms, and to prevent his wife and Judith's parents from finding out about their relationship.

Millie acknowledged that, in spite of herself, despite her natural alarm, she was growing more and more interested and involved in the lives of these people, just as some viewers are inextricably netted by the enthralling dramas of television serials. She knew that she should switch off, but was incapable of closing her mind. She had been jockeyed into being an unwilling eavesdropper and it had not been of her own choosing, and she began to fear that she might easily find herself slipping into the role of *voyeur* of scenes and also of actions that were for the eyes of the participants alone.

She remembered the first snatch of talk which she had overheard. There had been the slam of a door and the man had said to his wife: "*I don't know what you do with yourself all day, Nance, honest I don't. Lucy looks like a gypsy, and the house is no better than a slum. There's not even a hot meal on the table, and nought in the oven, I'll bet. Search me why I married you. Must have been off my rocker.*" He had spoken with unconcealed bitterness.

And Nancy had answered him: "*I'm out of sorts, Adam. Really I am. It's the headache. Somehow it don't seem to lift, no matter what. Lucy's been that trying, you've no idea. If it's not one thing it's another.*"

I'll be glad when she gets off to school." She had paused and there had been the sound of sniffing. *"And I'll be gladder still when she's old enough to go into service, 'tho that won't be for a long while yet, not for another nine years. I try to do my best, Lord knows."*

There had been a silence, then the man had said roughly: *"Just look at you! Like something the cat brought in. You might be fifty, not thirty. You can't be bothered with cooking or cleaning, and you're always tired out."*

The voices had grown indistinct, and Ida had come in and stripped off her gardening gloves and had said: "We must order some more coal so as to be ready for the winter. Do remind me, Millie. Oh, and Miss Findhorn—Monica, I should say—telephoned while you were at the chemist's this morning. I forgot to tell you. She wondered if we would take charge of the tombola at the church fête in July. I told her that we would be delighted to do so. Did I do right, Millie?" She had smiled kindly, aware that her friend enjoyed the companionship of such social activities.

Adam Loft's voice had been very different when he had been talking to Judith Cromer. It was slower and softer and took on a caressing and deeper slur. Not that he was in the habit of speaking a great deal when they were together. It seemed to Millie that it was the girl who did most of the talking. On each occasion when Judith called there were just the two of them. Nancy and Lucy were always out.

After they had made love, and Millie was perfectly aware that this was the sole object of Judith's visits, the girl would keep on pestering Adam about his leaving Nancy and going away with her to start a new life. *"Nobody would know us,"* she used to say, *"if we went overseas, we could make a fresh start. Nancy's no good to you, Adam, and you know it. She'll only drag you down to her own level. You don't love her, and she loves nobody but herself. She's not got it in her. She'll ruin you, mark my words. Don't I mean anything to you, darling? We could be someone if we went to Canada or Australia. Achieve something. There're wonderful openings in the Colonies for people like us. I had a letter from John only yesterday. He and Doris are doing ever so well in Vancouver."*

Adam had avoided replying directly to these urgings. Instead there had been sounds of kissing and half-hearted protests and the creaking of leather which, Millie thought, must have come from the old hide sofa which she and Ida had found abandoned in an outhouse, and which, the cost of repair having proved exorbitant, they had subsequently sold at an auction on the Green for ten shillings.

And so the story had unfolded. There were no twists, no unexpected developments. Adam's affair with Judith gathered momentum; his irritation with, and dislike of, his wife increased, as did the mounting tediousness of his child's behavior, which maddened him and frayed his nerves. Then, a few days before Ida's proposed visit to London, Judith had come to Adam and told him that she was pregnant. Millie had not heard this scene before. She did not think that the girl was unduly distressed by this occurrence, no doubt largely because the circumstance might enable her to force Adam's hand, and rather to her surprise the young man, after a brief outburst of impatient disgruntlement, had taken the news quite well and had made no effort to dispute her claim of his paternity.

The events which she overheard were not, to Millie's annoyance, always in continuity. She was anxious to know the outcome, but, on the next occasion when she was able to tune in, it was to a conversation that she had already listened to several times and thus she knew exactly what would happen. Adam had come in from work and had sat down to unbuckle his leggings, which he would throw over to Nancy to clean and polish for him while he went out to wash at the pump. Her protest at his request would be followed by the thud of his heavy boots as they too were tossed in her direction, and then would come her whining voice: *"It seems so silly and such a waste of time. They'll only get muddy again in the morning, and I've been on the go all day. Hardly been off my feet since you left the house."*

"So you want me to go down to the village all mucky, is that it?"

"I don't want you to go down to the village at all, Adam, and well you know it. Wasting your money in the Pelican with that Bill Haskins and all the rest, and then stumbling back home with a skinful and a face as black as thunder, so that I'm afraid to open my mouth."

"Well, I earn the bloody money, don't I?"

"I'm not denying that it's your money, and I do wish you wouldn't swear in front of Lucy. It's how you spend your wages that riles me. Lucy's not had a new frock this year, and come to that nor more have I, not for a twelve-month. After all, we are your wife and child . . . your own flesh and blood."

"Why can't I have a new dress?" It was the little girl. *"Why must you drink so much beer, Daddy?"*

"For Christ's sake, shut up, can't you?"

It was by now the second week of June, and it had been during March that Millie had just seen the hazy outlines of the speakers, outlines which had grown increasingly detailed until she had been able to discern their features.

Adam Loft was about thirty, clean-shaven and broad-shouldered, dark and sullenly handsome, with the strength of one of the shire horses with which he worked. Nancy had once been pretty, but discontent and fatigue had left their mark, sapping away the good looks which she had formerly possessed. Her reddish hair was streaked with gray and hung in wisps which she was forever pushing away from her forehead with the back of her hand. Lucy was a miniature replica of her mother at the same age.

Judith Cromer could not have been more than eighteen or nineteen. Millie had imagined from her voice that she would have been older, a bold and probably buxom hussy, but she was nothing of the sort. On the contrary, she was tall and slim with beautiful hands and feet, and had an exotic charm which was almost oriental and which was unexpected to come across in the wind-swept plains of the Norfolk countryside.

The next happening of which Millie had not been previously aware had taken place after tea on the day following the one on which she had learned of Judith's pregnancy. She had no means of knowing if it had occurred before or after that event.

Adam had been shrugging on his jacket preparatory to departing for the Pelican, when Nancy had said: *"Lucy, run along, dear. I want to have a word with your father alone."*

Adam had paused with his fingers on the door latch. *"Can't it wait?"* he had asked tersely.

"No," Nancy had been unaccustomedly firm. *"Do as I tell you, Lucy."* The small girl had left the room.

"*Well, what is it?*" Adam had demanded, and he was holding his watch in his hand to underline his impatience.

"*I met Lily Rickett this afternoon,*" Nancy had said quietly, "*and she told me.*"

"*Told you what?*" Adam had asked brusquely.

"*About you and that Judith Cromer.*"

"*What about me and Judith Cromer? What did she say? Are you daft? You ought to know better than to gossip with an old faggot like Lily Rickett.*" Even to Millie's ears, let alone Nancy's, it was obvious that he was put out and was stalling.

"*She told me that every time I took Lucy over to Watton to see Mother, Judith Cromer creeps in here to whore with you. That's what she told me. She says it's common talk.*" Adam swung arrogantly round towards her. He slipped the watch back in his pocket and stood with his thumbs tucked behind the long links of its silver chain, rocking slowly on his heels. "*And did you believe her?*" he had asked expressionlessly. "*And if you did, what do you think you can do about it?*"

"*If she comes here again,*" Nancy had said, "*I'm going straight to her parents. That's what I'm going to do about it. She's a dirty lustful little tart, that's all she is, coming into my house as soon as my back is turned, and carrying on like a bitch in heat.*"

There had been a silence before Adam had said in a voice thick with anger: "*I shouldn't act foolish, Nancy, if I were you. I really shouldn't.*" He had turned abruptly on his heel and the door had banged behind him, and Nancy had stood staring after him until the picture had faded.

Ida had gone to the station. There had been no flurry, no last minute checking of what she might have forgotten. She was too well organized and experienced to indulge in such behavior. Millie had received a peck on the cheek and had been told that Ida would be back in good time for supper on Monday, and would Millie please plant out the zinnias and dahlias, and she was not to forget to cut down on the milkman's delivery for, as Millie well knew, she abhorred waste.

Millie had arranged to have luncheon with Miss Findhorn, but otherwise she had made no social engagements for the week-end. The afternoon was hot, with a hint of thunder, and the flower beds were dry, which had necessitated a lot of watering in case the storm did not break, which was questionable as the clouds were slowly drifting in the direction of the coast and would most likely spill themselves into the sea.

It was when she had finished the task of bedding out, and had washed her hands and taken the tea tray into the neat drawing-room with its chintzes and lime green walls studded with gilt framed water colors that she heard Nancy Loft's voice. She had stationed herself not more than three feet away from where Millie was sitting with the tray on her lap, and she was as clear and as real as if she had been there in the flesh. Millie had the odd feeling that it was she herself, and not Nancy Loft, who was in fact the ghost. She glanced quickly from the stiff figure of the woman to the doorway which framed Judith Cromer.

"Won't you come in, Miss Cromer?" Nancy said. *"Adam's not home yet. Perhaps you would like to wait?"* she suggested with heavy sarcasm. *"I expect you're taken aback to find me here. When you have called before I've never been in, have I?"* She spoke with venom.

Judith did not seem at all put out by this reception. *"It was you I came to see today, Mrs. Loft,"* she said with composure. *"Adam told me that he would be working late."*

Nancy was by the side of the table which had been laid with half a loaf of bread and a slab of margarine, together with an opened tin of sardines and three slices of cold pork that had been arranged on a chipped willow pattern plate. She waited for the girl to continue. *"He did?"* she said at last.

"Yes. I wanted to tell you that I am going to have a baby, and that it is Adam's."

"Does he know?"

"Yes." Judith stepped forward into the room. *"He is going to ask you to give him a divorce."*

Nancy laughed. *"There's no harm in asking, is there?"* The hatred between the two women was palpable. *"Does he admit responsibility? A bun in the oven might be the work of more than one baker!"*

"If you don't divorce him," said Judith evenly, *"he will come away with me just the same. He hates you. You are repulsive to him. He's told me so frequently."*

"So you've decided not to face the music," said Nancy. *"You're going*

elsewhere to have your bastard. I can't say that I blame you. It's your parents that I'm sorry for." Her face was pinched and white. *"But I may as well tell you, Judith Cromer, that I will never divorce Adam, not for you or any other slant-eyed slut from the village whom he may have seen fit to pleasure. He's no better than a randy bull. And now get out of my house,"* she said, her voice rising. *"Get out before I do you and your disgusting brat an injury."* She snatched up the bread knife from the table and stepped forward.

The two women grappled desperately with each other for possession of the weapon. Their struggle seemed to Millie to last for an interminable time. Their feet scarcely moved, but their breathing grew loud and stertorous. Then Judith Cromer took a sudden pace backward holding the knife which had become steeped in blood up to its bone handle.

Nancy Loft sank to her knees, her mouth open as if in astonishment. As she fell she clutched at the tablecloth, bringing the cups and plates crashing around her to the floor. Judith stood over her, gazing down in horror.

There was a step on the oilcloth in the narrow hall and Adam came in. He stood stock still, taking in the tableau. *"Good God, Judith!"* he said. *"Good God!"* The girl let the knife fall as she turned to him.

Millie's hands were clenched. Over Judith's head the young man was looking straight at her, and when he spoke his words were slow and distinct and his dark eyes held hers. *"So now you know, Miss Ackland,"* he said. *"You have been watching us, and now you know the truth of what happened although I took the blame. You're on to us, Miss Ackland, aren't you? And you will be the next, if you talk. And talk you will! We'll get you one of these days, just you see if we don't."*

Millie closed her eyes to shut out his livid mocking face, and she was tense with terror, and when at last she dared to open them again the room was empty and exactly as it had been, and she was once more alone.

Upon her return from London Ida was most distressed to find Millie in what she could only describe as a state of near collapse. After considerable pressure as to the cause Millie was at length persuaded to talk, and Ida listened patiently and anxiously as her friend poured out the whole story.

It was pure imagination of course, but poor Millie appeared to believe every word of what she said. She must take her away for a holiday and then she would realize what nonsense it had all been. Otherwise, unless she was able to put her groundless fears into proper perspective, in all probability she would want to sell Rosemary Cottage, which would be sheer foolishness.

It was decided finally that they should book on a two weeks cruise to the northern capitals at the end of the month. Millie had proposed that they should go to Greece, with all its beauty and ancient culture, but Ida had objected that it would be intolerably hot at this time of year, and besides which they would not be able to afford to stay away for so long. Millie quite understood and was pleased with, and grateful for, the Scandinavian compromise. When they had been quite young women they had gone together on a vacation to Rome and Venice, and Ida had proved herself a most entertaining and well informed travelling companion.

The next morning, however, brought an unexpected complication, for Ida received a letter from her brother, Francis. She was in the habit of saying that she was more like his aunt than his sister, since he was twenty years her junior. He ran an art gallery in Manchester, and somewhat to Ida's surprise, a few years after his wife's death he had married *en deuxième-noce* a girl not long out of her teens, a competent sensible and nice looking girl whose father had been his friend. Now it transpired she had met with an accident and was laid up with a slipped disc, leaving him to cope not only with the running of his business but with the management of the house and also of their two-year-old son. Could Ida conceivably come and stay for ten days to help him out? They were expecting an *au pair* girl from Madrid, but she could not be arriving for at least another week.

Ida read through this *cri de coeur* twice. She was very fond of Francis and knew how utterly helpless he would be in such a dilemma. She could not go for the whole of the ten days, but she would have to put in an appearance and try to find someone to tide him over. Men were so unenterprising, they accepted defeat so readily in any domestic crisis. She wondered how she herself would make out with a male two-year-old. It would be so different from her girls!

But what was to be done about Millie? If she were to leave her by herself she wouldn't know a moment's peace. She could consult Monica Findhorn, who was a tower of strength. Perhaps she might know of some woman locally who might be bribed or persuaded to come in and oblige. It was both extraordinary and inconvenient that Francis's request should have arrived so soon after her London trip. It had been months since she had stirred from Rosemary Cottage. And now twice within a week!

When Ida broached the matter to Miss Findhorn that lady looked dubious. There was really no one in Swaffam, no one at all. Any available daily help was so quickly snapped up. She realized the urgency and would certainly make inquiries and she would telephone Ida at lunchtime. She was sorry to hear that Millie had been unwell. It had been rather naughty of her not to have let her know. She would pop round and see her as often as she could, but that was by no means the same thing as having somebody living in, was it? She would have been delighted to ask her to stay, but at the moment the spare room was being redecorated. Wasn't life difficult?

Ida walked back to Rosemary Cottage torn by conflicting loyalties. She would say nothing to Millie until the afternoon, but if she was to be of help to Francis she could not long delay the answer to his S.O.S.

At five minutes to one Monica Findhorn telephoned saying that she had heard of someone who might be willing to move in for a short while. She was not acquainted with her personally. She was a Mrs. Tarriman, and she was by no means young. As it happened, she was here on a visit from Tasmania and was a great aunt of Mabel Smith's, who lived in one of the new Council houses in Ramsden Road, and Mabel had told her that the old lady was becoming rather bored with nothing to do. She was nearing the end of a month's visit, for which she had practically invited herself. Mabel had not previously known her, but she had loyally decided that blood was thicker than water, and Mrs. Tarriman had written that she had saved up for a long time to pay a visit to the Old Country.

Ida went for an interview as soon as Millie had been settled down for her *siesta*, as she liked to call it. Mrs. Tarriman was not young, but she was not as ancient as Miss Findhorn had implied. She must, thought Ida, be roughly her own contemporary, maybe a little younger, a woman in her middle sixties. Still, she seemed pleasant and was prepared to be of assistance. She could start tomorrow if Miss Rankin wished that she should do so, and could remain until Saturday or even Sunday. She must be in Southampton by Tuesday to catch her boat. As to remuneration she would leave that to Miss Rankin. It was agreed that she should come to Rosemary Cottage on the following morning.

Ida telephoned Francis to announce that she would be in Manchester the next evening. Millie accepted this arrangement cheerfully. She was aware that Ida did not want to let Francis down and declared that as she would have a companion her friend must not give the matter a second thought. There was no problem. She would look forward to Ida coming back as soon as she had made the necessary arrangements for her brother. Mrs. Tarriman sounded excellent, and it would only be for a few days.

"She has good bone structure," Ida had added. "When she was young she must have been quite beautiful. You'll get on together like a house on fire. Don't worry, Millie." But when the taxi had come and had driven Ida to the station Millie felt some of her old fear return. She hated Ida going away and wished that the time would come for the beginning of their cruise.

Doctor Cripps had been insistent that she take things quietly, so Millie stayed in bed until noon and retired again directly after the news at a quarter past nine. She hoped that she was not giving too much trouble—but Ida had been adamant that she should carry out the doctor's orders. Millie comforted herself that by Sunday or Monday, when her friend would be back, such self indulgence would be no longer necessary.

At half past seven on the evening of Mrs. Tarriman's second day at the cottage Millie could hear her preparing supper. The doors which gave from the drawing-room and kitchen on to the passage were both ajar. Millie was lying on the sofa, an unopened copy of the *Spectator* beside her. She was scrutinizing the *Queen*, which she pretended to despise. It was Ida who was the subscriber, as she liked to be *au fait* with the activities of her "old girls", although Millie maintained that the publication was a frivolous extravagance.

She put the magazine to one side and began a polite, if rather loud, conversation with Mrs. Tarriman. Nowadays you had to treat domestic help as human beings, try to make them feel a part of the family. It was no use being aloof. The supper would be simple; a cup of hot *consommé*, some cold beef and pickles left over from luncheon, and perhaps an apple. The beef had been far too rare for Millie's taste, almost blue, but she had not liked to comment adversely on it.

Had Mrs. Tarriman, she inquired, ever regretted having emigrated? Life in Tasmania must be very different from that in England. It had a marvellous climate, or so she had heard. Had she many relatives living there?

Mrs. Tarriman replied that on the whole she liked it very much. She had one son and two grand-daughters in Hobart. When their mother had died the girls had been nearly grown up, and they had married early, so after she had lost her own husband she had moved in to housekeep for their father. It was a fine country for the young, what with the sunshine and the space and all and, if Miss Ackland would pardon her for saying so, there were no class barriers, which was nice. Her visit "home" had been enjoyable, but she was getting to be an old woman these days and it would be unlikely that she would be making another one. Of course, Tasmania had its snags, like all places, but there was plenty of scope out there and people could get on in the world.

Millie continued to talk. She had realized, ever since Ida's departure, that tonight would be Midsummer Eve, and she had no desire to participate again as an eye-witness of the long ago murder. If she went on chatting to Mrs. Tarriman there would be less likelihood that she would be swept in, and when she went up to bed she would take a sleeping pill.

"And did you know this part of the country when you were a girl?" asked Millie. "Or did you come to Norfolk just to visit your great niece?"

"I was Norfolk born," said Mrs. Tarriman, " 'tho they've all gone from hereabouts, that is . . . all of my immediate relations. I lost touch with them these many years back. Mabel is the only one that's left. The two wars took a heavy toll of the menfolk, and Mabel's brothers went off in their turn, same as I did, one to New Zealand and the other to South Africa. She tells me they've done very well for themselves." She hesitated and then added: "You might say I used to know this village well."

"All the same it must be sad," said Millie, "to see all the old places passing into new ownership." She paused, and asked: "What was your maiden name?"

Mrs. Tarriman came to the doorway and Millie saw that the big carving knife in her hand was red with blood. "My name?" she asked. "Why do you ask me that, Miss Ackland? It would mean nothing to you. As a matter of fact it was Cromer . . . Judy Cromer."

A chill breeze seemed to play over Millie and she shivered. Judith Cromer had come back. She was here in this room beside her, and on Midsummer Eve. Millie studied her nails. She must not allow herself to look up. Was that the sound of the front door opening? Who was it that was coming in? She knew with a sudden ghastly certainty who it would be that she would see. Against her will she raised her head. "Is there anybody there?" she called.

Framed in the door behind Mrs. Tarriman stood the burly figure of Adam Loft and his expression as he watched Millie was one of triumph, and she heard once more his whispered words: *"You're on to us, Miss Ackland, aren't you? And you will be the next. We'll get you one of these days."* And she had talked. She had told Ida.

Millie was gripped by a searing pain, as if a mailed hand was squeezing relentlessly at her heart. She found it impossible to get her breath. This was death that had come to claim her—and she recognized it as such. She gave a strangled cry and her head fell forward on to her chest.

Mrs. Tarriman had moved away, her thoughts in the past. Judy Cromer had been her maiden name. It had been curious how drawn her mother had been to the letter "Jay." James . . . John . . . her elder sister Judith, who had drowned herself on the day of Adam Loft's execution . . . poor tragic Judith . . . it had been in this very cottage that the young man had lived . . . and Julia. Why, instead of Judith, had it been herself, Julia, who had been the one who had always been known as "Judy"? It had been a family quirk which had had no explanation.

Hearing a sound of distress from the sofa Mrs. Tarriman hurried back into the room, the carving knife with which she had been slicing the beef still held in her hand. She knelt down by Millie. "Miss Ackland," she said with concern. "Miss Ackland, dear . . . what is it?" She felt for her pulse. "Miss Ackland, dear," she said once more. Then with her face starched with worry, she went across to the telephone to call Doctor Cripps.

THE SERUM OF DOCTOR WHITE

"At what time did you say that his train was due?" asked Humphrey.

"A quarter to six," said Alathea.

Her husband took out his watch and got to his feet. "Then perhaps I should start." He kissed Alathea on her forehead as she clung to him tightly. "There's no alternative, old girl," he said. "It's not only for Rachel's sake but also for that of other children."

"You truly believe that it is the right course to take? Hasn't the poor child suffered enough?" She pushed him away from her gently. "Are you honestly sure that you haven't asked him down here out of hatred?"

"My dear Alathea!" he said. "There *is* no one else except White." He hesitated. "What he has done to Rachel he may be able to ameliorate, even if no more than that."

Alathea did not argue, but came with him to the door and stood at the top of the flight of shallow steps, where she looked after Humphrey's large black car until it had turned out of sight around the corner of the drive.

As she was going back into the house she caught sight of Nanny coming up the path from the water garden, on the far side of which the folly had been built. The word was misleading, for it was not an ornamental baroque tower that served no useful purpose, but a miniature three-roomed Regency building that gave on to a wide exquisitely proportioned verandah which was semi-circular and colonnaded. Humphrey had installed plumbing and electricity and had made of the summer house a comfortable self-contained dwelling, and to there it was that Rachel and Nanny had been transferred.

Nanny had been with Rachel "from the month"—nearly seven years. She was a plump good-natured Irishwoman from the County Mayo, and she had attached herself to the Deckers with a love that verged on the fanatical, and since the child's illness, except for her church-going, she had refused to leave her side for longer than an hour or so, brushing away any suggestions of a holiday or of days off with a determination which brooked no discussion, nor would she permit the other servants either to visit Rachel or to go near the folly to disturb her refuge.

From the start she had set herself against Doctor White's treatment, declaring that a visit to Lourdes would prove much more beneficial for the little girl, and she had been forever pressing pamphlets and copious newspaper cuttings from the Irish press upon her employers, eye-witness accounts that told of the miraculous cures which had been effected by the power of prayer and the grace of Our Lady in that Holy Grotto. She still maintained that it was not too late for a pilgrimage to be undertaken.

Alathea reluctantly retraced her steps to meet her. She had informed her already of the doctor's imminent arrival and told her that he would be staying with them at Welford for the night, and Nanny had pursed up her lips at the news. "And hasn't that man been after doing harm enough?" she had demanded indignantly. "Isn't it time, wouldn't you think, that he'd be leaving the darlin' crature alone?"

The yellowish gray stone of the pleasant Georgian house was touched by the last rays of the sinking sun, gilding the windows and glowing lingeringly on the portico, around which in spring there hung the heavy cream and lilac swags of a venerable wistaria. Welford crouched mellowed and secure in its surrounding parkland, up to the walls of which had crept the remorseless and probing tentacles of the new housing estate.

"How is she this evening, Nanny?" Alathea asked. "She wouldn't speak to me when I was with her after luncheon. She sat there all hunched up and refused even to look at me."

"Sure and that don't signify a thing," said Nanny robustly. "It's nothing personal. If it's conversation you're wanting, Madam, it's not from Rachel that you'll be after getting it. She talks less and less, but then don't the rest of us talk a sight too much? The effort seems to pain her. I keep on asking her if she's losing her tongue." She gave an impatient sniff and then said in a quieter voice: "I light candles whenever I go to Mass, but the response is slow in coming. But it will tho', it will! And it's all the doing of that Doctor White. If I had my way it would be nailing him to Christ's cross I'd be, and that's God's truth."

"If it hadn't been for Doctor White," said Alathea, trying to speak kindly, "Rachel would have been dead. He's only human after all. No one claims to be infallible."

"You're right there," agreed Nanny forcibly. "If he'd kept his hands off her the poor soul would likely have been resting in the bosom of the Blessed Virgin by now with all the Saints for company." She stared over Alathea's shoulder, not giving an inch. "She was a good child, whatever she may be like at present. She was a real little doat." Alathea's gaze blurred with tears as she looked at Nanny, dedicated and partisan, with her blue eyes challenging and brilliant with defiance. "She's the same darlin' doat as she always was," Nanny repeated, "even if she may be changed a trifle . . . outwardly."

"Of course she is," said Alathea. She dreaded making her twice daily visits to the folly. They were becoming increasingly unbearable. She had to steel herself to undertake them, force her legs to carry her forward; and when Humphrey accompanied her it was more than she could do, to have to see his drawn and rigid face. "Of course she is," Alathea said again. Her thoughts fled back to nearly a year before, when Rachel's illness had begun. It had been sudden and dreadful, totally unexpected, and extremely frightening.

They had spent the following weeks, after the initial shock, in and out of Harley Street consulting rooms and hospitals, arranging for X-rays and blood tests to be taken, seeking conflicting expert advice and finding none that was encouraging. It had been diagnosed finally that Rachel was suffering from astrocytoma, that awesome and fatal tumor of the brain which was resistant to both treatment and surgery.

It was when they had known that time was rapidly running out that Alathea had heard about Doctor Max White. It had been Cathleen Bower who had been her informant. Mrs. Bower prided herself on being *au courant* with the new advances made by medical science, and it had to be admitted that in most cases she usually knew who would be the best man, or woman, to consult.

She had taken pains to make it clear that Doctor White was not known to her personally, nor had any of her friends actually been to him, but she had heard that he had made a considerable name for himself on the Continent, and he had received a lot of favorable publicity in various American publications. And Americans were so much more go ahead than we were, were they not? Nobody could deny that! She had fixed Alathea with her somewhat prominent gray eyes, and had made her point against a background noise of jangling Vogue jewellery with which she was always burdened, the cacophony being engendered by reason of her vehement gestures.

The origins of Doctor White were dim. Obviously he had changed his name after he had become naturalized. Cathleen believed that he had been born in Hungary and had made his way to England immediately after the war. It was rumored that he had been an inmate of a concentration camp, but no one seemed to know the exact details. She herself had glimpsed him but once, and that had been some years previously at a party given by Derrick Nott. He had been middle-aged and rather self-consciously dynamic. Observing him she had thought him a striking personality, who, in her opinion, relied for much of his effect on his undeniable sex appeal.

Randell, her husband, had been introduced to him by Derrick and had taken an instant dislike to him, but that was due, she was sure, to their being anti-chemical to one another and had had nothing to do with his professional activities. Under further questioning Mrs. Bower had been forced to admit that upon inquiry none of her medico friends had been at all enthusiastic about him, not that their knowledge of the subject appeared to her to have been very profound. She always said that doctors were as jealous of each other as were actors or musicians, conservative to a ridiculous degree, and closed their ranks in a grim protective unity whenever a talented foreigner started to enjoy a measure of approval.

Doctor Max White was apparently something of a mystery man. He had set up a research laboratory, staffed mainly by mid-Europeans, in a remote part of Yorkshire. Although he seemed to have no lack of financial backing the source from whence it came was unknown, and his qualifications were equally obscure. In addition to the laboratory he ran also a small clinic in the house where he lived, which was called High Hall, and where he took a maximum of three or four patients.

There had been a boy, or so Cathleen had read, who had been brought over from the States to see Doctor White and he had been cured. His name had been Lodge or Dodge or Hodge. Anyway, he was from one of the leading families. It was worth a try anyway, wasn't it? Cathleen had not added "since all else had failed", but her meaning had been clear. Humphrey, after a great deal of pressure from Alathea, had at last allowed himself to be persuaded into giving his consent and taking a chance.

Max White's clinic had been situated on the moors some ten miles from Pickering, and it had been in that bleak town that Alathea had made her headquarters during the dreary interminable months when Rachel had been under his care, Humphrey coming up for short periods to join her whenever his business commitments would permit.

The treatment had been prolonged and complicated and painful. Alathea had gathered that extracts from the tumor had been prepared and injected into animals, which in turn produced other tumors in their sex glands, and it was from these that a serum had been obtained for injecting back into the patient which, the doctor had had every reason to hope, would prove beneficial. From the beginning he had stated that he could not guarantee complete success, but on several past occasions he had achieved startlingly satisfactory results, although it was as yet too early to announce an efficaciousness of one hundred per cent.

At the end of eleven weeks, towards the end of January, the child's health seemed to have improved to a remarkable extent and immediate danger had receded, and Doctor White had suggested that she could return home, since he had administered the total number of injections that safety allowed and that they must now await results. "We can only hope, dear Mrs. Decker," he had said. "We can only hope, wait and see. Fortunately Rachel has encouraging stamina and powers of great physical resistance."

So they had brought her back in an ambulance, driving carefully through the snow shrouded countryside until they had reached Welford, where at first she had been tended by a nurse from the clinic and later on, in March, when the nurse had made her departure, Nanny had taken over for, apart from a weekly administration of a capsule containing a milky liquid, of which they had been sent an adequate supply, quiet and rest and watchful dieting were all that could be done for the little girl.

Shortly after their return Doctor White had left on a world tour which was to be part holiday and part research and during which he was to give several lectures. He would be away, he had said, for more than eight months. Miss Vanna, his secretary, would have a list of forwarding addresses, but he was afraid that he himself would be constantly on the move, and there was nothing more in the near future that he could do for Rachel. He would communicate as soon as he came back from his travels. By the same post Miss Vanna had sent Humphrey a bill for a thousand guineas.

Alathea was recalled from her reverie by Nanny's voice. "It's a shame right enough," she was saying, "tampering with nature and interfering with God's will." Her blue eyes rested on her employer's face and they were compassionate. " 'Tho it's sure I am that you and Mr. Decker acted for the best . . . according to your lights," she qualified grudgingly. "Although I'll not deny that it's enough to crack your heart in two."

"I hope that we have done so, Nanny," Alathea said. She wondered how long Nanny had been talking and what she had been saying. "Doctor White should be here at a quarter to seven," she went on. "I'll bring him straight down to you."

"Then it will be bathing my darlin' and giving her her supper that I'll be doing," Nanny announced. "She's never off her food, that's one good thing. She's not pernickety, I must admit. She's got an appetite as hearty as a priest's, and she's full of energy even if she's not talkative, scampering around and putting her nose into everything. She's that inquisitive!" Nanny brightened up. "It's been good-bye to Doctor White's diet sheet for a long while now, I can tell you. The poor pet always seems to be half starving. I was just on my way in to see if Mrs. Glazebroke would be obliging me with a slice or so of cold beef. Scrambled eggs and fruit won't satisfy Rachel, mark my words. Not these days, they won't! Half the time I suspect Mrs. Glazebroke thinks I'm after wanting all the extra food for myself. Imagine!" She bridled at the imputation. "That woman can be a regular ijiut when she's a mind to!"

Alathea frowned. "But Nanny," she protested, "that's very naughty of you. When Doctor White lays down . . . a routine; it is up to us all to see that it is properly carried out."

"Easier said than done." Nanny shook her head in disapproval.

"Rachel loses weight shockingly if she doesn't get enough. And her temper! When she's hungry she gets quite vicious, and it's no fairy tale that I'm after telling you." She paused. "The little angel!" she added inconsequently.

"Well, you must stop it," declared Alathea severely. "I'll ask the doctor this evening if it will be all right to increase and vary her diet."

Nanny did not answer. She nodded, suddenly aloof, and went on her way, straight-backed, down the overgrown path that cut through the shrubbery to the back door. Alathea sighed. Darling Nanny! She would not face up to reality. She clung obstinately to candles and prayers and miracles and a blind pinning of her faith on to the impossible.

It was twenty minutes to seven when Humphrey got back from the station. Alathea heard his finger on the horn as he negotiated the gates into the drive, and she hurried out to meet him. The car drew up and he jumped out, his country clothes arrogantly shabby, and walked round to open the boot from which he lifted a suitcase and a canvas K.L.M. carrier bag.

As he was doing so Doctor White emerged from the other door. He came over to her, smiling and with his arm outstretched in greeting. "Mrs. Decker! This is indeed a pleasure!" He gripped her hand too hard and held it for too long. "I trust you will not mind," he continued, "but I have brought Alexis with me. He is in the car." Alathea glanced past him and saw an enormous brindled lurcher sitting in sedate dignity on the back seat. "I do apologize," said Max White, "but really I had no alternative. I acquired him yesterday afternoon. He is for Conrad, the young son of my assistant. You may remember him? The boy adores what he calls 'the English sporting life'! I am taking Alexis back with me tomorrow to Pickering."

"Are you?" said Alathea. She refrained from remarking that waiting an extra day before collecting the dog would have made but a minor difference.

As if he had read her thoughts Doctor White said: "I am not returning via Sussex, from where he comes. I am taking a train from Oxford to York." He shrugged his massive shoulders. "A tiresome journey . . . *mais c'est la vie!*"

"It is perfectly all right," said Alathea. "We have no dogs of our own."

Max White bowed and smiled again and turned away to open the car door. She had not noticed before that he was so stocky and had such large hands. The big lurcher bounded out and stood for a minute with muzzle pointed upward sniffing the air with interest before he trotted staidly to the rear bumper where he smelt around inquiringly before lifting a leg against the shining chromium.

"Alexis!" said Doctor White reprovingly. "A hundred apologies, Mrs. Decker. It is the journey. He is not an experienced traveller. What one has to do in the name of friendship!"

Previously Alathea had seen the doctor only in his clinical white uniform or in the Lovat tweeds which he wore in Yorkshire. He looked very urban in his beautifully cut striped navy suit with a hard collar and a pale gray tie that was anchored by a pearl pin. He must have come from a conference in London that afternoon. His hair was curly and blue-black and it was clear that he needed to shave twice a day. "It doesn't matter at all," she said. "You must take him for a proper walk before dinner." Humphrey joined them carrying the doctor's luggage, and Alathea said: "I'll show you your room, and then we will go and see Rachel." She preceded them through the hall and up the curving staircase.

Tentatively Doctor White made a courteous, if abortive effort to take his cases from Humphrey. "And how is she now?" he asked her. "Your husband was not very forthcoming on the subject during our drive." The two men had in fact come from Oxford in nearly complete silence.

"You'll be able to judge that for yourself," said Alathea. Even to her own ears her voice sounded like that of a bad actress floundering in a pre-war comedy.

Max White glanced at her sharply. "I heard from Miss Vanna that progress had not altogether been maintained," he said. "Also I received letters from you in Rangoon and Suva and Bogota. Alas, by the time they had reached me they were out of date, so there was no point in answering them. When one is engaged in doing such long . . . hops, do you say? . . . as I have been doing since last we met, even air mail is unreliable. I came here as quickly as I could. I reached England only on Tuesday." He favored Alathea with a piercing look from under his thick eyebrows. "You perhaps found it necessary to call in other advice?"

"Yes," said Humphrey. "We found it necessary. No one was anxious to touch the case. Your methods seem to be unique and peculiar to yourself."

Doctor White inclined his head. "I think that I may say that they are." He did not feel at ease with Humphrey. He had never done so. His reaction to him, like that of many other people, was that Humphrey was summing him up with lazy dislike and disapproval.

Alathea opened a bedroom door. "Your bathroom is opposite," she said. "We will wait for you downstairs."

As they were once more crossing the hall they could see Alexis sitting on his haunches at the top of the flight of steps, his head cocked to one side, as motionless as a basalt statue of an animal-headed Egyptian deity. "Ugly great brute!" Humphrey said. His expression was grim as he went on: "I could kill that bastard, White," he said. "I can hardly keep my hands off him."

Alathea did not answer at once. Then she said: "We went to him of our own volition. Nobody forced us. It was my fault for having listened to that verbose fool, Cathleen."

"Our fault," Humphrey corrected her.

"That was kind of you," said Alathea. She smiled briefly, momentarily her face lit up and took on an endearing charm like that of a surprised bush baby. In recent months she had smiled rarely.

They were in the drawing-room and Humphrey crossed over to the drink tray. There was the clink of glass on glass and the sharp sibilant splash of soda. Then he stood by the window with his slim tapering back rigid, turned towards her, and looked out into the garden which was already losing its color to the night.

Alathea thought of Max White's question and Humphrey's abrupt answer, remembering when *la ronde* of doctors had begun again, although after a preliminary talk the majority of those they had consulted had found it more convenient to make the journey down to Welford rather than have Rachel call at their places of business. None had been able to offer the slightest help or consolation. They had been definitely unwilling to get themselves involved in the case, pleading the excuse of professional etiquette. She recalled that Gilbert Adler, as he was leaving after his examination, had muttered under his breath: "White is no better than a criminal. He should be deported." He had thought that he had not been overheard.

The atmosphere was tense with waiting. It seemed a long while before they heard the doctor's footsteps cross the marble floor.

Humphrey swung round as he came in. "A drink?" he asked, but there was no warmth in the invitation.

"I think not," said his guest, "not, that is, until after we have seen my patient." He pushed back his cuff. "It will soon be her bedtime." Doctor White had made a leisurely change into a country suit and had washed his hands and combed his hair.

Humphrey did not insist and they walked together through the fading light across the driveway to the lawn and past borders burning with the bright defiant flowers of autumn. "Rachel and her old Nanny have been installed in a small house in the garden," said Alathea, ". . . on their own. She likes it better there, and it is easier that way."

Max White halted. Ahead of them the big dog circled, delighting in his liberty. "It might be wiser," Doctor White said, "if I were at first to see Rachel by myself. For five minutes only," he added, "then Mr. Decker and you can join me."

Alathea opened her mouth to remonstrate, for she did not want the child to be alarmed, and doubted too the manner of Nanny's reception, but she caught Humphrey's barely perceptible nod and did not speak.

"Just as you wish," Humphrey said. "You follow the path at the end of the rose garden and then turn to your left."

"Thank you." Doctor White whistled the dog to heel and began to walk on.

"I think it might be better if you left Alexis in the house," called Alathea after him. "Nanny is the president of the Anti-Dog League!" She made it sound like a joke. "Will he follow me if I take him?"

"I doubt it," said Doctor White. "He is an independent character." He walked back with her without speaking and the lurcher was shut into the flower room.

When they had rejoined Humphrey Alathea put a hand on Max White's sleeve. "Rachel may be rather frightened when she sees you," she said. "She had a rough time at High Hall, so please be very gentle with her."

The doctor laughed softly. "Mrs. Decker," he said, "I have an easy manner with children. Also much experience. You need not be alarmed. I have no threatening syringes with me this evening." He made a gesture of farewell. "*A bientôt.*"

"Why did you agree to his suggestion?" Alathea asked when he was out of earshot. "Why shouldn't we have all gone down to the folly together?"

"Because," said Humphrey with bitterness, "Rachel's impact on him will strike him more forcibly if he is alone and knows that in a few minutes he will have to face us." They stood where they were until the doctor's neat figure had been swallowed up among the bushes and then very slowly they began to walk after him. "It may not be impossible even now," Alathea said. "He may still be able to do *something* for her. We must not forget that he has had his successes. There was that boy from America . . ."

Humphrey flicked away his cigarette stub. "He must have taken a new line with Rachel," he said with suppressed violence. "Maybe he found his *penchant* for experimenting during his Belsen days."

Through the thickening dusk they entered the dark tunnel of the pergola, the petals of the rearguard of the summer's white roses gaining in substance and brilliance as night fell, and the air was saturated with the scent of the flowers. Alathea's mind was filled with memories of Rachel as she had been before the onset of her illness, so appealing and lovely and with an infinite capacity for spontaneous enjoyment and affection, and her heart was heavy.

When they had brought her back from High Hall she had for a time made progress and Alathea had felt a humble gratitude, but gradually she had relapsed. The child had not become weak or listless, quite the contrary, but Alathea had feared that her brain had been affected, and that the terrifying tumor was growing again. As the weeks passed and her speech had become increasingly difficult, words had grown meaningless. Her hair had dulled and dried up into brittleness and had fallen out, and in its place had come a brownish down, while scaly scabrous patches had made their appearance on her skin. Her soft child's body had hardened and grown curiously muscular, and her features had sharpened

and changed until she was grotesque in her little girl's frocks, and
Alathea had dressed her in jeans and long sleeved shirts to disguise
the travesty of a human being into which she was degenerating.
And then . . .

Alathea shuddered and endeavored to force her thoughts into
other channels. There must be a way to save her. There had to be
a way. If there was not there was no justice in the world, nor any
God in heaven.

As they followed the path towards the folly they heard the barking of a dog, a high frenzied note of hysterical excitement. "It's
that bloody great tike of White's," said Humphrey, and he quick-
ened his pace, "How in the hell did he get out? I wonder what it
can be that he's put up."

A stretch of rough grass sloped down to the point where the
stream had been dammed to form a small lake mottled with brown
islands of the moored leaves of the water lilies. At its narrow end it
was spanned by a humped wooden bridge that gave access to the
folly on the further side, and as they stepped out from the shadows
of the trees on to the grass they realized that the barking of the
dog had ceased.

In each of the rooms of the sculptured building the lights had
been turned on and they were streaming through the open door
and windows, illuminating the verandah, and it was against this
backcloth that the group of actors were struggling in dark and
chaotic silhouette.

Rachel and Nanny must have been waiting under the colonnade for the doctor's arrival, and when he was pushing through
the swing gate Alexis must have rushed up and brushed past him
and must have leapt straight for the child. Now he had her down
on the flagstones and was savaging her, the man and woman bent
double and unable to get a hold, trying in vain to pull him off.

The slatted floor of the bridge beat a drum-like tattoo as Alathea
and Humphrey tore forward. As they neared the scene they saw
that both Nanny and Doctor White were spattered with blood, and
that there was a long tear in the sleeve of Nanny's uniform.

The child was twisting and turning desperately in an effort to
escape the dog's jaws, her lips drawn back from her teeth in an
animal snarl, her bright eyes glittering balefully. Her hands with

their clawed nails and her feet, one of which was in a pink bedroom slipper, struck impotently upwards in automatic and savage retaliation, raking without effect against the dog's chest and belly. The shrill squealing, degradingly exciting, that issued from the little girl's mouth was like that of a doomed rodent engaged in a hopeless death struggle, rather than any sound that could have come from the body of a member of the human race caught, however tightly, in the grip of deadly fear.

The dog's deep growl rumbled from the base of his throat while he worried at the child, exerting all of his strength as he tried repeatedly to lift her from the ground in order to swing her furiously from side to side so that her neck might be broken, as a terrier will break the neck of a rat, cleanly and with despatch, for it was in the guise of a huge rat that she had appeared to him.

It had been from the living bodies of young sewer rats that the cultures for the serum had been made, rats that were the strongest and most voracious of all, and while Max White wrestled with the lurcher he knew with horrid certainty that its potency, and that of the capsules, had been beyond dispute.

As her parents reached her Rachel's twitching ceased and the mutilated body in the torn Jaeger dressing gown lay limply splayed out in death. After nuzzling the head to make certain that life was extinct the lurcher raised his muzzle from the mangled bizarre corpse. His jowls were dripping with blood, for it had not been at all a clean killing. The quarry had been too heavy.

He shook himself and wagged his tail, and the liver colored lips curled back from his teeth in anticipatory pleasure as he waited in the pool of light, confident and expectant, for the customary murmured words of approval and the congratulatory pat on the back which would be his merited reward for a job well done.

"DANCE LITTLE LADY"

THERE had been a scene of the greatest confusion outside the Golden Plover. The imperious blasts of police whistles, the shouts and cries and curses of the combatants, the shrieks of the women and girls had all combined to shatter the enjoyment of the Saturday night.

For the main part the mêlée had been composed of immigrant Irish and colored men, but a number of the local boys had weighed in on the side of the Micks, egged on by the clamor of the girls who had been with them.

Buzz and Lofty had managed to make their getaway just in time, taking Rosie with them. They had walked off with long unhurried strides, supporting the protesting girl between them, for she had wanted to remain to see the outcome. At the first side turning which they had reached they had broken into a run.

Buzz had been the one to instigate the break away. He had no desire to be picked up by the coppers, not for the second time in six weeks, he hadn't, not on your ruddy life, not with knuckle-dusters and a flick knife on him. The police could be proper buggers when they got you inside, especially where racial incidents were concerned, and with a record like his. Sometimes he thought that they sided with the black bastards.

He hadn't intended to get mixed up in anything tonight. Not really. He'd just been having a few drinks with Lofty before closing time to round off the evening like, when who should drift in but Rosie, and after that they'd stayed until the end, and had plenty.

He knew her slightly. One of Spike Logan's lot, she was, somewhat on the fringe of his mob—but she went along with them. Said she was eighteen but he doubted it, more like sixteen, but that hadn't put the fellahs off, and after all there was no telling, was there? When she was in the mood, or so he'd heard, she'd been known to take on four or five a night. Real hot stuff.

The surprising thing about Rosie was that she did not look at all tarty. You might have mistaken her for a straight girl if you hadn't known better. Not much make-up, no kinky clothes. It was her eyes and mouth that gave her away after she'd got outside a few gins, when she became all sort of moist and clinging and couldn't seem able to keep her hands to herself.

You didn't have to pay her or anything of that kind, or so they said; not, that was, unless you felt like doing so, and then, of course, she wouldn't say no. But she never asked. She was an odd one in a lot of ways.

It was Rosie who had got them involved. She had a thing about the West Indians. Couldn't stand them. Buzz wondered why. From all he'd been told about them he'd have thought that they'd have been right up her street. But perhaps it was only a lie. Propaganda put about by those strutting show-off bucks. The black girls weren't no different, he knew that for a fact; and the smell when they got hotted up! Enough to fair turn your stomach up it was. Talk about the cat house at the zoo!

An ambulance shrilled its alarm and a police car tagged along close behind it. They'd all be converging now on the Plover. Here came a second of them. Vultures, that's what they were, a pack of bloody vultures.

Buzz muttered to Lofty and they slowed their pace to a careful walk. He thought that Lofty was rather overdoing the nonchalance. In his stained duffle coat and with that scruffy beard he looked as shifty as could be. Buzz halted and lit a cigarette with the last of his matches, shielding the flame in his cupped hands. Rosie giggled and Buzz felt a flash of irritation. He wasn't going to let himself be picked up, not carrying these "offensive weapons". Lofty had a knife too. He'd seen him use it on a great slob of a nigger. "Shut up!" he said curtly to Rosie.

As it went by on their side of the road the police car was crawling along at no more than seven miles an hour. The pale ovals of the officers' faces were turned inquiringly towards them. After a short close scrutiny the car increased speed. The trio stood where they were until it had turned away into Blakeney Road.

"Now," whispered Lofty. "Come on!" They must put as much distance as they could, and as quickly as possible, between themselves and the scene of the disturbance. He had made no plans ahead. They couldn't go to Rosie's house, she lived with her mother and brother. And so did he and Buzz, that is, they too were cooped up with their families. That was always the trouble. No place to go. They'd have to find an archway. Parky, but better than nothing.

From the end of the roadway behind them there came the patter of running feet. They looked back apprehensively over their shoulders. A knot of jostling shouting youths was surging towards them, and further back they glimpsed blue uniforms.

"Get a move on," urged Lofty again. They broke into a run. On their left was a narrow alley, little more than a passage, and they doubled down it. It was long and straight, its sides unbroken by doorways, a depressing canyon, claustrophobic and moldering. They had covered more than half of it when the sound of the shouting grew louder.

"We'd best leave 'er, Lofty," said Buzz in a matter of fact voice.

"That you don't!" Rosie said. She was beginning to sober up in the cold night air. "If you think you're going to scarper off and leave me to that there bunch you've got another think coming." Her hands tightened spasmodically on the boys' arms.

They made a dash for it to Latham Street from which radiated a maze of small and ill lit roads. They darted across the thoroughfare to get away from the passers-by. A car hooted at them indignantly, the driver reviling them obscenely from his side window.

Once in Logwood Grove they stopped, all of them panting and out of breath. Their immediate danger passed, the boys at once forgot all about it. Buzz tugged out a bottle of whisky from his overcoat pocket. He took a deep swig and handed it to Rosie. "Here," he said, "have a go—but don't drain it, mind!"

"Haven't you got no gin?" she asked querulously.

"Lofty's got the gin," Buzz said. "One thing at a time as the sailor said to his mates!"

They walked slowly on down the street. Logwood Grove consisted of two-storeyed houses backed by the hoarding bordered cutting of the railway line. The dwellings grew increasingly squalid until, at the end of the residential area, they petered out altogether into a down-at-heel district of warehouses and small factories. Against the skyline loomed the obese bulk of a gasometer.

Buzz wondered who should be the first with Rosie, Lofty or himself. Not that he minded. He wasn't particular. Rosie was wondering the same thing. She was equally indifferent. It was a part of her evening routine, going with boys, that was, when she could get away.

She thought that she could go for Buzz. His heart would be in it, unlike so many of the weeds who did it just to bolster up their own silly egos. She liked his thick shoulders and quick smile. A bit stocky, but then you couldn't expect everything. He dressed smartly too, took trouble with himself, and his finger nails were clean.

When they had been in the Plover she had asked him why he was called "Buzz". It had seemed such a funny sort of a name. Apparently he had been christened Roy, and "Buzz" had been his Mam's idea. He had told her that when he had been little he had never been able to keep still, was always dashing about all over the place. A regular buzz bomb his Mam had called him and the nickname had stuck. He'd said it was gruesome really, as later on his Mam had been killed by one of them . . . one of them buzz bombs. Rosie, too, had had a nickname when she'd been a tiddler. "Lady-bird" her father had called her. That was before he'd gone off that Saturday night about six years ago. He'd gone off and they'd never heard from him since.

They walked on and Logwood Grove fell behind them. The streets became increasingly emptied of lights save for those of the widely spaced standards sentinelled along the pavements. The high walls blurred into dreary lines of featureless sooted brick.

They pushed on purposefully, just as if they had some fixed destination. Lofty began to press against her breast with his arm, rubbing his elbow up and down. She didn't care much for Lofty. A tunnel leading to the loading yard of a warehouse gaped at them on their right from across the road. They all stopped and regarded it speculatively. "How about it, Rosie?" Buzz said.

She shook her head emphatically. "Too cold and dirty." She gave an encouraging laugh. "Come to that, how about giving us another drink? And coming to *that*, Buzz, what do you think I am? Some sort of a public convenience?"

"I wouldn't say that, Buzz, would you?" asked Lofty innocently. "It wouldn't be polite. 'Mr. Manners'—that's me!"

The boys guffawed at this witticism and Buzz passed over the bottle. "Don't know so much about the 'public'," he said to Rosie, "but you're certainly convenient!" A thin drizzle began to blow into their faces and he turned up the collar of his coat. His eyes went again to the dark opening. "We might do worse," he said at last. "At least it's got a roof!"

Rosie wrinkled her nose. "It smells," she said. "It must be a tannery." She took another gulp of the whisky. "I won't think all that much of you two if you can't find somewhere better than that! Reg Mullion once took me to a hotel."

"Reg Mullion!" said Lofty. "The Savoy, I suppose?" he ended with heavy sarcasm.

Her small eyes in the childish pudding face hardened. "No," said Rosie. "I never said it was up West." Her expression grew mutinous, her podgy hands tightening on her red plastic bag.

"Oh, all right," said Lofty. "Tell you what, we'll go on for another five minutes and if nothing better turns up we'll come back here. Fair enough?" he demanded.

"Fair enough," agreed Buzz.

Rosie said nothing.

They walked on more briskly in the direction of the gasometer. Suddenly Rosie tugged at Buzz's sleeve. "Look down there!" she said.

They were standing at the top of a short flight of stairs which led to the entrance of a squat single-storeyed building. On either side of the doorway was a ponderously barred window and, what had caught her attention, was the fact that there was the glimmer of a key that had been left in the lock.

Buzz whistled softly. "Shelter from the stormy blast!" he said. "This calls for another slug!" He took out the bottle of Haig and passed it round. When it came to his turn he drank for a long time until it was finished and then slung it across the road. There was a thud as it struck the wall opposite, the fragments of jagged glass tinkling as they starred down on to the pavement. They found this immensely amusing, for they were more than a little drunk and their laughter was prolonged and meaningless.

Lofty was the first down the steps, then came Rosie holding cautiously on to the handrail. Buzz paused for a moment before he followed, looking automatically up and down the road to see if they might have been observed.

The key was a Yale and the door swung open easily. The interior of the building was stygian, the blackness almost palpable. They stood bunched together, hesitating on the threshold. Buzz pushed the other two aside, his hand searching for a switch.

Seemingly from their midst there came the eerie throb of ghostly dance music. "What the hell . . ." said Lofty, looking up to the level of the road.

Rosie gave a hiccup. "It's only me, stupid," she said. "I brought my transistor."

Buzz found the switch and at the end of the white tiled room glaring strip lights sprang to dazzling life. Rosie blinked around her uncomprehendingly. Her feet tapped on the glazed surface of the floor. She clicked her fingers, her pin heels stamping out a flamenco rhythm, her young mouth puffed out into a reddened trumpet. "Let's have a ball!" she said. She began to dance, still snapping her fingers, her tight skirt molding her rounded buttocks. Buzz strutted towards her in time to the music and struck an attitude.

The room was square and there was an opaque and dusty skylight built into the ceiling. The only furnishings consisted of a metal trolley on one side of the entrance and a desk and a chair of tubular steel on the other. At the end, away from where they stood, was what looked to them to be an enormous deep-freeze. The walls and floor were of unrelieved and clinical porcelain slabs.

Rosie turned up the volume of the transistor radio. The acoustics in the bare aseptic room amplified the sound to the same deafening degree as they would have experienced had they been in an empty swimming bath. Abruptly Lofty told her to modify it. He was staring round and frowning. He could have imagined no more bleak and uncomfortable surroundings for love making than those in which he now found himself.

"Oh close the door do, Lofty," said Rosie impatiently. "It's like an ice box!"

Without thinking Lofty obeyed, giving it a violent jerk, and the key, which had been left in the lock on the outside, dropped unheard on to the rain washed flagstones of the area.

Buzz took Rosie in his arms and they moved away to the music. Lofty sat down in the utilitarian chair and watched them through the smoke of his cigarette. He took out his bottle of gin and put it on the table in front of him. "You don't half look ghastly under them lights," he said. "You put me in mind of Dracula and his bride. That's what!" He looked at them, grinning, playing with the ornate ring on his middle finger. "You might both of you be made out of green cheese or something!" he mocked.

"You don't look no heart throb yourself, Lover Boy," Buzz called back. "More like something the dog didn't fancy and brought up on the parlor carpet, if you asks me."

"No one's asking you," Rosie said. "And no one's asking for no uncalled for remarks either! See what he's doing, Buzz?" she went on pertly. "He's scoffing all the booze, that's what!" She broke off dancing and pulled Buzz over to the table by his lapel. "Share and share alike is my motto!"

"All right, all right," said Lofty. "Keep calm! Come and get it; but there's no more where that came from when it's gone, so I'm warning you."

"Oh, isn't there?" said Rosie. "That's all you know. How wrong can you get?" She picked up the scarlet bag. "I've another half stowed away in here." She smiled broadly. "You can't expect the boys to pay for everything all the time, can you?" she said. "Leastways that's what my Mam taught me."

"Is that all she taught you?" said Lofty. "Maybe now you could teach your old lady a trick or two?"

"That's right," said Buzz. "Maybe she could at that!" Lofty gave him the bottle. "One for you . . ." Buzz said. "One for me . . ." he tipped back his head, "and one for little Rosie," he finished. His breath reeked of spirits as he handed her the bottle. He gave her a slap on the bottom for good luck.

"Well, what about it, Rosie?" said Lofty, wiping his mouth with the back of his hand.

"What about what?" she said eyeing him.

"What about our having a twirl?" he asked innocently.

She put the tiny radio set down next to the gin bottle. "Okidoke," she said. She held out her arms. Even when drunk they were all of them expert dancers.

Buzz settled himself in Lofty's place, tilting his chair and resting his elastic sided boots on the table's top. "'Not me'," he sang, "'not me . . . not me . . . not me . . . not me . . . but *you!*'"

The room was all at once plunged in darkness. "Hey!" came

Lofty's voice. "What's the big idea? Don't act so silly, Buzz. You crazy sod!"

Buzz gave a laugh. "None of my doing," he said. "Power cut!" He listened to the uninterrupted slither of their feet on the polished tiles.

"No you don't, Lofty!" It was Rosie's voice raised in protest. "No you don't. Give over!"

Buzz gave a shout of laughter and the beam of a torch cut through the gloom, freezing the dancers in alarm. "Carry on, kids," Buzz said. "It's only yours truly. Thought we'd been raided?" He smiled, benevolently playing the beam round the walls until allowing it to come to rest on the big dual doors of what he took to be some sort of a refrigerator. "I'd like to know what they keep in there," he said thoughtfully. "What about it, Lofty? What about a look see?"

Lofty and Rosie came over towards him, one side of the girl's purple coat touched by the shaft of light. "Why not take a look?" she said. "After all, it's their carelessness! But first let's all have a little drink. It's on me later on, don't forget. Do you think it's stopped raining?" she asked. "It must be getting ever so late." She stood on tiptoe trying to peer out of one of the grimy barred windows. Unable to see anything she went to the door by which they had entered. "Flash it over here, Buzz," she said. He did so and she flicked idly at the small circular guard over the keyhole. There was a significant silence, but when she spoke she sounded frightened. "We've gone and locked ourselves in, Buzz," she said rather breathlessly. "It must have happened when you slammed the door, Lofty. Whatever shall we do?"

Lofty went across to verify what she had said. "We've had it," he announced, "so far as getting out of here is concerned." He waited for his friends' reaction.

Buzz directed the torch on to the massive rolled gold watch bracelet on his wrist. "It's after midnight," he said, "and we ain't done no harm. Someone will be along to let us out in the morning. An old caretaker, most likely, and if he tries to make any trouble Lofty and me can dot him one and run for it." He smiled. "Meanwhile we've got each other and something to drink, so what's the worry?" He held up the Gordon's by the neck. "Let's have ourselves a good time and enjoy it. Wine . . . Woman . . . and Song!"

"Tomorrow's Sunday," said Rosie. "Perhaps he won't come at all."

"He'll come," Buzz said. "He'll be along as soon as he misses the key."

Seeing that Rosie continued to appear anxious they all had another round and Lofty said: "Well—aren't we going to have a look?" He nodded towards the huge cupboard. "Maybe it's not even locked." Hands in pockets he lounged off, kicking out at the metal trolley as he passed by and causing it to move smoothly on its castors. "Hi, Rosie!" he said "Want a ride?" Picking her up, and despite her struggles, he dumped her on to its enamelled top at the same time giving it a hearty push.

Rosie squealed as she was carried away into the darkness. The trolley jarred to a halt against the far wall. The young men followed it, walking together in step to the wide closed doors, the beam of the torch focusing down to a smaller circle as they approached.

There were two handles, one on each panel, and they pulled it open with no difficulty. Inside were ranged five long deep trays on rollers. Buzz tugged experimentally at the one on the top. It slid forward. Upon it lay the corpse of a woman, shrouded in a sheet. They stared at it with incredulity.

Rosie gave a stifled shriek. "Push it back, Buzz," she said, fighting panic. "It's a stiff. You know where you are, don't you? We're in a morgue, that's where we are! And what's more we're shut in! Locked up in a mortuary!" She started to shake uncontrollably. Lofty thought uneasily that she was about to have hysterics, and Buzz, to quieten her, obeyed.

"Stiffs can't do you no injury," he said. "For Christ's sake take a pull on yourself, Rosie. Nothing's going to happen to you." He fell silent, following her train of thought and then said: "There's another door in the side wall. I noticed it earlier on."

They took the torch and crossed over to investigate, but again there was no key. Had they but known it, it gave access to the Coroner's Court.

Curiously, the circumstances of their being immured with the dead gave both Lofty and Buzz a thrill of peculiar excitement.

They returned to the table. Buzz took possession of the bottle. "Ladies first!" he said, handing it to Rosie. She drank and the color began to come back into her face. The boys followed suit, the spirit burning their throats. Lofty coughed. Buzz held the empty bottle upside down. "Another dead man!" he said.

"Don't!" said Rosie.

Buzz opened Rosie's bag and took from it her liquor contribution. "We've enough left to keep us going 'til morning, so cheer up, all. Let's have some fun. We're alive and kicking," he added, "which is more than that poor bitch is!" His words were slurred and his laugh thick. "Get with it!" He turned up the radio. "You suggested we should have a ball, Rosie . . . well, here goes! Ladies and gentlemen," he commanded, "take your partners! Lofty—you can have Rosie."

"Buzz," she said, "what do you mean? What are *you* going to do?"

He waltzed over to where the dead woman lay and began to pull out the metal shelves, no more of which, he discovered, had any occupant. "Oho!" he shouted. "Party's complete. Even numbers! Two girls and two chaps." He eased out the top shelf and carefully lowered its burden into his arms. By now he was very drunk. "Howdy, m' darlin'," he said. "Time to shake a leg!" Laughing, he threw back his head. "It's knees up, Mother Brown!" The body he was embracing was young and in life must have been quite pretty.

Lofty and Rosie stood beside the table watching his antics bemusedly. They passed the bottle between them from hand to hand. "Buzz!" shouted Lofty, flushed and swaying slightly. "Action stations! Change partners!" His mouth, above the straggling reddish beard hung loosely open. He belched loudly.

The light from the torch was beginning to dim and the darkness crowded closer. "Not on your life," cried Buzz. "I'm capable of finding my own bleeding dates without your help. And see this one dance!"

Lofty ran forward, sliding over the floor towards the cabinet, his arms flailing wildly. "We'll make this an 'excuse me!'"

Rosie remained by the diminishing light watching them dance, her expression fatuously vacant. Although afraid, she was beginning to be affected by the boys' bravado.

"Why be a wall flower when there's a gentleman in the stag line?" Lofty called, pointing to himself. "Do you suffer from B.O.? Won't your best friends tell you?" He grinned over at her. "Come along and join us, Rosie." He tapped Buzz on the shoulder, at the same time making a low bow.

"Don't be scared, Rosie," Buzz said encouragingly. "Somebody may do the same for us one of these days!"

Rosie walked slowly and reluctantly forward towards them. The transistor's music changed from pop to a waltz. It was an old classic. "If you were the only girl in the world". . .

Dancing across the fading path of the torch their shadows were enormous and distorted as they passed brokenly over the tiled walls. Fuddled by alcohol and numb with fright Rosie could scarcely force her legs to move.

"Tell you what," said Buzz, "what do you say to our giving this here mademoiselle a break? Doctors can make mistakes same as the rest of us, can't they? You read about it every day. Let's give 'er the kiss of life. It's worth a try, isn't it? She's got nothing to lose, and if we succeed then we'll be smashing heroes. Might even get a mention in the *News of the World*."

As he spoke he was revolving within a few feet of the trolley, and with exaggerated care he stopped and propped his partner up against it. Rosie was within a short distance of the tubular table. She had broken away from Lofty who was isolated in the middle of the room.

There was a strained silence broken only by the labor of heavy breathing. Minutes went by. "Phew!" said Buzz. "This is too bloody much like hard work. You 'ave a go, Rosie, then if it's no damn good I vote we pack it up."

Rosie leant forward, and suddenly she screamed. "It's alive! It's . . . I mean her . . . eyelids fluttered. I swear that they did. You're wicked. Why can't you leave her alone? Why can't you? She's not dead at all. Oh, my God!" She released her grip of the body and it slumped forward, spreadeagled across the table, and upsetting the torch in its fall. The torch rolled to the edge and toppled down on to the floor, breaking the bulb. They were in total darkness.

Rosie continued to scream, long ear piercing monotone notes of terror. Batting around, unable to see where they were going, the boys could do nothing with her. Then they closed with her, and after short periods of exhaustion during which they held her tightly she would begin anew, the knuckles of one hand pressed against her lips. She quivered with horror, racked by her shuddering.

"Strike a match, Buzz," said Lofty.

"Got none left," he said. "Aint you got no lighter?"

"No, God blast it! Needed a new flint."

"Let me go. Let me go. I must get out of here. Please let me go." Rosie said the words over and over again like an incantation.

It was ten minutes past eight before the man arrived to open up the mortuary and daylight was probing half heartedly through the dirt of the windows.

As it was, Buzz would be late for work, and Lofty wasn't going to be left behind holding the baby, not for no teenaged nymphomaniac he wasn't, let alone letting himself in for God knew what trumped up charges. Body snatching . . . breaking in . . . rape . . . they'd throw the book at them if they got nicked.

As they had surmised, the caretaker was old, and Buzz and Lofty had no difficulty whatsoever in evading him. One blow in the chest had sent him reeling back against the iron railings, and another in the face had been enough to temporarily blind him and splinter his spectacles.

When the old fellow had pulled himself up and had gone painfully through the doorway the sound of the boys' running feet had already faded away.

He found Rosie crouched in the chair behind the desk, clasping with desperation at the hand of the dead girl. The old man had spoken to her gently. He could get no sense out of her, no sense at all. She kept on repeating: "It's morning, and I've been out all night. What can I say to my Mam? What can I tell her? She'll be ever so mad at me. Ever so." On the floor at her feet the radio was chattering away to itself.

In the course of the dark hours, and in spite of Rosie's frenzied struggles, the boys had made the most of their opportunity. It had been necessary to keep warm and they had had to make the time pass in some way. She'd known well enough what was expected of her when she had come along with them.

They did not anticipate any retaliation from Spike Logan. Their lot was more than a match for his any day of the week, and Rosie didn't count. She wasn't important. She wasn't anybody really, and they could deny everything if she turned nasty. But she wouldn't. She would know better. She was only a little tramp, a tagger-on. It wasn't as if she'd been someone special, like Rene Harper or Kitty Walters who were Spike's own property.

No, Rosie wouldn't open her trap, not if she knew what was good for her. If she so much as gave a cheep they'd "do" her properly, and she knew it.

And she'd put away a fair share of their drink—hadn't she?

The old man was able to do nothing with her. She refused to let go of the dead girl. She kept on stroking her hand and pressing her own lips against the set ones, trying to breathe into her lungs. "She's not dead," she kept on saying. "I saw her eyelids move, really I did. And corpses don't go fluttering their eyelids, do they? She's foxing, that's all. Can't you see she's only foxing? If you give me time I can bring her back." She gazed up imploringly at the old man. "But what about my Mam?" she said. "She's ever so strict with me, really she is."

The caretaker looked sideways at her flushed face, uncertain as to what action he could take. His glance took in the torn clothes, the trembling lips and inward unseeing stare. She'd gone round the bend proper and no mistake. It was no use asking who her Mam was or where she lived. She'd never tell him that. He'd best fetch a policeman—or policewoman—and they'd know what to do. He'd have to report the break-in anyway.

Poor little trollop! Some girls didn't have a chance these days—not with all those young hooligans around with money to spend and no discipline. She wasn't no more than a kid, and the one lying there on the floor hadn't been much older. It was a shame right enough.

"No," said the old man, "you can't leave her all alone. You stay just where you are. I won't be gone long—not above a few minutes."

He climbed painfully up the steps, steadying himself with the handrail. He was very handicapped by the loss of his spectacles. He'd get a constable to come back with him. That body sprawled there on the chipped tiled floor . . . he couldn't move it without help. Not at his age, and with his bad back, he couldn't.

LITTLE BOY BLUE

MOIRA LATTEN had not herself stayed at Stonethorpe. When, as a child, she had first been taken for a holiday to Cleeness the house had been pointed out to her, and on subsequent occasions she had gone there to tea. It was her mother who, in her youth, used to be sent to the Misses Wallace to recuperate after various infantile ailments, under the care of the three kindly ladies who owned the house, which they let out as lodgings.

Stonethorpe was one of a row of semi-detached Victorian villas that faced the sea. There was a road which separated their neat and formal front gardens from the bowling green, now seldom used, behind which lay the sandhills and the beach.

Cleeness had expanded a good deal since the war, but the expansion had taken place at the other end of the town, beyond the shopping center and the clock tower and the Amusement Park, until it had petered out at the new Butlin's Holiday Camp, and the vicinity in which Stonethorpe was situated was hardly changed. It had become more of a backwater and it was shabbier, but otherwise it had remained much the same as when Moira had last seen it.

For several years, when her two children were growing up, Moira's mother, Mrs. Soskin, had chosen to take a bungalow in Cleeness for the summer, preferring it to the more select resorts. It had been usually the same bungalow, The Look Out, and it had been rambling and white stuccoed and had stood on the edge of the sandhills, surrounded by a defeatist garden in which practically nothing but sea-thrift and marigolds and surges of nasturtiums would grow. To remedy this floral sparsity there was a lot of gravel drive lined with whitewashed boulders. The town was on a bleak part of the Lincolnshire coast and was considered to be bracing, and certainly the bathing there had been more of an endurance test than a genuine pleasure, necessitating as it did brisk rubs down with towels and reviving cups of Bovril which had been forced between chattering teeth.

Moira had retained a strange nostalgia for these somewhat

Spartan holidays and so, with the passage of time, when her own son, Oliver, had been recovering from a severe attack of measles, she had remembered the Misses Wallace's establishment and had written on chance to inquire if they still received guests. Their reply had said that they did so on occasion, but since they were well advanced in years they could no longer undertake to provide dinner at night.

Moira and Oliver arrived at Stonethorpe late on a Friday afternoon, and immediately upon entering the house, so unchanged was the atmosphere, that Moira had felt that she had stepped back not only into her own nursery days but even into those of her mother. They were the sole visitors and had been given the front sitting-room for their exclusive use, and the room across the hall was to be set aside for the serving of their meals. Their bedrooms on the first floor faced the sea and were adjacent to the only bathroom.

Miss Dolly Wallace had been delighted to see her. Yes, she well remembered the days when they used to meet, when Moira had been "so high". And how was dear Mrs. Soskin? Keeping in good health, she hoped. How time flew! It seemed like yesterday! She and her sister Connie had been saying so last night, and to imagine that Moira herself now had a child of her own, and such a big boy for eight. Quite the little man! No doubt Moira had heard that they had lost their sister Annie? She had been the youngest of the family, seventy-one, and the first of them to go. It only went to show, didn't it? Moira must come down after tea and have a word with Connie. She was keeping very well really, had retained all her faculties, but nowadays could not manage the stairs.

Yes, it was strange to think that between them they had run the house for close on eighty years, ever since Mrs. Wallace had been brought to Stonethorpe as a bride by her husband in eighteen eighty-eight when it had been newly built, and all their family had been born there. Until a short while back the management of the establishment had been no trouble, but finally they had been reduced to a single girl as staff, and now they had no one. Girls could pick and choose, couldn't they, and they didn't seem to fancy domestic work.

Miss Wallace patted Oliver on the shoulder and told him to

make himself at home and then left Moira to settle in, telling her that tea would be ready in ten minutes and that there would also be a snack at a quarter past seven.

Oliver adored Cleeness. It had all the basic requirements for a boy of his age. Miles of sands studded with rockpools, and the dunes in which he could dig caves and roll down their sides. It was the beginning of May, and except for Saturdays and Sundays the beach was practically empty. Spring had come late, but when it had arrived it had been an exceptionally warm one, and paddling and sunbathing could be indulged in as well as the building of sand-castles for the incoming tide to attack and obliterate. They spent nearly all their day in the open air, and right from the start Oliver's strength had improved.

Moira had planned to stay at Cleeness for two weeks. She did not mind the uneventfulness of the routine, for in the evenings she was able to continue with her work. She was a contributor to several of the women's magazines for which she wrote articles and short stories, and she was glad to be freed from all domestic chores.

It was at the end of their fourth day that Oliver had come running in to her in a state of gleeful gratification. Since Stonethorpe commanded the bowling green and sand dunes Moira used to allow him to go out by himself after tea, with the proviso that he should not stray too far, and that at half past six she would emerge to retrieve him. On this Tuesday evening, pink with excitement, he came jumping down the sandhills with the news that he had made a friend. His name was Sammy and, being seven and a half, he was a year younger than Oliver. He was staying nearby, although he had not mentioned the name of the house. Moira must come immediately and meet him, and could he please ask him to lunch tomorrow?

"Of course you can, darling," Moira said. "We'll go and find him now and invite him, and I'll see if Miss Wallace will give us chops and ice cream."

Oliver led the way, pulling her along behind him in his eager-ness, but there was no sign of Sammy and the happy anticipation faded from his face. "You'll meet him again in the morning," said Moira comfortingly. "We've got the beach almost to ourselves, so you can't miss him and you'll be able to ask him then."

After Oliver had had his bath and was in bed Moira went up to his room to say good-night to him and, as always, he was loath to let her go, choosing for delaying tactics to give her a detailed account of his encounter with Sammy. "He's going away to boarding school next term, and he lives at Uxton, which is a village outside Nottingham, and he has sixpence a week pocket money—which I don't think is very much, do you?—and he wears a sailor suit with a ribbon on the hat saying H.M.S. *Valiant*, which I think is rather babyish and I told him so and he didn't seem to mind a bit and said lots of boys have them and that I was dotty, and he's got a bucket and a wooden spade, and his father's got a big grocer's shop, and there's an older sister who's called Mavis." Oliver paused for breath before he went on: "He knows an awful lot, the names of all the different kinds of seaweed and shells and anemones, and all about the tides and the stars, and he told me a story about a ghost ship called the Marie something or other, and he collects stamps and fossils and his mother makes him go to dancing class and he can't swim yet." Oliver sounded rather reassured by his lack of this latter accomplishment.

Moira laughed. "Neither can I," she said, "and neither can you! Maybe there are some baths in the town where you and Sammy could have lessons. I'll find out. It's still a bit cold for the sea." She bent down to receive his hug. "I'm so pleased you've made a friend. There're another ten days during which you can play together. Good night darling. Sleep tight!"

Her hand was on the door-knob when Oliver was in full spate again. "And he knows all the songs the pierrots sing. They have competitions for the children. I've never seen any pierrots. Can we go one day?"

"If you like," said Moira. "They used to be an attraction in every seaside town, but I thought they'd been dropped these days except on the big piers. We'll go on Friday if you want to. I wonder where they are? I expect on the other side of the Amusement Park."

Oliver held out his arms and she could not resist going back to give him another kiss. "Good night, Mummy," he said. "It is all rather super, isn't it?"

Wednesday, however, brought a disappointment. It was a glorious morning and a few people made their appearance on the

sands, but Sammy was not amongst them. Oliver spent most of
the morning and afternoon looking for him but without success.
A small girl with rabbit teeth and spectacles, by the name of Freda,
tried to scrape acquaintance, but it was not the same thing and he
gave her no encouragement. Oliver experienced a sense of anti-
climax. Perhaps Sammy's mother had been called back suddenly to
Uxton and had taken him with her and he would never meet him
again.

Moira was delighted by Oliver's progress. He was already a different child from the pallid little boy of the previous week. Cleeness, she thought gratefully, must indeed be as health giving as
its publicity claimed, and at this, the quiet end, it was really ideal
for children. No dangerous currents, no steep cliffs and no traffic
except for an occasional tradesman's van. There were, it is true,
buried strands of rusted barbed wire concealed amongst the hummocks, relics of forgotten defenses erected against invasion by the
Germans in World War One, and there were, too, some scattered
patches of quicksand when the tide was out, but all the residents
knew their exact locations and they took care to brief the visitors
so that they could keep away from them. Otherwise there were no
perils for the unwary.

Sammy's withdrawal from Oliver's life lasted until Sunday evening and then, when the last of the trippers were trailing back to
their cars, Oliver found him again. He was solemn and shy and
was unwilling to say where he had been or why he had kept away
from the beach, and Oliver forbore from pressing him. Parents, as
he knew himself, could be odd and unpredictable and their actions
difficult of explanation, and he did not wish to cause him embarrassment by persistent questioning.

It was Sammy's suggestion that they should leave the dunes and,
as the tide was turning, build a castle near the water line which
they could strengthen and defend defiantly and breathlessly against
the siege of the waves. He proved to be an expert builder and
under his tuition a most intricate and impressive fortress was con-
structed which they decorated with a pattern of pebbles and oyster
shells.

When Moira came across the dunes to collect Oliver she was
rather vexed at being forced to walk for such a long way before she

could shout to him. He was a tiny dot between the arc of the sky and desolate sweep of the sands. He came to her reluctantly. His shorts and gym shoes were soaked, and he made no protest when his mother told him that he had gone beyond their agreed boundary and that he had stayed out too late.

Rather to his surprise she did not include Sammy in these strictures and, since Oliver saw that she was annoyed, and suspected that if prompted she would probably put the blame on to Sammy for having led him astray, he neither looked back nor referred to him, especially as his friend had shown small pleasure on receiving the invitation to lunch at Stonethorpe, but instead had said firmly that it would be better if they were to meet each other away from the company of grown-ups, who were frequently bent on spoiling everything. His veiled ultimatum had implied that if their friendship were to continue it would have to be a secret one, and on his own terms, with no adult interference.

As Oliver volunteered nothing more after this concerning Sammy, Moira had taken it for granted that the boy must have left Cleeness, and had decided that it would be wiser not to make inquiries through Miss Wallace how he could be traced, for Oliver did not seem to miss him. In fact he appeared perfectly content and self-sufficient. When they came back to the house he sat bright-eyed and smiling and seemed vaguely constipated with some suppressed and unshared pleasure. He could hardly wait to finish his tea before rushing off to resume his interrupted play, but she could not help but wonder why it was that he so preferred the evenings when the warmth of the sun had gone and there was very often a chill wind.

On Sunday night Moira sighed and put the cover on her typewriter. She crushed out her cigarette. There were already half a dozen stubs in the ashtray. It was ten o'clock and the article which she had just finished was abysmal in its banality. It epitomized all the dreary and rehashed triteness that she had read so often and at which she had so readily mocked. Tomorrow she would make herself tear it up and start afresh. She should have thrown it away at once but here and there there had been a phrase or two which had pleased her and which she considered might have some future potential.

Miss Wallace's over-furnished sitting-room was stuffy, for one of the by-products of the dislike of girls for domestic service had been the replacement of the open fire which had formerly blazed there by a cheerless, but labor saving, arrangement of electric logs which she had switched on. This was made to appear even more unwelcoming by the background of black tiles with hand painted water-lilies that had surrounded the old grate. Moira lit another cigarette and thought that she would walk to the gate for a breath of fresh air before going up to bed.

She stood looking out on to the deserted road and wondered how Jeremy was making out while she and Oliver were at Cleeness. On the whole their marriage had been a happy one, but when, for one reason or another, they had to be apart, they were both tacitly relieved, although their subsequent reunions were appreciated by both.

The night was as warm as June and a full moon hung in a sky of light grey silk, and while Moira lingered by the gate, unwilling to go in, she heard Oliver's voice speaking cautiously and quietly as if he did not want to be overheard. "All right, Sammy," he was saying. "I'll be there, and I'll bring some sweets and my sailing boats. I've got two and they're super and so there'll be one each. Same place. Same time."

Moira looked quickly over her shoulder. Naturally there was no one there. Little boys wouldn't be allowed out so late at night. Oliver must be talking in his sleep, and his bed was pushed up against the open window which made her able to hear him. Or else he was awake and playing—which was very naughty of him. He ought to have been asleep hours ago. She glanced up at the façade and caught the flash of a striped pyjama sleeve as it was whisked back behind a curtain. She returned to the house and hurried up the stairs. Oliver was fast asleep. She scrutinized the heart-breakingly innocent face and the closed eyes with their fingers of dark lashes. Or was he just pretending? Moira tucked in the sheets and he did not stir, and closing the door softly behind her she went on to her own room. Tomorrow would be their final day. It was so hard to remember how vivid the games of childhood had been and how real the imaginary companions. Perhaps he had been missing Sammy all the time and had been putting up a brave front.

She smiled wistfully as she started to undress, for so soon it would be childhood's end.

It was the following evening, and Moira straightened up from her packing. It was all finished except for the few things which they would need in the morning. She looked with a jaundiced eye at the collection of souvenirs which Oliver had painstakingly accumulated during their stay, limpet-spotted strands of bladder-weed, smoothly frosted fragments of glass of white, blue, green and brown, which had been ground by the action of the waves until they had acquired the beauty of uncut jewels. There were scallop and razor shells, and some with exquisite pink shading that had housed minute bivalves such as she clearly remembered having collected during her own long ago foragings. In a bucket there were other shells containing live or moribund winkles and whelks, which would promptly die and smell to high heaven, but she knew that Oliver would insist on taking them all back with him to his home near Guildford.

She saw from the Mickey Mouse watch by Oliver's bed that it was almost seven. As their holiday was finishing she had asked Miss Wallace if she would put back their supper until a quarter to eight as a treat for Oliver, so she would not have to chase him up yet but could leave him to enjoy the extra time. She closed the cases and went down the precipitous stairs with their worn oilcloth and into the sombre hall that was dominated by the ponderously ticking grandfather clock and the big brass gong, and which always smelled of yesterday's roast mutton and cabbage.

As she entered the sitting-room Miss Wallace came up from the basement with a bulky album cradled in her arms. "Oh, there you are, Mrs. Latten!" she exclaimed. "While I was having a turn-out yesterday I came across this book of photographs and Connie said I must show it to you, so I've brought it up as she suggested. There's a sweet one of you taken when you used to come to see us as a little slip of a thing." Miss Wallace followed Moira into the room and dumped the heavy book on to the tablecloth. "It's quite a comprehensive record of our lives here," she said. "My parents began it and after they died we three girls kept it up. Of course these are only a selection in this, from the years nineteen fifteen to thirty-eight." She carefully turned the thick gilt-edged leaves.

Moira, who topped her by a head, peered down over her shoulder. "But what fun!" she said politely.

"There!" said Miss Wallace, pointing in triumph with a wrinkled finger. "There you are!" She displayed proudly the photograph of a skinny and singularly unprepossessing child who was making hideous grimaces above a shrimping net that she extended towards the camera. "Connie declares that you haven't changed at all!" enthused Miss Wallace contentedly. "She told me that she would have known you anywhere. And so would I!" Moira's smile was a trifle bleak. "And what is more," Miss Wallace went on, "in an earlier book I have one of your dear mother when *she* was a kiddy! I'll just pop down and fetch it. It's no trouble," she said as Moira began to protest, "only carrying more than one album is too heavy for me. I'm not so young as I was."

"We none of us are," said Moira automatically.

Miss Wallace gave a primly appreciative laugh. "You cannot bracket yourself with me, Mrs. Latten!" She pattered out of the room, with evident enjoyment, leaving Moira to thumb through the pages.

The dreadful thing was that none of the names that confronted her rang any bell at all, so that it would be hard to show satisfactory enthusiasm. She stared at a forbidding "Miss Hill and Ivor," who had probably been staying at Stonethorpe when she had been taken there, but she had retained no recollection of them.

Miss Dolly Wallace returned. The second volume was even more massive than its predecessor, and had once been secured by a large brass lock, but this was now tarnished and hung open disconsolately. She was panting from her exertions and her pince-nez were askew. Her yellowish-white hair was also in need of tidying.

Moira suddenly remembered how much her grandmother had laughed when she had told her of her own early visits to Cleeness, which had always been to Stonethorpe and which had taken place shortly after the turn of the century. The Misses Wallace had been young women then and the personifications of Edwardian respectability but, according to Grandma, their lavatory had, for utilitarian purposes, been stocked with sheaves of neatly cut up newsprint from an obscure Bolshevist publication which had prophesied, and indeed advocated, bloody revolution. "As if," the old lady had told her, "the poor dears would have liked to have packed all of us into tumbrils and sent us off to the guillotine!" Fortunately this economy had long been discontinued and more normal amenities were now provided.

The oldest of the photographs had been printed in that delightfully soft sepia that is now seldom used. These were for the most part stiffly posed tableaux of the Wallace family, steadfastly hypnotized by the lens. Then, with the coming of black and white processing, emerged the more informal "snaps" of the guests who had come to Stonethorpe on annual holidays. Miss Wallace found the one of Moira's mother and it bore a striking resemblance to that which Moira had been shown of herself. It could not be denied that it was fortunate that the looks of the female members of her family had invariably improved with puberty.

She put the book down and as she did so it fell open at a page which was headed in intricate script: "Summer Season, 1912". The lady lodgers of that year had worn long white skirts and busy high-necked blouses. Their hair had been arranged in a fashion which Moira mentally labelled as "cowpat", or else they had pinned on elaborately trimmed hats. The men had worn choking collars with their blazers and boaters and had displayed a wide variety of moustaches.

In one corner was the picture of a small serious boy in a sailor suit leaning bashfully against the side of a young and pretty woman. The caption underneath read: "Mrs. Mortlock and Sammy. July."

Miss Wallace could not fail to notice Moira's fascination as she studied it. "That poor little boy!" she said. "It might have been yesterday. Such a tragedy! He was the Mortlocks' only son, and he met his death on the last evening of his stay with us." She shook her head. "He was sucked under by the quicksands. A fearful calamity! He had been cautioned about them continually, as all of our visitors are always cautioned, but he managed to give Mrs. Mortlock the slip, and in spite of the fact that as soon as he was missed we all of us went out to search for him, it was too late. It was terribly distressing. Poor, poor Mrs. Mortlock! I thought she would go out of her mind! Sammy was a charming child who won everybody's heart with his winning ways. Such a friendly little fellow, although in some ways he gave the impression of being shy and lonely—or

shall I say reserved? We used to call him Little Boy Blue." Dolly
Wallace was looking back through the long tunnel of the years.
"Such a lovable little fellow," she repeated. "I feel haunted by him
to this very day, and even after all this time! It's funny but it's true.
And so does Connie. He seems so real, he might never have left
us."

It came with dreadful impact to Moira that she had never met
Oliver's "Sammy". Up to this moment, without troubling to think,
she had accepted alternative explanations concerning him. Either
he had been granted scant liberty until the evenings, or else he
had never had any existence except in Oliver's imagination. He had
been a "dream friend", such as solitary children often invented and
adopted. But how could Oliver have dreamed up the sailor suit and
coupled it with the correct Christian name? And why had Sammy
only come to him at the close of day . . . when he would find him
alone?

Without a word of explanation to Miss Wallace Moira hurried
out of the sitting-room, brushing past the branched hat-stand in
the hallway on her way to the door. She crossed the road and,
squeezing through the railings which protected the bowling green,
dropped down and ran across the dark patchy grass to the spiked
hummocks of the dunes. "Oliver!" she called. "Oliver . . . where are
you?" There was no answer. Driven by a sense of panic urgency she
climbed up the hillocks, the loose sand slipping down and filling
her shoes.

At the top she paused. The boundless sweep of the deserted
beach stretched out before her. Away to her left were the forsaken
fantasies of the Amusement Park; the figure-of-eight, the phal-
lic tower embraced by the curving path of the helter-skelter, the
Ghost Train, whose gaping fang-fringed entrance was closed by a
barrier. The distance dwarfed them all into toys, and they would
be untenanted and silent until Whitsun.

"Oliver!" she called again. Her voice in the vast emptiness was
thin and tinny. "Oliver . . . where are you?" A strong breeze was
blowing in from the sea and it flung her words back to her, flatten-
ing her skirt against her body and tangling her hair before her eyes.

Across the expanse of the sand a scattering of gulls, startlingly
white, strutted and pecked in search of food, or rode on the swell

of the waves before they broke and forced them to take flight, and their plaintive strident cries were both harshly angry and forlorn.

The sea was racing in, flooding over the hard corrugated ridges which the receding waves had carved earlier and which were so painful to hastening naked feet. There was a network of creeks which at low tide became stretches and lakes of sand-locked water, but which swiftly joined together with alarming speed when the tide turned.

At what seemed to her to be an incredible distance the flowing together of the creeks had combined to leave an island around which the encroaching waters lapped and nibbled, and marooned in this low lying hump of sand stood the figure of a little boy. Moira's heart leapt until it seemed to stick in her throat. From where she was standing it must be a quarter of a mile to the water's edge, and beyond that was a stretch of sea which was nearly as wide. She stumbled forward, kicking off her shoes, in the grip of paralyzing terror. The cold of the water struck at her ankles and calves as she splashed through the shallows. For a hundred yards the shelving of the beach was gradual, although the water was rising steadily until it became waist high. When she judged herself to be within hailing point of Oliver she shouted his name once more. This time the child, who had been looking out to sea, heard her and turned his head, his delicate arms planted with heroic bravado on his hips as he tried to swivel round.

The island on which he stood had in a few minutes shrunk to half of its former size. "Stay where you are," she called, "and I'll try to get to you." She staggered into a hollow and almost fell, but managed to struggle to her feet, the salt stinging and smarting in her eyes. Battling on determinedly she realized that very soon she would be out of her depth and would be able to go no further. Oh God, why had she never been made to learn to swim? Oliver was too far away for her to see his expression, but she knew that he must be afraid.

"Sammy brought me out here," Oliver called. "He said that we could dig up buried treasure. And now he's gone. He disappeared and left me all alone, and then I found that I was surrounded. He disappeared under the sand and left me. I thought he must have found a secret tunnel and had gone to look for the treasure, but

I couldn't find one, and I'm frightened." His voice grew higher. "The sand is getting all wobbly and shaky. It's up to my knees and I'm stuck. I can't lift my legs. Hurry, Mummy, and find somebody with a boat." Oliver tried to move round towards her but the effort only made him sink the deeper.

Moira tried to remember what little information she had ever heard about quicksands. You must remain quite still. Best of all you should lie down flat to distribute the weight as evenly as possible. But Oliver was too frightened to do that. If only she had a plank. But there was no plank, and very soon there would be no island. "Keep still darling," she shouted. "I'm going back for help now. Don't try to make a move. I know it's hard, but don't do it. You understand? Whatever happens you must not struggle." The impossibility of her being able to reach him appalled her. If she could have done so somehow she would have managed to pull him clear. On the horizon a tiny cargo boat was chugging northwards.

She fought desperately back to the shore and ran blindly up the beach and over the dunes to enlist aid, and the knowledge that the water was rising with each passing second pounded like hammers in her brain.

> "Oh Little Boy Blue
> Come blow on your horn . . ."

Oliver watched his mother's retreat as she made her way back to dry land. He was afraid, terribly afraid. Right at the beginning, playing and laughing with Sammy, he had not been at all frightened. When the sand had started to quake a little he had regarded it as funny, and had prodded at it jokingly with his spade. Soon afterwards Sammy had dared him to collect the sailing boats which had overturned and had drifted some way out, and he had chased after them, and it was while he was on his way back that his legs had become stuck in the sand and he had not been able to free them, and he had noticed that the sea was all around him and that Sammy was no longer there.

He had sunk up to his thighs. The sea was closing in on him from every side, and through the sands, not six feet away, bubbles were rising, bubbles which grew and pulsated before they burst.

The movement he gave was involuntary, and immediately the suction was increased. He must remain absolutely still as his mother had told him to do, until she could return to him with help. She would not fail him, she had never done so. He must be courageous and calm.

Despite his resolutions he pushed down with his hands at the melting sand and it offered no resistance, but when he endeavored to withdraw them he found that he could not do so. A wave darted in and, having spent itself, gently touched his arm. The wind had turned colder with the fading daylight, and a gull flew low over his head, and the sea began to slap against him in a regular and rhythmic caress. He was being drawn down inexorably by the enveloping sand.

It was as if eager arms were dragging him down, a small boy's insistent arms, arms that were covered by the navy blue sleeves of a sailor suit, and he thought that he could hear Sammy's urgent whisper: "Come and join me, Ollie. I'm lonely and I want you, and it will not hurt for long."

He made one last effort to free himself and the sand welled up to his chin and was forcing itself into his mouth and nostrils. He twisted back his head and started to choke and gave a retching spluttering cry as he tried to spit out the sand and water which were suffocating him. All he could see now was the cloud smudged sky. His small round face was stricken. On what, at his age, should have been an unsullied canvas, there was stamped an incredulous horror, the realization of what was about to happen, a hopeless and rebellious despair that no human being, least of all a child, should have ever known.

The ripples lifted his fair hair so that it floated in the sea, and presently the remaining vestige of the sand bar was submerged and the surface of the water was untroubled.

Miss Wallace had kept her head admirably and had rung up the police who were already on their way and who had in turn immediately alerted the Cleeness lifeboat. The two young men with Moira were the Melvilles, who lived in the house next to Stonethorpe, and who were powerful swimmers.

They were standing beside her at the water's edge and, gazing out over the smooth grey waste of the sea, and she realized that she could no longer even be certain of where the island had been. As she scanned the water it seemed that for an instant two children rose above its surface, and that one of them had on a yellow jersey and flannel shorts, while the other was wearing an old-fashioned sailor suit.

THE CORNERED BEAST

THERE were several gaps, as depressing as those of missing or broken teeth, in the semi-circle of electric bulbs that outlined the entrance to *Funland*. For many months the management had intended to remedy this defect, but somehow they had never got around to doing so, and the spirit of failure and decay which permeated the interior had also claimed the façade; for no amount of invitation, they comforted themselves morosely, would be likely to entice back their clientèle in its former numbers, so why throw good money after bad?

Funland was situated on the fringe of the theatrical district. Its red plush and gilt had become sadly shabby and tarnished, and a worrying proportion of the slot machines which lined the passages leading to the main halls and galleries were almost permanently out of order.

During the afternoons unemployed youths lounged or barged against one another, and small urchins scampered among these down at heel attractions, hopefully pulling the levers and pressing buttons in case an obstinate coin had lodged, unused, from the previous evening; but usually it was not until two hours before closing time that the paying public—or that small and faithful remnant of it—arrived to kill time for a short while before rounding off an evening.

The reason for this lack of support was not hard to find; the crushing competition of bowling alleys, bingo, television, and dog racing, together with the more stimulating enjoyments of all-in wrestling and X-films, had been too great and, with the coming of the affluent society, a pleasure and sensation jaded generation had little time to waste on the Halls of Mirth, the Haunted Houses or the Tunnels of Mystery, which now had retreated mainly to the coastal resorts.

Lovers, who could find mutual relaxation and ease, unobserved for three hours or more in air-conditioned luxury, in addition to the privilege of intermittently watching their favorite stars in double features, were no longer tempted by the prospects of a few furtive minutes on the broken-springed seats of the Romance Express.

The Freaks, it is true, retained as yet something of their former appeal, ranged, as they were, around a wide and shallow bowl sunk into the floor of the second hall; and a small additional charge could still be made for admission into this inner sanctum. The Giantess; the Half-Man-Half-Woman; the Inseparables; the World's Largest Rat; Leonard, the Dog-faced Boy; the Smallest Man on Earth; Goliath; the Hairy Ainu; and the Seven-legged Lamb—all stood, or sat, on their baize-covered platforms, or cowered in the back of their cages, week after weary week, indifferently eyeing the file of spectators as it made a slow tour of the arena; until, by closing time, there would be quite a number of cigarette stubs, lolly sticks and empty chocolate wrappings to be swept up and thrown away before fresh sawdust was put down in preparation for the morrow.

Leonard had spent all his life in similar surroundings. At irregular intervals he would be transferred to a manager in a different city or, occasionally, to a travelling circus, but the routine was always the same. He was uncertain of his age but reckoned that he must be in the early thirties. Tonight he would be glad when it was time to sleep. His head was aching from the blare of the juke boxes and his eyes felt hot and gritty. Impassively he watched the barker usher in the knot of slightly self-conscious sightseers through the curtains that masked the arched doorway. Two weedy youths, one of whom was patchily bearded, an old lady with her daughter who, in turn, led a small child by the hand, a curly-headed young man with a pretty fair-haired girl hanging on his arm, three soldiers, full of camaraderie and beer, and spruce in neatly pressed uniforms, and a well-built lad in a leather jacket swinging a "skid lid".

They gazed uneasily at the hermaphrodite and the midget. As they drew level with the giantess, Gargantua, one of the soldiers whispered a joke to his companions and they all three guffawed loudly. The young mother lifted up her child so that it should miss nothing of the entertainment.

The Freaks were not impervious to this scrutiny. It was, after all, the reason of their being. "Look at us!" was their mute appeal. "Look at us! Laugh if you like, be disgusted if you must, but look at us, we beg of you. That is why we are here. We are different from you. We are members of an exclusive club. We are unique. And this is the way in which we must earn our livings."

The child was waving its hands at the monstrous mass of female flesh. "Say 'good evening,' duckie," the barker said. The fat woman obeyed. Her voice was high and tiny for so vast a carcase. The wide expanse of her face creased into pleats of an answering smile, inane as a half-wit's.

"She spoke to me," exclaimed the child delightedly. "Did you hear her, Mummy? She said 'good evening'."

The group shuffled on to Leonard. The little girl regarded him with frightened eyes. Suddenly her face puckered up and she began to cry. "I don't like it, Mummy," she complained. "It's horrid."

"It's not right to show children things like that," said the blonde girl indignantly. "Some people don't seem capable of bringing up a child. They don't know what's right!" Her voice was intentionally loud and self-righteous. Her escort grinned awkwardly, and the women exchanged hostile looks.

"Don't be such a baby, Bella," the mother said sharply. She dragged at the little girl's arm and hurried on, flushed with anger and embarrassment.

Leonard stared at the young man with the curly hair and the blue suit. It must be nice to have a smart suit, he thought, and to have a pretty girl on your arm who kept on looking up at you so admiringly. He wondered if the young man thought it was nice, too. He'd never really noticed people before—not as individuals, but just as a shuffling queue. He had always been on the receiving end of stares. Without turning his head he followed their progress with his eyes to the limit of his vision. He could hear Manshaw, the barker, trying to sell his post-cards by the exit.

"The most remarkable gathering of human curios ever brought together," he was saying. "Twelve post-cards in a souvenir folder, or sold separately if you prefer it. Now, sir, how about a memento of Gargantua, eh? She'd make a nice armful for some gentleman!"

Again Leonard heard the suggestive laughter led by the soldiers, and the chorus of polite tittering that spattered from the remainder of the party.

Vera was very nearly pretty, but the fresh appeal that she had possessed at seventeen had, ten years later, blurred and faded. Her eyes were large and blue, and her legs were slim. She had excellent teeth, but they were too prominent and gave her a mean, rather rodent expression. Her taste in dress was regrettable. She had a small neat figure, and a small dull mind. She possessed also an incurable sense of the romantic, which was perhaps fortunate, since it helped to deaden the tedium of her unlovely life.

Vera had made up her mind to make one more sortie before "retiring" for the night. Not that it was necessary, she comforted herself; she was still doing all right; but it was only twelve o'clock, and this seemed to be her lucky day. She had once read a story in a paper-back about a girl just like herself. "Ladies in Shadow" she thought the title had been. It was all about a girl whose real soul had remained untouched by her way of living. Really beautiful, it was, even if it had made no contact with reality.

She planned to walk along Lancaster Street, do a little cover up window shopping and then, if no adventures offered themselves, she would walk up to Clemont's Hill and return home to Hanover Mansions, just like anybody else taking the air. It had been raining earlier in the evening, but now it had cleared up and the night was clean and cool. She felt pleased with life and confident of her own charm. She gave a friendly but dignified inclination of the head to a titian-haired vision who swayed past her as she turned the corner into Lancaster Street. She didn't hold with getting too intimate with the other girls, it always led to trouble in the end, but there was no harm in being polite, and *she'd* been raised properly and knew how to behave. No Coloreds. And no kinkiness.

Vera hesitated in front of a dress store and gazed into the window at the group of models, headless and dramatic, symphonies in violet and mauve, which were draped modishly, if eccentrically, on their stands against a background of soft gray hangings.

She was genuinely interested, and it was only gradually that she became aware that a man had paused behind her, and that he also was assuming absorption in the cunningly arranged display. She moved a step and twisted her head to try and study his reflection in the plate glass. It would be silly to face him until she knew more about his appearance. Girls like herself were fair game for . . . for anything. She was fully conscious of the dangers of her profession.

But it was no good. She moved along to the next store. Here she was more fortunate for, behind the hats, rakish on their steel supports, was a sheet of mirror. And now she could get a glimpse of him. He would be, she considered, about forty-two or -three, and he was ever such a handsome fellow, she thought, with those big shoulders and that broad chest; rather on the plebeian side maybe, but for all that a real man—not like some she'd taken on lately! He was wearing a dark suit and a black hat, and she noticed he favored a starched white collar, and that a thick gold watch-chain hung in a ponderous curve across his waist-coat. Old-fashioned touch—but perhaps it was an heirloom. Even when freshly shaved, she saw, his beard would shadow his skin. His shoes were brilliantly polished, and his tie was sober and carefully tied. "Real class" she told herself. "Or if not exactly class—at any rate dependable."

She favored him with a shy glance and the barest suggestion of a smile as she minced away along the pavement. He followed. Each was aware of the other's interest, but they had covered a block before he spoke.

"Good evening." She thought his voice lovely. Gave her a real thrill. Sexy. She allowed him to draw level.

"Good evening," she answered.

"Where are you off to in such a hurry?"

"Nowhere in particular. Minding my own business, unlike some people!" she replied, and immediately regretted her pertness. It wasn't his line. He'd think she was no lady.

"On the loose, too?" he asked, not in the least put off. "Like to join me in a bite of supper?"

She gave him a summing up look, and grew pink with suppressed excitement.

"I don't mind if I do." They didn't often feed you first. She took his arm, allowing her hand to slide up his sleeve and caress the muscles of his biceps, formidable even under the serge of his coat. It wouldn't do to be *too* ladylike. He pressed her arm against his side.

"Where shall we go?" he asked.

She pondered the question, then she said: "Why not The Warrington? It's only just round the corner."

She wondered if she could take him home with her, or if he

would prefer her to suggest a hotel—but she could decide that later, after supper . . .

"What's your name?" she asked shyly, as they walked along.

"Tom," he replied. "What's yours?" No surname, naturally. Almost certainly married.

"Vera. Tho' my friends all call me Vivi."

Perhaps he's in Telly, she thought. Immediately she imagined herself as a part of his life, queening it at Show Business parties, gay and sparkling and sophisticated. Tom's new discovery.

Actually, he was an efficient chauffeur, up in the city for a few days, and having a night off while his employer was attending an important Company dinner.

The Freaks were housed, under the chaperonage of their manager, in a down-at-heel apartment house now about a half hour's walk of *Funland*, a sleazy lodging which had been taken over for them in the season. A special closed van called at their place of work when it was time for their departure, so that they could be transported back to their destination without the risk of causing any shocks to such dilatory pedestrians whom they might otherwise have encountered at zebra crossings or in traffic blocks.

Leonard was fortunate in the fact that he had a room to himself; a narrow stuffy cubicle of a room, but still one of which he was the sole occupant, and which gave him the blessed solitude that he prized so highly, and which was so seldom his.

After they had been given their suppers in the room that had been allotted to them for the purpose, Leonard and his fellows were packed off to bed, while Manshaw, in whose charge they were, enjoyed a drink or two with the owner of the house.

Leonard, when he thought of the matter at all, liked Manshaw better than some of the men to whose mercy fate had entrusted him. It was only on the comparatively rare occasions when he had had too much whisky that he was unintentionally brutal, and Leonard had learned to keep out of his way when he saw the signs; at other times he treated them like a conscientious keeper who had an affection for his valuable animals. He saw that, as long as they behaved themselves, they had enough to eat and drink, and the strictly necessary amenities, even sometimes little luxuries. Beyond their material needs he never thought to trouble himself.

Leonard lay staring into the darkness. In spite of his fatigue he could not sleep, and for the first time experienced the nagging torture of insomnia. Against the blackness he saw moving figures: the young man in the blue suit and the laughing golden-haired girl—always the golden-haired girl. Leonard felt stifled. If he did not get some air he would go crazy. A bold plan crossed his mind. He would go out for a while and walk by himself in the streets; be free like anybody else for half an hour; be his own master like the young man in the smart suit.

Cautiously he climbed out of his camp bed and dressed himself in the darkness. From a hook in the wall he took his waterproof and hat. He opened the door. At the foot of the stairs a bar of light showed the room where Manshaw and his companion were still talking, the rumble of their voices intermittent. He waited a moment, and then with extreme care he started his descent. One of the treads creaked . . . and then a second. Breathlessly he halted, but apparently the sounds had passed unnoticed. The front door, he knew, was not locked until the men went to bed, which would not be for some time yet. He could see them through the crack of the door sitting by the table, a bottle and glasses and a half-emptied plate of sandwiches placed between them. Manshaw's chair was tilted back, he was smoking a pipe and was listening to the other's talk. His vest and the two top buttons of his trousers were undone to accommodate his belly in greater comfort, and his shirt sleeves were rolled up, showing his black-haired arms.

Leonard tiptoed past the danger zone. He found that the latch gave noiselessly to his touch. He was outside the house. The street was deserted and the night air was refreshing on his hot skin and he crammed his hat down over his eyes and turned up the collar of his waterproof as high as it would go, so that the minimum of his features would be visible. Quickly he slunk away, keeping wherever possible to the shadows. He had covered about fifty yards when he heard a shout. Turning, he saw Manshaw, who had been alerted had Leonard but known it, by the draught from the door. He was calling after him, ordering him to come back. His gesticulating body was silhouetted in the light from the hallway behind him, like a cut-out.

Leonard started to run towards the end of the road to where it joined a brightly lit main thoroughfare. Behind him he could hear the pounding of the man's feet in pursuit. Hearing his shouts, a figure courageously stepped forward with outstretched arms barring his way, thinking that he was a thief. Leonard's lips curled back and he bared his teeth in a snarl as he found himself battling with this unexpected antagonist. In the struggle his hat fell to the ground.

"Good God!" He heard the terrified exclamation as his opponent sprang hastily aside, and then he was free. Snatching up his hat he ran blindly, turning and twisting down by-roads, away from the populous street across which he had been forced to dash. He could hear no sound of continued pursuit. His pace slackened; here no one paid any attention to him. His breathing was labored. His heart hammered painfully against his ribs and a fierce pain burned in his side. Gasping, he leant against a wall to get his breath. He must hide. If they caught him they would probably beat him and put him on short rations—or take away his room and put him in with the hermaphrodite. The moon silvered the windows of the house fronts and glimmered on the rain-washed tiles. As he stood there a deep desolation filled his soul. Without thinking, he raised his head towards the sky and a cry of torment welled from his throat as he bayed to the gleaming disc above.

Once again he hurried on—this time in a quick walk, afraid to run lest he should make himself more conspicuous. He was completely lost. After what seemed like hours he drifted to a dark doorway at the end of a cul-de-sac. He crouched down exhausted on the doorstep. From the end of the street he heard the approach of a measured tread and a young policeman approached, an impassive Olympian, his light probing inquisitively into the dismal secrets of the areas.

Fearfully Leonard scrambled to his feet and hastened into the gloom and up the flight of steps that spiralled the building from the squalid entrance. Here he felt more secure, and lay panting in the darkness. After a long time a door below him opened and he saw a man and a woman come out, the light from the room shining on her blonde hair. They went down the stairs out of his sight. He could see into the room which they had left—all glow-

ing warmth and color and intimacy, of a luxury which he could
scarcely have imagined.

Flattened against the banisters he edged his way towards this
sweet-scented oasis. His feet slipped and slithered on the worn
wood and, panic-stricken by the noise he was making, he darted
into the refuge. In one corner he saw a screen. Behind that he
would be safe.

Vera shrugged herself into her dressing-gown and, thrusting her
feet into moulting mules, accompanied her visitor as far as the
bend in the staircase. She held up her face and received a perfunc-
tory kiss. "Good night, darling," she whispered. He had been like
all the others. It always puzzled her why they set such store by
it. And he had had nothing to do with the Telly, which had been
another disappointment. Said he was in the car trade.

Tom Hutton snapped open his cigarette case, and the flare of
the match lit up his head and heavy shoulders. He bent the cigarette towards his strong, cupped hands with their nicotine stained
fingers. From above them, from around the bend, came faintly
the sound of scuffling. Tom dropped the match and looked at her
inquiringly.

"Mice?" he asked.

Vera laughed deprecatingly. "There may be one or two. This is
a very old house."

"You ought to get a cat," he said. "Then you could have a great
bit of sport, like I used to when I was a kid. They have a fine old
game with 'em before they finally get round to eating 'em up."
He stood grinning down at her, his hands jingling the coins in his
trousers pockets, the cigarette stuck to his sensual lower lip, and
his stomach stuck forward.

Vera shuddered. "I call that cruel!"

Tom laughed. "Why? They're only vermin, aren't they? I tell you
it's good sport! They're that artful!" He winked at her and, half lifting his hand in farewell, went on his way to the street entrance. The
patter of the mice was so loud that it might have been the shuffling
of feet.

Vera stood for a moment looking after him and indulged in
a meaningless sigh before climbing the half flight and returning

to her bedroom. She was perfectly familiar with its appearance, but automatically she glanced around to see if everything was as it should be. The tall screen which cut off the wash basin in the corner, which he had not used, the chest of drawers, the wide rumpled bed, her dressing table with its triple mirror, the stool, and a large rather battered Panda doll completed the furnishings. Locking the door, she threw off her kimona and crossed to tidy up the litter of bottles and cardboard boxes that were scattered on the plate-glass top of her dressing table.

As she did so she saw the glint of gold. Among the clutter of spilled powder, tissues and manicure requisites lay three crumpled pound notes and Tom's large hunter watch and chain. She picked it up, fingering the massive links. Lovely, it was, a proper gentleman's possession. Snatching up her kimona again she ran to the window and peered down. There he was, oddly squat and fore-shortened from this height, pausing to relight his cigarette. She flung up the sash and called to him. "Tom!" Without waiting for an answer she withdrew the key from the keyhole and threw it down. He had started to walk away.

"Tom! You've forgotten your watch and chain," she called. "Come back and get it. I can't come down like this. Come on back up, dear."

Apparently he had not heard her. She looked after his retreating back. The key lay unnoticed on the kerb.

Vera was greatly nettled. "A fine thing!" she said aloud. "The stupid bull-necked bum! Who does he think he is, I'd like to know! And now I've gone and put myself in purdah! It would be just my luck if the house should catch on fire. A fine thing, I must say! A nice way for a gentleman to behave!"

Tom decided to walk home. The dawn was paling the sky above the roof tops. It would, he calculated, take him the best part of half an hour, and the walk would do him good; and, in any case, he hadn't to report for duty until ten. Overhead he heard a window being raised and his name called. He would not listen to her. He grinned as he began to walk away. Wanted more money he supposed. His jaw jutted sullenly. He'd be damned if he'd give her any more. These women were all alike. Did not seem capable of appreciating generosity. He'd left three quid, which was generous really as there hadn't been anything fancy. He rubbed his chin, his fingers rasping against the dark wiry stubble of his beard for he hadn't had a chance to shave since early morning. When he'd been abroad in the army he'd had a dozen better at a quarter of the price who'd really known their job! It was all rather a waste of time, but you couldn't eat the same pudding every day. You needed variety in the sex game as in other things. Something tinkled on the asphalt behind him. His powerful body swung along through the fresh morning stillness as he drew deep contented breaths into his lungs.

It was not until he reached the house where he was staying that he discovered that his watch and chain were missing, for on one end of it he always carried his latchkey, in the lower right-hand pocket of his waistcoat, together with his penknife.

He stopped in his tracks. Hell take the little slut! Fortunately he remembered the address, so she wasn't going to get away with it this time. Belonged to his father that watch had, and the chain must be worth a tidy bit too, gold being the price it was. The barman at the Warrington had said only tonight that he wished that he had had one like it. All of three ounces it weighed and every link was marked. His loss made him feel inadequately dressed, almost as if he'd come out without his tie. He remembered seeing it on the dressing-table when he'd been pressing the bone stud through his starched collar and while he had been adjusting his tie knot in the leprous-looking glass. He'd go right back and find a copper and they'd force their way in together if that little tramp tried any funny business. His face flushed with pardonable anger, hot in righteous and surly outrage at having been robbed by a cheap little whore who hadn't even been good at her work.

What had been the name of that girl who had called him "Mr. Atlas" and who had said that he could have it for free? Maisie? Daisy? Something of the kind. It was so long ago that he could no longer recall. She'd been a bit of all right, that one, reminded him of Betty Grable. Quite a dish!

He wondered what she'd think of him now. He'd always been a heavyweight, and in his Army days, during his twenties, he'd known how to use the gloves. Been rather a glamour boy too, or so they used to tell him, although with the passing of the years he had to admit that he had thickened out and was becoming all belly and arse. So far as women were concerned he was none the worse for that, for they appreciated something substantial fore and aft. It made a nice change from all those wasp-waisted sissies.

It was daylight when he got back to the turning which led to Hanover Mansions. A bored young patrolman was standing yawning at the corner of the street. Tom Hutton crossed over to him and related his grievance. Rocking gently from toe to heel the man listened to him attentively.

"Isn't that too bad!" he said, grinning, when the story was finished. Then he smiled. "O.K. I'll come along. The girl sounds like our Vera—although it's the first time I've had a complaint about her. She must be slipping!"

They walked off together, their footsteps echoing on the deserted pavements. As they neared the house the policeman's foot struck something which clinked softly. He bent down and saw it was a key. Mechanically he dropped it into a pocket. Without speaking they climbed the hollowed wooden stairs.

Leonard heard their approach and, straightening up, padded back to his hiding place.

The young policeman knocked on the door. There was no answer. He threw Tom a questioning look.

"Number 18," Tom said. "Yes, that's the flat right enough."

"Come on, Vera," said the patrolman loudly. "Open up. It's Dick Casey here." His voice was slow and gruff. "Want a word with you to clear up a misunderstanding."

There was no reply from within although they could see a streak of light struggling with the day through a slit in the warped panel.

"If you don't open the door I'll have to break in," Casey said reasonably. "I'm afraid you're in trouble, ducks." There was a certain kindly tolerance in the way he said the words. "A gentleman here says he has been robbed."

Silence was the only answer. The two big men looked at each other in the early morning light. Casey shrugged. Again and more insistently he knocked on the panel. "As you like, Vera," he called, "but we're coming in!" He seemed worried by the lack of response and glanced at Tom questioningly. Of course she might have gone out again, but it was unlikely at this hour. There was a quality in the silence that seemed to bode no good. He rapped peremptorily on the wood once more.

Then he put his shoulder to it. The door swung open with surprising ease, for the woodwork was rotten and worm-eaten and, caught unawares, he stumbled forward into the room. Beyond him Tom saw Vera lying across the bed. She was naked, and her throat was torn and her thighs deeply gouged, as if she had been savaged by a mad dog. Nearby, on the threadbare carpet, lay the gold watch and chain.

Casey twisted his head and looked at Tom Hutton grimly. At first glance the room appeared to be empty, until from behind the screen there started the sound of an exhausted panting and whimpering as if from an animal in distress, a desperate cornered beast.

THE INTERLOPER

GILLIAN WOODSTOCK had lived on Saint Dominique for most of her life, since, indeed, she had been eighteen months old. The island was tiny and remote, a pinpoint on the larger scale maps, and it was midway between Saint Vincent and Saint Lucia.

Saint Dominique had been purchased by Lavinia Mason shortly before the outbreak of war for what would now be considered as having been "a song." Lavinia had returned to England for the war years, in the process of which she had collected several outstanding decorations for her services with the Maquis and in other parts of Europe where she had done much invaluable work in liaison with the Résistances.

Hermione, Gillian's mother, had met Lavinia Mason during the last year of the hostilities. Hermione had been recently widowed, for her husband, Mervyn Woodstock, had been a casualty in Normandy while landing on D-Day, leaving her with very little money with which to bring up and educate their daughter. Hermione should have been heartbroken by his death but, in fact, the only sensation that she had felt was one of relief, tempered by worry about her financial future.

She had never really loved Mervyn. She had endured his amorous advances with concealed distaste and had married him solely for the prospect of a modicum of security when peace might finally come. After he had been killed she had no income of her own, apart from her pension and what she made, and she was bored with her job in the typists' pool in a hush-hush Government department. She was as pretty and flaxen as a china doll, and possessed a streak of hardness combined with an ability for self-preservation which were denied by her appealingly fragile looks.

Mervyn had been in the Commandos, a tough and uncomplicated character who had revelled in the cloak-and-dagger activities to which he had sometimes been assigned. He was thickset and dark, and was inclined to drink far more than he could carry, when he invariably became aggressive, which Hermione had found a

great trial. In civilian life he had been, oddly enough, a minor exec-
utive in a leading cosmetics firm. He had been hardworking and
a thruster, and upon his enlisting it had been understood that his
position would be kept open for him, so although he had no capital
his prospects had been good. He was, as Hermione had realized at
once, rather common; and had looked better in his uniform, with
the glamour of its green beret than he would have done when he
returned to "Civvy Street".

Hermione had encountered Lavinia Mason at a cocktail party
given by Mike Bland, who was her boss and who had labored with
considerable success in the network of M.I.5, although the work
which Hermione performed for him was at a distance, since it fil-
tered through to her by way of the alert and elderly Miss Duncan,
who herself attended to all confidential matters. Major Bland's
manner was deceptive, for behind his lackadaisical effeminacy there
was a keen brain and iron determination.

The gathering had been held in Mike's flat in Albany, and had
been what Miss Duncan had described as "high powered". Miss
Duncan had not been best pleased by Hermione's inclusion on the
guest list, and had rightly put her invitation down to her baby face
and emphatically feminine personality which, when off duty, her
officers were likely to appreciate. Lavinia Mason had arrived in
England only that same afternoon and her attendance at the func-
tion had been in the nature of a surprise.

Lavinia was elegant and poised and as detached and self-sufficient
as a Harper's model. She was also extremely talented, speaking perfect French and German, and was imbued with the courage of a
lion, without which she could not have carried out her tasks. Unexpected though her arrival had been, she assumed immediately the
role of Major Bland's guest of honor, and he was somewhat taken
aback when for most of the evening she devoted herself almost
exclusively to Hermione Woodstock. Following that first meeting
Lavinia had spent the bulk of her time with her during the short
periods when she had been recalled from France for the delivery of
reports and further briefings. Miss Duncan had confided that she
had already become something of a legend.

It had been Lavinia who had happened to be with Hermione
when she had received the news of Mervyn's death, and it had

been Lavinia who had said abruptly to her once her tears, which had been from shock rather than sadness, had dried: "You never loved him, darling, did you? It is unnecessary to pretend with me. You can't have loved him because . . ." she had hesitated for the space of a few seconds, "because you don't like men any more than I do." There had been a moment of tension, and then Lavinia had kissed her very tenderly, and the barriers had been down.

On the next evening, after Hermione had finished work and when they had been out together to dine, they were sitting in the uninspiring surroundings of Hermione's furnished flat, which was really a bed-sitting room and a bathroom-kitchenette. Gillian had been evacuated to her grandmother in Torquay to escape the bombing. Hermione was darning a stocking. She put it down on her knee and glanced across at Lavinia. "Were you always . . . like you are?"

Lavinia smiled. "I knew almost from childhood . . . what I was. I suppose in that way I was lucky. There was no need to pretend to myself." She stretched out in her chair and lit a cigarette, her long legs pointing to the gas fire. "It was not until after I was taken by the S.S. that my aversion to the male sex became what I must admit has grown into a phobia." She narrowed her eyes against the smoke of the cigarette, and when she spoke again her voice sounded impersonal. "I have always hated men if they tried to be close to me in any way. I have never been able to bear one to touch me, even my own father. Then, in the summer of 'forty-two I was pulled in by the Gestapo. They tried their customary routine to extract information, beatings up with truncheons, solitary confinement and starvation—followed by hour upon hour of incessant questioning —and burning with the stubs of their cigars and cigarettes, but they were unable to make me talk.

"A woman named Françoise Melun was the one who betrayed me, and she it was who told them of my . . . character. The men of the Maquis had always respected me. You can well imagine how those bloody thugs of the S.S. enjoyed themselves after they had talked with Madame Melun. Seven of them systematically raped me in turn in a cellar under their Avenue Foch headquarters. Two orderlies stripped me and held me down while the officers stood in a circle in their gleaming jack-boots and tight black breeches, watching and laughing and making jokes.

"The first was of course their senior, a Major Fallada, a big blonde brute of a man whom some, I suppose, might have considered handsome. The last was a lieutenant in his early twenties, a Baron Erik von something, I never heard his surname. He was thin and wiry, and lustful, as vicious as a ferret, and I loathed him the most of all. I hope even now that he was not killed but that he will die of cancer." Her lips were a tight scarlet line.

"Françoise Melun stood in the background egging them on and offering revolting advice, and screeching throughout like a peahen." Lavinia crushed out her cigarette with a stab and her eyes hardened. "During the days of the liberation many old scores were paid off, and I found her, the filthy bitch, and had the pleasure of slowly garrotting her with my own hands."

She fell silent, and then continued: "Those delightful debauches went on every night for a week, but I managed to remain sane. At exactly a quarter past nine, when they had finished their dinner and brandy, they would all of them file into my cell and we would have a repetition—with variations! A few days later I was rescued while I was being transferred to the prison at Fresnes, and in due course I discovered that I was pregnant, which was the final humiliation. I tried unsuccessfully to get rid of the baby. It was a boy, and when it was born I wanted to kill it, but the couple who were hiding me on their farm and to whom I had confided a part of my story were sentimental fools, and too quick, and they took it away from me. They told me afterwards that they had left it on the steps of a church with a label pinned to its coat bearing the name of its probable father. Probable!" Lavinia laughed. "They saw fit to choose that of Fallada in preference to Baron Erik! But then, they were Communists! Perhaps now you will understand why I detest all men. Those officers behaved worse than they would have done had they been in the lowest brothel. It must have been infinitely more fun for them outraging a creature of my sort than raping a nun or a cripple, for they were violating not only a body but a soul. I was a taunt to their masculinity because they knew I despised it."

From under her lashes Hermione looked at the woman who was sitting opposite to her, and who had told her story so calmly. She felt humbled. It was incredible what people could suffer and still survive. "And yet after that you twice went back to occupied France?"

Lavinia shrugged. "I have never hated my country. It was my duty."

They had gone together to Saint Dominique early in 1946, and apart from Lavinia's occasional business visits to Saint Lucia or Saint Vincent they had never left it since. Hermione had discovered that Lavinia, or "Larry" as she preferred to be called, was immensely rich, and she had turned the island into a luxurious and forbidden territory, an "Adamless Eden," as she had herself described it.

In the years immediately after the close of the war a number of women of similar outlook to her own, but of a different class, had been encouraged to join her colony. There were six in all, who acted in various capacities, and who were addressed always by their surnames, a custom which they employed also among themselves. Springfield, Hulze, Paulot, Groves, Dumby and Hibbersley. They occupied three bungalows within sight of the big house. In addition there were twenty or so colored women who tended the banana plantation, looked after the garden and kept up the road to the little jetty.

Larry had grown deeply attached to Gillian, whom she had come to love as much as if she had been her own daughter, with an affection that was more possessive even than that of her mother. Groves, under Larry's supervision, had been allotted the task of Nanny, progressing to that of governess, and she kept strictly to the itinerary which her employer had laid down.

Hibbersley, who had been an ex-Staff-Sergeant in the W.A.A.F.s was the mechanic of the launch, was responsible for the electric light plant, and also piloted the helicopter. Hulze and Springfield, tall and athletic types, looked after the livestock; and Paulot, the personification of gentleness, combined her secretarial duties with those of a doctor, for which she had studied. Dumby, who was a South African, occupied herself with the overseeing of the colored labor, three of whom worked in the house. The colored women were signed on for five year contracts, but many of them stayed for ten, for the conditions and pay were excellent. It all worked out very well.

With the exception of Larry they had no contact with the outside world, and wished for none. The mail, which was collected weekly from Saint Lucia, was taken direct to Larry's office. There was a radio, but Gillian was not permitted to listen to it, nor was she shown any newspapers or magazines. Books she was allowed, but they were carefully chosen and vetted by Hermione and their range was not extensive.

It was understood that Gillian would be Larry's heir and that Saint Dominique would eventually pass into her keeping, and with this end in view it had been decided that a time was approaching when suitable friends for her should be asked on visits, Larry having gone so far as to announce that shortly she must take a trip to New York, or even to London, to seek out worthy companions.

Gillian was now nineteen, and it was agreed that she should meet a hand-picked selection of her contemporaries. Gillian was perfectly content. She had known no other life save that on Saint Dominique, she had kept no other company than that of the bluff camaraderie in which she had grown up, and the women among whom she had lived were kindly and amusing, although she sensed obscurely that in some way they were members of a club, and that their community was a closed and secret one which had been cut off deliberately from their fellow human beings.

The male world had no existence for her. When she had been small and had inquired about men she had been made to feel that her interest was lewd and indelicate. Larry had told her briefly that men were necessary for the procreation of children. They fulfilled the roles of farm animals, and were equally boring and disgusting. They created all the sadness and trouble in the world, they were dirty and selfish and predatory and could be dispensed with very well.

Larry had crossed her slim legs in the flawlessly cut linen trousers, twisted the massive gold signet ring on the little finger of her left hand, and had given her a short dissertation on typical masculine behavior in such places as concentration camps and prisons generally, and in such historical occupations as witch burnings and the Inquisition. She touched on the activities of noted murderers of the genre of Heath and Christie. Venereal disease was also mentioned, but she forbore to enlarge upon the topic. She wound

up her discourse with a wryly amused smile: "And so you will realize, darling, why we are so lucky here. We have managed to keep
Saint Dominique as an oasis, unique—maybe it is the only one of
its kind in the world, completely uncontaminated by men. And
we most strongly hope that when it belongs to you it will be the
same."

Hermione nodded her agreement and rested her hand on Larry's
knee, her pekingese prettiness only just beginning to fade. "I am
quite certain, Larry, that it will," she said. "I hardly think it necessary to extract a promise on that score!"

They had never again spoken together of men.

Gillian lay in utter contentment on the soft white sand. Her naked
body was the burnt ivory of an almond shell. It was the habit of
those on the island to dispense with bathing suits. She spent a lot
of her time in the water and was so at home in it that Hermione
had once told her that she was amphibious. Gillian kept, however,
to the lagoon, for beyond the reef, which was pierced by a single
narrow opening, always carefully netted, there were many barracuda, those voracious wolves of the sea that are as dangerous as
any killer shark.

She sighed with sheer and lazy voluptuousness before she scrambled to her feet, her young figure as smooth and firm as tinted ala-
baster. There was still some time before luncheon and she thought
that she would go back to the house and take a shower to wash off
the salt, and then she would relax on the verandah and listen to the
new records which had arrived on the previous day, and of which
they had built up an extensive library. Light or classical, they were
all either played or sung by women.

A path zigzagged through the sentinel coconut palms and
crossed a ridge which separated the lagoon from the rock-peppered
bay whose far boundary was the jutting headland behind which the
house was situated. Gillian walked slowly through the cushion of
the caressing sand, pausing now and again to pick up a shell which
she would examine with interest and then discard.

It was when she was nearing the rock spur, where the stream
ran into the sea, that she found the man. He lay by the water's
edge, the wavelets lapping timidly round the lower part of his

body. He was young and fair and was clad in a pair of tattered white cotton undershorts. A faint blur of beard shadowed his face and thicker hairs clung to his muscular legs and wide chest. On one arm a snake had been tattooed and on the other were the initials H.F. A deep gash ran from one corner of his mouth to his jaw line, and from it a red trickle still oozed. There was a second and more savage one at the side of his neck and he was weak from loss of blood. He eyes were closed and he was unconscious from exertion and fatigue, but from the rise and fall of his chest she could see that he was breathing. An upturned rubber dinghy floated at a little distance from the shore.

Gillian stood in the hot sand staring down at him. He was the first male that she had seen since she was a baby, and she regarded him with an apprehensive fascination. She knew nothing of such matters, but she thought that he must be of an age with herself, perhaps a year or two older. She remembered the tales and warnings that Larry and her mother had told her. As she studied the boy's strained and exhausted face it was hard for her to believe that all the stories could have been true. She had imagined that a man would have been very different, far more coarse and primitive. She had had a vague idea that men resembled gorillas. But this boy, in his way, was beautiful.

She knelt down beside him. Round his neck hung a plastic medallion. As she lifted it the worn cord, to which it had been attached, broke, and when she had risen to her feet the medallion was clutched unnoticed in her hand. He muttered to himself, but she could not catch what he said.

She wondered what she should do. It was quite obvious that this boy had nearly drowned, and that he had paddled and struggled to the shore after many weary hours in the leaking dinghy. She must run back and tell Larry and her mother, for he would be too heavy for her to try to move by herself. As she turned away she glanced back. The young man's eyelids fluttered and for a fleeting instant his blue eyes opened, to shut again at once in protest against the glare of the sun.

Gillian ran back to the house, spurred by urgency, the bleached page boy cut that reached halfway to her shoulders bobbing as she jumped across the ditch which irrigated the garden.

She found the two women in Larry's office. They were intent on checking the accounts which Paulot had brought to them and raised their heads in good-humored surprise at Gillian's sudden entrance. "Hello, kid," Larry greeted her, "what's all the panic?"

Gillian told them of the young man whom she had encountered on the beach and of the critical condition in which he had been, and when she had finished her story her mother glanced at Larry and their eyes seemed to hold one another's for at least a minute before either of them spoke.

It was Larry who finally broke the silence. "You were perfectly right to come to us, Gilly," she said gently. "We will see to him. You stay here in the house. I do not wish you to go down to the bay again while he is there. You understand? It is most important that you should not do so."

"Very well," said Gillian. "But he will be all right, won't he? I mean you don't think that Paulot should go, too? After all, she is a trained doctor; and he doesn't speak English. The few words he murmured seemed to be in German. Let me go and find her."

"No," said Larry shortly. "I intend to handle this. We can manage perfectly well, your mother and I. From what you have told us our uninvited visitor seems to be in a bad way. Should he be alive when we reach him you can rest assured that I will know what to do."

"He's not an ordinary man, Larry." Gillian spoke breathlessly. "He's not at all the sort of man you described. He can't be. He's . . . he's most attractive."

"Gillian!" said her mother. "Have you taken leave of your senses? How can you possibly say such a repellent thing!" She looked across at Larry apologetically. "She doesn't know what she's saying!"

Larry's face might have been carved from marble as she pushed back her chair. "You will stay here until we return," she repeated, "and you will say nothing of this miserable happening to any of the others. Not one word." She was rigid with restrained emotion as, followed by Hermione, she went out of the room.

When they had gone and she was alone Gillian stepped out on to the veranda which commanded a vista of both the headland and the harbor where the launch was moored, and she stood there in a haze of worry, grasping at the smooth wooden rail. For a while nothing happened to disturb the quiet scene, and then she saw her mother and Larry passing through the garden together and separating at the gate, Hermione taking the path to the bay and Larry going on down towards the jetty. Presently there came the chugging of the engine.

Gillian was uneasy and bewildered by the reception of her news and rebellious at the terseness with which she had been ordered to remain in the house, and the memory of the young man who lay helpless in the tideless shallows disturbed her strangely. She waited until her mother had disappeared into the cover of the coconut palms, and until the launch had moved away from the sharp side of the quay before she hurried along to her own room and snatched at a linen dress. On her way back through the office she took up a pair of binoculars that had been left on Larry's desk and started off through the landscaped clumps of flowering shrubs and over the piece of waste land in the direction of the peninsula to a point on it where she would be able to see what would happen without herself being seen. She was facilitated in this by the chaotic rock formations, and she concealed herself in an eroded tunnel that she knew well, and which at one end had a low natural parapet that overlooked the bay.

Her mother had reached the spot where the young man was sprawled, and she was kneeling down beside him half facing Gillian's hiding place, which was about twenty yards away. Hermione's expression was a curious blend of hostility and unaccustomed pity. The boy's head was twisted sideways and the cut on his cheek showed up like a livid scar against the pallor of his skin.

As Gillian watched, the launch nosed its way around the point and stopped a short distance from the shore. Larry climbed out and stood thigh deep in the water, a vivid and piratical figure in her scarlet shorts and white shirt with a spotted azure handkerchief knotted round her neck. The closely cropped dark hair that was now starting to go grey showed off the fine shape of her head and emphasized her clear-cut features.

She waded ashore to where Hermione was waiting for her. Gillian could not hear what they were saying, but the murmur of their voices came to her over the water. Larry seemed to be insistent on some course that her mother was being reluctant to pursue, and

Larry's face was angry and Gillian had never before seen her in a fury that was the more frightening since it was tightly controlled.

Finally they bent down and hoisted the young man to his feet, his arms hanging limply over their shoulders as between them they supported him out to the launch. His weight was making them stagger. They had difficulty in getting him aboard but after a lengthy struggle they eventually succeeded in so doing.

The engine sprang to life and the boat speared its way towards the middle of the bay, to where it shelved to a considerable depth. Larry was steering, and Hermione had the young man's head resting in her lap. When they were a quarter of a mile from the shore the phutting of the engine ceased and the boat stopped. Larry was curved over where the boy lay. She moved her arm violently several times, and the sunlight caught the flash of the knife which was kept in the launch for the gutting of fish. Larry straightened up. She must have been leaning directly over the young man's body. Hermione did not move and her hands were clamped over her eyes. Gillian watched them, hypnotized.

Then, to her horror, and at a word from Larry, her mother got up and, by a concerted effort, the corpse of the young man was eased overboard. In the basking stillness of the morning Gillian could hear the splash as it hit the water. Larry tossed something into the sea with a contemptuous gesture and wiped her hands on the red shorts. The launch remained where it was, quietly rocking, and the sparkling surface of the bay was unruffled as the occupants of the boat waited for what might happen, for the net at the entrance had been removed. After a minute the calm of the sea was broken by the ploughing approach of gigantic fish. The barracuda were gathering and barracuda, as Gillian knew full well, were attracted by the presence of blood.

As the barracuda converged, there came the throb of the engine and the launch made out to sea, leaving in its wake a widening trail of wash as it circled to circumnavigate the tongue of rocks to reach the quay.

Gillian could not believe what she had seen. It had seemed like a scene from a nightmare; the flash of steel as Larry had slashed at the young man, the callousness with which he had been thrown into the water to certain death at the evil jaws of the man-eating fish. She was gripped by a nauseous fear that she would not have thought to exist.

She went blindly back to the house in a stumbling run, trembling with terror and hardly conscious of what she was doing. She must have turned on the gramophone, for she was sitting near to it when her mother and Larry returned, the glorious voice of Maria Callas insulating her from all reality. Gillian refused to dwell upon what she had witnessed. It had been the cold-blooded murder of a defenseless human being. She jumped up from her chair as the two women came out of the office, but she could not force herself to look at them directly.

Larry was as confident and unruffled as she had always been, coolly arrogant and armored by her charm. Hermione was shivering, and when she began to talk she did so too fast and in too high a voice, and she smiled too often. "Gilly," she said, "I'm afraid that we were too late. He was dead, so we buried him at sea. He was a sailor and he would have liked that." Gillian might not have heard what she was saying so uncomprehending was her regard, and Hermione rattled on: "Larry thought that it was the best thing to do . . . for all concerned. And she was right. You see, had we buried him on the island there might have been talk and endless tiresome inquiries as to who he was and how and why he had come here, and we don't want that, do we? We don't want officials—men—coming here to ask us questions. He must have been a victim of a yachting disaster, although there was no mention of one on the radio." She was looking anxiously at her daughter for some sign of approval. "There was nothing that we could have done for him, Gilly, really there wasn't. And under the circumstances only the three of us will ever know that he landed on Saint Dominique, only Larry and you and myself. And it must remain our secret. We have no desire to court trouble, and it isn't as if any of us even knew who he was."

"Some deckhand or steward," said Larry.

Gillian saw that the palm of her right hand was stained carmine. She threw the identity disc on to the table, and Hermione reached over and switched off the gramophone. "I can tell you who he was," Gillian said, and her voice was strident in the silence. "His name is stamped on that."

Larry leaned forward and incuriously picked up the drab plastic circle. For a moment she did not speak. "Hans Fallada," she read out. "Fontainebleau, 22 April, 1943." She stood gazing down at it, her face inscrutable, until Hermione snatched the disc away.

"Larry!" she said, and Gillian might no longer have been present. "He must have been on his way to find you when . . . when he was wrecked." Her plump fretful face crumpled in distress. "Who could have told him? . . . Who could possibly have known?"

"It would not have been difficult." Larry looked at her friend coldly. "At one time I had a certain . . . notoriety! But why should he have crossed the world to find me?" She was challenging Hermione to answer her. "The idea is absurd."

Gillian felt the sudden tortured crisis which had sprung up between them. Under her tan Larry was taut, a bitter tormented ghost. Hermione's fingers were clutching at the back of a wicker chair and her nervous laugh came out more of a sob. "I don't know, Larry," she said. "I just don't know."

Larry Mason was driving herself on, and in spite of the smile that curved her beautiful mouth her listeners were aware of it. "Even if your wild theory were true, Hermione," she said, "I have only finished what I should have done in that farmhouse all those years ago. It is no more than payment deferred." Her stricken glance passed from Hermione and rested upon Gillian, and as it did so it softened. "You have been protected here, Gilly," she said, "and as I have told you many times I hope that you will always be so protected. You have not seen death before or any unpleasantness and death can be very unnerving; and so far as I am concerned, so far as it may lie in my power, you shall never see it again. That unfortunate boy was dead. Your mother has already explained to you why we had to do what we did." She turned back to Hermione. "I would like you," she said, "to throw his identity disc into the bay. It can be his . . . memorial." She took a cigarette from her exquisite Fabergé case. "It has been a great shock to Gilly. It has been a great shock to us all." She clicked at her gold lighter before she went on: "We must now turn our thoughts to pleasanter things. I think that I will not delay any longer but will go next week to New York in search of some congenial friendships for her. It would not do for Saint Dominique to became claustrophobic."

Gillian made herself meet the serene loving stare that was lev-

elled at her, a stare that tore at her heart, and she heard herself
saying in a loud voice that she did not recognize as being her own:
"But why, Larry, why, before you . . . before you threw him in . . .
why in God's name did you have to use a knife?"

THE CROSS

"HE doesn't look at all well," said Chaora, "you can't pretend that he does, Balton. He looks perfectly dreadful, and if I lose another one it really will break my heart."

Her husband regarded the pet that lay trembling in one corner of the vast room, shivering in spite of being bathed in heat rays which came from a cone-shaped device positioned only a few feet away. His look was one of pretended concern overlaying an ill concealed distaste. "He's certainly lost most of his hair," he commented, "and is much too fat. I must admit he doesn't seem too good."

"I don't know what to do," Chaora said. "So very little is known about them, that's the whole trouble. I've asked Dara, who pretends to be such an expert," she went on acidly, "and all the advice she could offer was warmth and nursing and plenty of liquid; and he won't eat or drink anything at all. I've done my best but he doesn't seem to respond."

Balton tried hard to look suitably worried and sympathetic. Secretly he would be relieved if the animal were to die, but he could scarcely say so. These dilazos, or "bibikis" as the women called them, were most unattractive to an adult male mind; they were feeble physically, had horrid habits and were thoroughly insanitary. La-li was the third of them that Chaora had chosen to introduce into their lives. He found them most tedious and embarrassing. Given the chance they copulated as shamelessly and as eagerly as insects, in the most repellent manner, were always clamoring for attention, and were possessed of the most rudimentary intelligence. He had no patience with those of his friends who claimed that they had even an embryonic intellectual capacity. It was whimsy of a nauseating character, degrading to its perpetrators, and done to bolster up their own egos. Suppressing a yawn he contemplated his own sleek and handsome appearance in the looking-glass which completely covered one wall. "I expect he'll pull through," he said, "but you must face the fact that he is, well

. . . mature. And if he shouldn't do so," he offered generously, "I'll try and find you a replacement." This, he realized, would not be easy. The climate did not suit dilazos, they ailed and they became sluggish and they died, and very few of them were able to breed successfully, and even when they did so, normally they achieved only one offspring, the majority of which expired before they were even weaned, which was yet another of their repulsive habits.

"Perhaps his collar's too tight," said Chaora. She hurried across to her patient who was stretched prone on a miniature air-filled mattress. "I'll take it off altogether. Oh, my poor darling!" She unbuckled the flexible collar, woven in a silvery metal and studded with huge sapphires, and laid it down on a low table. Her lovely eyes were tear-filled. "Oh, Balton," she said, "we've only had him for two years and already he's graying and senile and, as you pointed out he's losing his elegant figure. Why don't they live longer? It is so unfair."

"To give your heart to animals," Balton said pedantically, "is a great mistake, for they will break it every time. You should try to be more like Dara," he advised, "have them, but resist growing too fond of them."

"Dara!" said Chaora. "You wouldn't like it one bit if I were like her! She's ninety per cent masculine; and her dilazos are all fighters." She shuddered. "That horrible Krask! He's absolutely hideous. An awful mud color, so clumsy, and in every way unappealing." She was working herself up, mounted on a favorite hobby-horse. "As far as Krask is concerned," she went on, "Dara is a disgrace to her sex—if anyone has ever been able to discover what it is! Dilazo fighting should be prohibited by law," she said vehemently. "They cut each other to pieces or else batter one another to death. It's cruel and revolting. I can't think how you can bear to attend one. You, who are supposed to be a civilized being!"

Balton laughed. "It's quite amusing when you understand the technicalities," he said.

"It's loathsome and barbaric and bloody," Chaora contradicted, "and I hate you for supporting it."

Balton was standing by the windows gazing out over the expanse of plain, dotted with giant trees and patterned by a checker board of irrigation canals, many miles of which were his property. Soon he would have to go back to the laboratory, but he did not like to leave his wife while she was so distressed. He glanced over at the panting animal in the corner, wishing that he could have been moved by its sufferings so that he could have shared her anxiety. Dilazos came in three colors, off-white, black, and yellow. There were brown ones too, like Dara's, but these were not so highly prized. Some people held a theory that dilazos had a language of their own, that they were able to communicate with one another, but personally he doubted it. They made gabbling and rather disagreeable sounds, those of the females being particularly shrill, but that was all. One day Dara and he had tried to carry out an experiment, using the swarthy Krask and a young yellow female, but there had seemed to be a complete lack of understanding between them. They had just stood there making unintelligible noises at each other, until Krask had flung himself on her, his intentions plainly discernible. Dara had sworn angrily and cuffed him and dragged him off and put him back on his lead.

Unselfishly Balton hoped that he would be able to obtain another of them for Chaora but they were becoming hard to come by; he'd been told that their numbers on Alogia had shrunk to less than five hundred, and one had to pay through the nose for one. A little while ago when they had been plentiful there had been a cult for clipping them, shaving the heads of the males, except for a few tufts, and leaving them with their beards only, which was, in its way, sensible, since they harbored vermin; while the hair of the females had been twisted into fancy plaits, which had made them appear even more fantastic and ridiculous. He could not say truthfully that he cared for dilazos, and he was certain that they were carriers of disease. Luckily they were only a passing fad.

"Well," he said, "I must be going. I hope for your sake that La-li will recover. If he does not," he added, fearing that he had sounded heartless, "contact me at the laboratory, not that there will be a great deal that I can do to help."

He kissed her quietly, and when he had gone away Chaora settled herself by the invalid. She noticed that a scarlet rash had begun to spread over his entire body, the eyes were closed and pus was oozing from their corners, and his breathing had become laborious. She realized that she was being unreasonable by permitting

herself to get into such a state of desperation, that it was unwise
to try to cling on to a dilazo, and sheer madness to love one. Their
life span was so short. They were unsuited to the environment, to
extremes of heat and cold. It was like transplanting shrubs into a
different and hostile milieu where they would have but a slender
chance of flourishing or even of survival.

She looked down at La-li. He had, from the first, refused the
vitamin pills, had chosen always to scavenge for himself, returning to the house after a foraging expedition with either vegetables,
that he would eat raw, or with the mangled corpses of birds which
he had managed to catch and kill, not that the latter was much of
an achievement, since they were mainly vavos, which were unable
to fly and which had been preserved solely for the brilliance of their
plumage. She should have insisted on his swallowing the vitamin
tablets, with their balanced diet, for they would have built up his
resistance, she should have fed La-li forcibly when it had been necessary. And now, she thought, she had left it too late.

She felt a deep depression. She remembered when he had first
come to her, how he had danced on his hind legs to please her,
how he had embraced her knees and made humming noises as if
he had been trying to sing, and how she had failed utterly to teach
him to walk on all fours, which he had been quite clever enough to
master, but about which he had been very obstinate.

She could not have explained why she found dilazos so endearing. They could be, and often were, disappointing pets, petulant and
of uncertain temper, which she found easy to understand, for their
pathetic interests were so limited, nor could she deny that it was a
nuisance having to take them out continually for the purposes of
exercise and so that they could fulfil their primitive natural func-
tions. They dawdled along so slowly, which was insufferably tedious,
and resolutely refused to be hurried. In many ways they were infu-
riating. She supposed that their delicate constitutions came from
their having no built-in adaption to changes of temperature; they
were like ozadozzas—those exotic flowers which had to be grown
in thermostatically controlled caverns.

Some of her friends had tried sewing them into little coats of
vavos feathers to keep them warm, garments which covered their
bodies while leaving their limbs exposed for free movement, but

they had been irked and ill at ease while wearing them and had clamored for them to be taken off.

The first dilazos to be imported had been used for biological study, but vivisection had shown them to be structurally uninteresting, and safe so far as alien contamination was concerned, and the next consignments that had arrived had been allocated to the various zoos, where they had been temporarily a novel attraction; then, when they were brought back in increasing numbers, they had been sold as pets and had become something of a craze, the black ones being held to be aesthetically the more pleasing, although they were more difficult to train.

Chaora sprayed La-li with a soothing lotion and wiped away the discharge from his red-rimmed eyes. Although he was so useless and tiny she loved to see him around when she came home. She was never lonely when he was there. Balton was unable to understand her love of animals. It was not a part of his make-up. She stroked the tufts on La-li's head and gently pulled at his grizzled beard that so short a time ago had been golden. She tried again to make him take his vitamins and the medicine which Dara had recommended, but he shut his mouth tightly and turned away his head and refused to eat or to drink from the dish of water which she held for him. She spent most of the day by La-li's side, stroking and encouraging him, but there seemed to be no improvement in his condition. Once he opened his eyes and his lips parted showing a glimpse of white teeth, but he could only move weakly and his face was glistening with sweat.

She was still crouched down beside him when Balton returned. He looked at La-li and then at his wife. "I'm afraid it's no use," he said. "He can't recover, and there's no point in going on torturing yourself. Darling, he won't feel anything, I promise you that. Please let me deal with it for you. Why don't you go over and see Dara and leave La-li here with me? It would be much the kindest thing to do."

Chaora nuzzled the little creature's hot cheek. Presently she raised her head. "Very well, Balton," she said quietly. She went out of the room without looking back.

When she had gone Balton pushed a button and a wall panel slid back. From the cupboard he took out his atomizer, which was similar in shape to a revolver. Going over to where La-li was lying he took careful aim. "Take it easy old man," he said. He pressed the trigger and there was a sibilant hiss, and then all that remained was a heap of ashes. He looked round the room and found a bowl of engraved crystal and into this he spooned the residuum of La-li. Perhaps Chaora would want to bury the ashes in the corner of the copse where she had made the animals' cemetery. She was so gentle and foolishly sentimental. Before he started on the work which he had brought home he pondered briefly on the mystery of dilazos, wondering what, if anything, went on in their minds, whether they were capable of coherent thoughts, and if La-li had realized what was going to happen.

Chaora came back as the long twilight began to close in. She saw the bowl immediately, and the jewelled collar which Balton had placed beside it. She picked them up without comment and left the room. After a while, from the window, he saw her crossing the garden. In one hand she held the bowl and in the other there was a slim metal excavating rod. He smiled tolerantly and watched her as she walked away until she disappeared into the spinney of scented flowering trees.

As she made the grave Chaora mourned for La-li. She could never bring herself to have another dilazo. Never. She had been told that there were not many of them left now, a few colonies remained in the more remote corners of their globe, little communities of tough survivors who had proved themselves resistant to the virus that had been used against them, and these had taken to the jungles and the inaccessible mountains.

She tried to recall what she had learned as a child about their remote planet. Their villages, or so she had read, had been built around spired temples where their dead were buried in the earth, left to rot in wooden containers, and marked by monuments of stone, usually in the shape of a short-armed cross, stark and simple. Why this was so she had no idea, but tomorrow she would have this strange device erected. She would have it fashioned out of the local purple stone from their quarry, which in the dark was faintly luminous. She knew that Balton would laugh at her, but La-li would have liked it, of that she was sure.

Inside the circular house Balton touched a switch and the room was flooded with concealed lighting. He pressed a second that worked the transparent shutters which contained also the source of heat against the arctic Alogian night, and while they were slowly closing he saw Chaora on her way back from her melancholy task. She was very beautiful, her silky azure fur set off to perfection against the banks of white flowers between which she walked, flowers that in a few hours would be blackened and cut down by searing frost.

Chaora told him immediately of what she intended doing, and Balton mocked her with a wry kindness and tolerance, as she had known would be the case. His unexpressed hopes were that when La-li was lying at rest beneath a symbol which, had Chaora only known it, had been largely meaningless in his own country, in future he himself would receive a greater quota of her devotion which previously had been squandered so abundantly on the well-being of the dilazo.

"It's a delightful idea of yours, Chaora," he said, "but why only for La-li? Won't it make his predecessors feel rather neglected?"

"No, I don't think so," she said. "A thing of that sort must be done at once, or not at all. Oh, I shall miss him! Dreadfully. He was so sweet. It won't be at all the same now that he's no longer here."

Balton held out his hand. "I trust," he said cautiously, "that I did right in atomizing him, and that you had not perhaps planned on having him stuffed?"

Chaora, to his extreme dismay, began to shake with sobs. "Balton, how can you make such a nauseating suggestion! Why, I'd . . . I'd as soon plan to have you stuffed, as darling little La-li." She half ran to the doorway. "I'm going to lie down," she announced. "How could you be so beastly? How could you!"

Left by himself Balton shrugged his herculean shoulders. It was difficult indeed to know what was the right thing to say to a woman.

Before La-li, or Dimitri Protov as he was then, had been herded aboard the space ship, although his owners were naturally ignorant of that fact, he had been a dancer in the Russian Ballet. Balton was reckoning that if the proprietor of the animal dealer's establishment had been correct, and it was well known that it was simple enough to determine a dilazo's age from the condition of its bones and teeth, La-li must have reached twenty-seven or -eight terrestrial years, or about four by Alogian reckoning. After the necessary quarantine he had remained in Chaora's pampered keeping for a further two years, which must total up, Balton thought, to some kind of a longevity record for their pathetic species.

Upon further deliberation he had decided against their embarking upon another dilazo. He would buy her a querante instead. They were less delicate, infinitely more attractive and amusing, and altogether more biddable, but then, of course, they originated from a planet which was in a state of considerably greater advancement than that of Earth.

Querantes had fur, at least, and did not need to make discordant squeaks or growls whenever they wanted to make themselves understood. Dilazos, on the other hand, if one could bring oneself to study their intimate behavior, were really revolting. Evolution had made many mistakes on a multitude of planets, but surely a dilazo must have been one of the crudest?

Chaora would soon forget La-li.

ALSO AVAILABLE FROM VALANCOURT BOOKS